RISE OF THE
SHADOW
DRAGONS

LIZ FLANAGAN

David Fickling Books

31 Beaumont Street
Oxford OX1 2NP, UK

RISE OF THE SHADOW DRAGONS
(Legends of the Sky: Book 2)
is a
DAVID FICKLING BOOK

First published in Great Britain by
David Fickling Books,
31 Beaumont Street,
Oxford, OX1 2NP

www.davidficklingbooks.com

Hardback edition published 2020
This edition published 2021

Text © Liz Flanagan, 2020
Cover Illustration © Angelo Rinaldi, 2020
Inside Illustrations © Paul Duffield, 2020

978-1-78845-146-8

1 3 5 7 9 10 8 6 4 2

MIX
Paper from
responsible sources
FSC® C018072
www.fsc.org

DAVID FICKLING BOOKS Reg. No. 8340307

A CIP catalogue record for this book is available from the British Library.

Typeset in Sabon by Falcon Oast Graphic Art Ltd, www.falcon.uk.com
Printed and bound in Great Britain by Clays Ltd, Elcograf S.p.A

For Christoph, of course xx

PROLOGUE

Two dragons flew in darkness. Their breath came in wheezing gasps. Their wings flapped heavily, straining hard with every beat. Their scaly flanks were streaked with blood.

'The dragons need to rest,' Milla yelled, black hair escaping from her blue scarf. Her face was caked in ashy dust. 'They won't make it.'

'They will! They have to,' Thom cried hoarsely, a grim look on his face. 'Milla, we've got to reach Arcosi, before it's too late.'

As if to prove his words, a huge jet of hot steam hissed up from the slopes below, narrowly missing his red dragon. She banked sharply, almost losing control.

'Thom!' Milla screamed. 'Are you all right?' She twisted sideways and urged her blue dragon lower, searching in the gloom.

His voice carried up from the darkness below. 'See? The

volcano is erupting. Right now! There's no time. We have to try!'

Sitting low on their dragons' backs, hunched and tense, both riders faced towards the west, urging their exhausted dragons to one final effort.

Milla whispered a constant stream of encouragement, 'Hurry, Iggie, hurry! If it's the last thing we do, we have to tell them of the danger. We have to tell them what to do.'

Behind them, the sky was streaked with red-gold sparks.

CHAPTER ONE

Six months earlier

*J*owan Thornsen was dreaming of flying. His hands gripped a purple scaly neck, the wind tugged his hair, the sea sparkled beneath him as his dragon sped through the air . . .

When he woke up, Joe was still smiling. The dream faded and he sat up with a jolt, remembering what day it was. Hatching Day fell on his twelfth birthday. His friends Amina and Conor had said it was lucky. And now a dream of dragons? That must be a good sign. Today was the day his life would change for ever. By that evening, he might have bonded with a newly hatched dragon. He'd be living in the dragonschool of Arcosi. His bag was right there, packed and ready. Excitement bubbled up inside him, and he couldn't sit still any longer.

He leaped out of bed and pulled on yesterday's crumpled shirt and trousers, leaving untouched the new white clothes that had been laid out for him; they were for the ceremony later. He wanted to run and sing and shout, but it was still early, so he crept downstairs, avoiding the creaky floorboards and jumping the last three steps. No noise came from his parents' room.

Outside, smoke curled from the kitchen chimney, up into a blue sky dappled with pink clouds. He peeked through the crack of the kitchen door. No sign of Matteo the cook, just a large plate of steaming cinnamon rolls on the workbench. His favourite. Joe went in and grabbed two, burning his fingers. He shoved them in his pockets, feeling the heat spread through the worn linen. Then he ducked through the back door, walked quickly through the garden and climbed the high stone wall of the practice yard where he'd spent hours working on his sword skills.

He perched there like a pigeon, looking down over the rooftops of Arcosi, the wind in his face conjuring his dream again. He spread his arms like wings and his heart took flight. He gazed past the ships docked in the harbour far below, and right out to the pale sea which stretched away in every direction. Today, he had his first chance to bond with a dragon. He looked at the sea and imagined flying over it. It was so close, he could taste it. It would be just like his dream.

Just then, everything grew dark as a dragon glided low overhead, sapphire wings spread. It landed just outside the practice yard with a *whoomph* of wings and a crunch of earth.

'Milla!' Joe sprang down from the wall and went to greet his cousin. 'I thought you were too busy to come today?'

'Never too busy for your birthday, Joe!' Milla tumbled

off her dragon and Joe threw himself at her. 'Dragons' teeth! I swear you've grown in a week.'

It was true. Joe was growing so fast his legs ached each night, and he kept banging into things, not used to this new body. That wasn't all that was new: strange intense moods blew in like storms. They passed as fast as they came, so he kept quiet and hoped no one noticed.

'You're tall enough to swing *me* round.' She pulled back from the hug, eyes shining, black curls framing her face. 'Don't you dare try, or I'll set Iggie on you.'

He laughed at her mock-serious tone. She might be one of the first dragonriders of Arcosi and almost twenty-five years old now, but she was always ready for mischief and he loved her for it.

Joe reached out for Iggie, his cousin's huge blue dragon, who greeted him enthusiastically with sparks and grunts, and lots of head-butting that nearly knocked him over. Iggie was at least twice as big as the largest carthorse on the island, and his wings were massive. Joe ran his hands over Iggie's scaly neck, realising that by sunset he too could have a dragon of his own. Real and breathing, here in his arms. What a birthday gift that would be!

'I used to sit there too,' Milla said, gesturing at the wall. 'Best view in the city. Shall we?'

They climbed back up and sat side by side. There was a shadowy full moon giving way to the rising sun, and the air was still cold.

'Happy birthday, Joe. This is for you.' Milla passed him a small leather pouch.

7

'Thank you,' he said, opening its drawstring. He tipped it carefully, and something small and shiny fell into his cupped palm. It looked like a coin and a mass of silver chain.

'It matches mine,' Milla said, tapping the medal she always wore round her neck.

Joe lifted up the silver disc. It had a device beaten into it: a circle to represent the full moon, and a dragon in flight beneath it. It was the symbol of their family, the ancient dragonriders of Arcosi. 'Oh, Milla.' He struggled for the right words. 'It's perfect. I'm going to wear it today, for luck.'

'Let me help you with that clasp.' Milla fastened it behind his neck, brushing his wavy black hair aside. 'There! Just as it's meant to be.'

He patted it, feeling the cold metal settling into place at his throat. 'And here's something for you: breakfast!' Joe passed her a roll and started ripping his own into shreds.

'Ooh, hot from the oven. Matteo's cinnamon rolls are as good as Josi's,' she said, nodding her thanks.

'You better not tell her that.' Joe grinned at her. Joe's mother's temper was as legendary as her cooking. Josi belonged to the island's highest society these days, recognised as a descendant of the ancient royal family of Arcosi, but when Milla was young, Josi had been the household cook, hiding her true identity.

'So,' Milla said next, drawing out the syllable. 'The big day?'

'Uh-huh,' Joe mumbled, mouth full of bread.

'Ready?' she asked.

'I feel ready.' He hesitated, and he was aware of his heart

beating faster, as he chose to tell her. 'This morning, I was dreaming of a dragon. A purple one. Did that happen for you, with Iggie . . . ?'

She smiled, remembering. 'Yes, a few times. I couldn't see him, not exactly. But I knew he was blue, and I knew we would fly together.'

'Yes!' Joe said, relieved. 'That's what it felt like for me.' And with a rush of eagerness, he begged her, 'Is there a purple egg? How many are there? You've seen them, haven't you? Tell me, Milla, please!'

'You know I can't tell you.' Milla's brown eyes held his, sparkling with life and humour.

He took that as a yes. There *was* a purple egg! He knew it.

Milla yawned widely, and Joe noticed the shadows under her eyes for the first time. 'Are you all right?' he asked.

'Didn't sleep much last night,' she said. 'Trouble in the lower town. Tarya had to send a few dragonriders to back up her troops.'

'Trouble from the Brotherhood?' Joe guessed.

'Who else?' Milla grimaced.

After the dragons returned, just before Joe was born, the army of Arcosi was halved in size – the island just didn't need that many soldiers when it now had dragons to defend it. Half the army had been paid off to leave their jobs, all those years ago. And some of them, the ones who resented it, had banded together and now called themselves the Brotherhood. They loitered around, causing a nuisance and calling out insults, but no one took them too seriously.

9

'It's not Tarya's fault!' Joe defended his sister, the island's general. 'She was generous to the soldiers who left.' He'd heard his father saying this many times.

'She still is. That's the problem.' Milla sighed. 'I understand she can't ban them, in case that makes them more popular, but—' She stopped herself.

'What do you mean?' He remembered seeing the men, still wearing their old black uniforms, tattered and faded. They gathered on street corners, drinking in the daytime, trying to get people to listen to them. 'They're harmless . . . aren't they?'

'I'm sorry, Joe.' Milla put one hand on his shoulder. 'I shouldn't talk about my worries, not on your birthday. Don't let this spoil Hatching Day. Your first time. How are you feeling?'

Joe paused, really considering that question. 'Excited? A bit nervous.'

'Don't worry – all the dragons are healthy now.'

'Are you sure?' he asked anxiously.

These were only the second clutch of eggs laid since the Great Loss. Two years ago, a terrible sickness had swept through Arcosi's dragonhalls, killing more than half its dragons. Joe's brother, Isak, one of the first dragonriders along with Milla, was the Head Dragonguard of Arcosi, and his hair had turned pure white overnight from the shock.

'Isak has been so vigilant,' Milla said now. 'He's nurtured these eggs as if they were his own.'

It must be a nervous day for them all too, Joe realised in a rush. When the Great Loss came, no one could save those dragons: not Milla with all her healing skills; nor Isak with all his wisdom; not Tarya with all her battle skills; nor Duke Vigo in spite of his power. He'd heard the rumours, everyone whispering that it was a sign that these youngsters didn't know what they were doing and that someone else should take charge of ruling the city. So they all needed this to go well.

Just not as much as him.

Joe looked down, and noticed he was gripping his silver medal tightly between his fingers. *Please let it be me today*, he wished. *Please don't let me be a waddler!*

That was a rude word for people who couldn't bond with dragons. Someone stuck on the ground: a *waddler*. Someone who would never fly on dragonback. It was whispered by the children before each ceremony. You weren't supposed to say it. Most people on the island were waddlers. Only a lucky few were dragonriders. It didn't stop every child praying, dreaming, wishing that a dragon would choose them.

Since the dragons returned, every young person in Joe's family had bonded with one. 'Oh, Milla, I hope all the eggs are healthy. Whoever they bond with.'

'It's all right, Joe,' Milla said, her eyes warm and bright with understanding. 'What's meant for you won't pass you by.'

He nodded, reassured.

'Come on, let's go down. It's time to get ready.' She wiggled to the edge of the wall and jumped off, landing lightly on both feet.

Joe followed his cousin, feeling his excitement building again. The air smelled of salt and woodsmoke, and he could

11

hear the distant calls of the fisherfolk down at the harbour, the sounds of the island city waking up.

Iggie clambered up from where he'd been dozing in the first rays of sunshine. To Joe's surprise, the blue dragon came to him first and placed his huge forehead against his chest.

'He is wishing you good luck,' Milla explained. 'From both of us . . .'

Joe scratched between Iggie's blue ears, grateful for his attention, but knowing that the dragon's heart belonged entirely to his cousin. 'Thanks, Ig,' Joe whispered, so only the dragon could hear. 'Later today, let's hope there'll be a new purple dragon for you to meet.'

Iggie half closed his huge green eyes and growled softly, sending tremors through Joe's whole body.

He relaxed. Today would be all right. Today would be the best birthday ever.

Joe could hear his parents discussing him as he ran up the main staircase of the Yellow House to get changed, the *stomp* and *clack* as his father paced with his walking cane.

'So why isn't he here, then?' his father was saying. 'What could be more important?'

'Nestan, my love,' his mother replied. 'Stop fretting. He won't be late. He's been so excited, he's been counting down the days! Perhaps he just—'

'I'm *here*!' Joe pushed his bedroom door open with a bang. 'Sorry, I lost track of time, talking to Milla.'

His mother swooped on him first. 'Happy birthday, Joe!' She wrapped him in a warm embrace, kissing his cheek loudly. She was already dressed in her best clothes: a crimson gown, a matching silk scarf over her black hair. 'Here's your gift from us.' She gestured at the bed.

There was a large parcel next to the white clothes for the ceremony.

Joe darted across and seized the package, unwrapping it eagerly. There was a fur-lined hat and long leather gloves, lined in silk, cosy and warm. You could get cold flying – he'd heard Milla say so. He'd be needing these, as soon as his dragon was big enough to carry him. Dragonriders always wore the colours of their dragons. And these ones were . . . *purple*! The same deep dark purple from his dream.

How did they know?

'Thank you,' he whispered, glowing inside with this evidence that they believed in him.

'You can try them on later, *after* . . .' Josi said.

'Happy birthday, Joe,' his father said, hugging him one-handed. 'And there's this, now you're twelve.' He had a large cylinder hanging on a leather strap from one shoulder. He swung it round, caught the strap and handed it to his son.

Joe took the cylinder. Its weight and smoothness seemed familiar. A memory rose up, from the days when he'd followed his father round like a little shadow, asking endless questions and receiving patient answers, all day long.

Standing in his father's study, still so small he could barely see over the desk.

'What's that?' Joe had asked, pointing at a smooth black leather cylinder.

13

'That's my shipwreck kit,' Nestan had told him. 'It's saved my life three times now.'

'How?' Joe asked, not understanding.

'When a ship goes down, you have no time,' his father explained, reaching for it. 'Three things saved me: luck, swimming skill, and this.'

'What's in it?'

'Flint and tinder, blade, fishing lines, hooks, oilskin, compass . . .' Nestan pulled it open and shook the contents out onto his desk. 'Everything you need to survive.'

And now Joe held his very own shipwreck kit. 'Wow, thanks, Dad,' he said, touched. And then he teased, 'Are you expecting me to need it?'

'It's traditional. Ours are sea-people,' Nestan said, a smile tugging at the corners of his mouth, his blue eyes wreathed in laughter lines. 'Once upon a time, every Norlander child received their own shipwreck kit on their twelfth birthday. You keep it close and hope never to need it.'

'Well, not today at least?' Joe put it on the shelf and turned back to the white robes he needed to wear this morning, like a blank sheet of parchment till his purple dragon bonded with him.

'I think we can be sure of that. Now, if you get changed quickly, we can still be on time.' Nestan ran one hand raspily over his white beard, while the other leaned on his walking cane. 'Your brother and sister will be waiting.' But he didn't move, not yet.

Joe's mother slid one arm round Nestan's waist. His

parents stood there together, both looking at him in a strange way, their smiles slightly wobbly and damp.

'What?' He stared back at them. 'Are we in a rush or not? What's wrong?'

'Oh, nothing's *wrong*, Joe!' Josi said. 'We're just so proud of you.'

That was a new thought for him. 'I haven't even done anything yet.'

'We're proud of you,' his father repeated, blinking hard and clearing his throat, 'whatever happens today.'

Joe's mother flicked a tear from her cheek. 'Oh, look at me! I'll spoil this silk, and it's not even the ceremony yet.' She sniffed loudly and wiped her face on her husband's shirt sleeve.

'Go on, I'll be down in a moment. We won't be late – promise!' Joe turned away to hide his face as it hit him: if today went well, he would never live under his parents' roof again. He'd been so busy thinking of his dragon, he'd forgotten that part. With another pang he realised he was ready for it all: ready to grow up and leave his home behind, ready to make his parents really proud, and, most definitely, ready for his dragon.

CHAPTER TWO

The island of Arcosi was abuzz. Humming with life like a giant anthill. Bells rang out, echoing up and down the steep twisting streets, summoning everyone to the marketplace near the harbour for the hatching ceremony.

Joe and the other Potentials gathered in a shady street just above the marketplace, waiting to be summoned. They were busy saying goodbye to their parents, under the watchful eyes of four dragonguards.

'Good luck, Joe.' His mother hugged him tightly, speaking into his ear. She pulled back and stroked his hair, where it always stuck up at the front.

He could see she wanted to say more, but he turned away, towards his father, who was searching for Isak and Tarya in the crowd. He noticed with a twinge of worry how old his father looked, leaning on his cane, his white hair bright in the sunlight.

'Bye, Dad.' Joe got in first with a quick hug. 'You'd better go down: don't lose your seats.'

Nestan nodded. 'We'll find you, *afterwards*.'

Afterwards. When, just maybe, he would be holding his dragon! Joe tried to picture that: a wriggling purple hatchling in his arms. His excitement built even further.

He watched his parents walk down to take their places in the hot, crowded marketplace below. There were no stalls today. Instead, the tiers were packed with people in steep rows, as if they were in a theatre, about to watch a play. Ceremonial flags fluttered, showing the symbols of Arcosi and Sartola. And there in the centre, like a stage, an empty sunlit circle waited for the dragons and the eggs to arrive. Joe's stomach started tangling itself in knots of anticipation.

'Joe!'

He turned to see his friends rushing towards him, also wearing white. They must have arrived earlier. He was glad they were all Potentials together.

'Happy birthday!' That was Amina, fizzing with energy, pushing her way towards him, wearing a new white headscarf to match the robes.

'Amina!' The day seemed even brighter to Joe suddenly.

Conor followed more slowly, and gave him a light shove. 'Just cos it's your birthday, doesn't mean you'll get the first dragon, all right?'

'Course not!' Joe grinned at Conor. 'But I might!'

'Potentials!' A dragonguard called them all to attention. 'The eggs will be arriving soon. Not long now: be patient and get in position.'

'Ah, this bit takes longer than you think,' Amina said impatiently, shuffling and bouncing on her toes. 'I remember from the last ceremony. They daren't rush the carriage in case they jolt the eggs. There's time to give you your presents!'

'Now?' Joe said. 'But they're about to call us through.' Nothing else mattered, next to that.

'Nah, last time they took ages,' Conor said. 'Happy birthday, Joe.' He took a bundle from his pocket and passed it over. 'Careful. Don't lose your thumb. I know how clumsy you are, mate.'

Joe unwrapped a soft leather pouch. He opened it and took out a small knife with a bone handle carved with a dragon's head pouring flame.

'Me and my dad found it on a trading trip last winter,' Conor said. 'I've been saving it for you.'

'Wow!' Joe tested the blade on his thumb. 'Ouch. It's sharp!' A red bubble of blood swelled up.

'Told you, idiot,' Conor teased.

'Oi.' Joe sheathed the blade and elbowed Conor.

'He means *thank you*,' Amina said.

'Thank you, Conor. I do mean it.' He tucked the knife carefully in the inside pocket of his white jacket.

'My turn!' Amina said, and took out a tiny parcel wrapped in purple silk. She handed it over. The sunlight turned her eyes amber-gold and made her brown skin glow against the pale scarf. Her smile was very wide and very white. She hugged him quickly and said, 'I made it for you.'

'Thank you.' Joe was touched. The bundle fell open in a

18

blur of jewel-bright colours. On the small piece of fabric was woven a purple dragon in flight against a background of deep blue, with a border of multi-coloured hexagonal shapes all interlinked.

Another purple dragon! It was a sign. 'It's amazing,' he said. 'Really!'

'When did you get so good, Amina?' Conor leaned over, sounding impressed.

'I've been doing it in the evenings when the day's work's done.'

'It must have taken ages!' Joe said.

Amina's cheeks grew rosy pink. 'That blue, that's made with indigo from the Silk Islands.' Her family of weavers had come from there and settled on Arcosi a few generations back. 'And I blended the red myself, from madder root . . .'

Joe folded it carefully, putting it in his other pocket. The day felt even more special. He wanted to say how lucky he was. How good it felt to have friends who knew him like Conor and Amina did. 'You two! It's . . . I'm . . . you know?' The words failed him, and he just stood there grinning at them. 'Thank you.'

'You're welcome,' Conor said, grinning back.

'Five minutes!' the dragonguard yelled at them. 'Final positions, please!'

In silence, they all stared towards the end of the street. They'd rehearsed for this. They knew what would happen, but it was still awe-inspiring.

Every head turned to watch the procession of dragons

and the egg-carriage rolling slowly down the wide main street that circled the island like a snake.

Joe caught a glimpse of Ravenna, the mother dragon, striding just in front of the dragonguards pulling the carriage. As she passed the end of the street, she filled the gap entirely. Joe saw her black wings folded, her long scaly back, her claws sparking against the cobbles. As if she sensed him, she turned her huge head, glared at him through yellow eyes and hissed.

He gasped. He'd known mother dragons were protective, but it was a whole different matter when it was aimed at him.

There was no time left: they started walking too, following the procession down the main street. Joe looked over the heads of the others, realising he was the tallest one there.

Conor was in front of him, his red-brown curls blowing themselves into new tangles as they walked. Behind him was Amina, jigging with impatience.

Now Joe could see his brother and sister down in the middle of the marketplace. Half-siblings, really, but there were no half measures about it in Joe's eyes. He adored them both.

His brother, Isak, was Head Dragonguard, famous for having read every book in the city library. Tall and calm, with white hair and black-rimmed eyeglasses, Isak stood now with the mother dragon and her covered clutch of eggs. They were circled by all the adult dragons on Arcosi – a dozen in total.

Next, his eyes fell on his sister, Tarya, standing next to

her husband, Duke Vigo. Tarya was the island's general, and she'd led its forces to victory in the revolution when Vigo had become duke, thirteen years earlier.

Joe noticed that his sister looked tired. Tarya's wild blonde curls were plaited close against her scalp, in the dragonrider style. She wore her sword at her hip, her ceremonial armour and arm-guards. She'd always been his fierce, capable sister, but now her face was grey-white. They all knew the reason for this: she'd just announced her pregnancy. She bit her lip as if she was fighting sickness. His mother had told her it was normal and she would start feeling stronger soon. Joe hoped for her sake that Tarya wouldn't be sick right here – she'd hate that.

Next to Tarya stood Rosa, her second-in-command and old friend, with her huge orange dragon, Ando. Everyone expected Rosa to take over from the general while she cared for her new baby; some were surprised it hadn't happened already.

'Wait!' the dragonguard with the Potentials called.

Joe and the others paused just outside the marketplace. Any moment now, the duke would start the ceremony, and then they would file into the empty space to take their positions.

He felt his whole body buzzing with excitement and impatience.

Just then someone wormed into the space between Joe and Amina, and leaned forward to murmur, 'Feeling lucky, birthday boy?'

It was Noah, from Joe's group at the city's school, where

all the children of Arcosi went for a few years at least. He was small and wiry, with a thin freckled face, and light brown hair that flopped over his eyes. He was also wearing the white clothes of a Potential.

'What are you doing here?' Joe's heart sank. 'I thought you hated the duke and my sister.'

Noah's father had been one of the soldiers out of a job when the dragons came. He'd been killed last year in a street brawl, and Noah blamed Vigo and Tarya for taking away his father's job, his pride and his life.

Joe and his friends had tried to be kind to Noah as he grieved, but he didn't make it easy.

'Yeah, so?' Noah narrowed his eyes and glared in the duke's direction. 'Why should I miss out on a dragon?'

Conor and Amina exchanged a wary glance.

'All right, Noah.' Conor turned to the younger boy, saying mildly, 'Well, it's up to the dragons now, they will choose who they want.'

'I'm a true Norlander, not a halfie like Joe, or incomers like you two. Of course a dragon will choose me.'

Before the revolution, under the old duke, people of Norlander descent had been the most privileged and wealthy.

'Ah, no one cares about that now,' Joe said, biting down a stronger retort. He'd inherited both his father's blue eyes and his mother's black hair, while his skin was light brown. Sometimes people guessed his ancestry wrong. But he'd never been insulted like this before, not to his face at least. '*Halfie?*' he repeated, trying to laugh it off. 'Did you think of that one?' It sounded ridiculous.

'That's what you think!' Noah said. 'You just wait and—'

One of the dragonguards was coming over, frowning. They all fell silent. None of them wanted to be excluded. Not now, at the last possible moment.

'What are they waiting for? Call us through already!' Noah muttered when the dragonguard had moved on.

Joe peered forward to see what was happening.

Isak was speaking to the eggs' mother, the fierce black dragon Ravenna, who was bonded to Lanys, the young woman who was hunched stiffly, scowling at them all.

Was there a problem? Joe studied Lanys: her freckled face was white with worry, purplish shadows under her eyes, auburn hair braided tightly back, tension in every muscle. He guessed it must be tough, watching your dragon incubating her clutch, unable to help, unable to go near her. Brooding mothers were dangerous, everyone knew that. Their protective instincts were powerful, and they would hurt or kill anyone who came too near their eggs.

There was a rumour that someone had once destroyed an egg in the early days of the return of the dragons. The mother dragon had reacted, lethally, before anyone could stop it. Looking at Ravenna, Joe realised with a shock that the other dragons were there to protect the Potentials, not the eggs.

Let us through, he thought as he looked at Lanys. *Just let us bond with the baby dragons, and you can have your Ravenna back.*

As if she heard him, Lanys turned and frowned more deeply at all the waiting Potentials.

Finally Isak stopped speaking to Ravenna, straightened up and raised his voice. 'Welcome to the Sixth Hatching Ceremony of Duke Vigo's reign . . .'

Applause rang out then, and cheers echoed around the marketplace.

This was it. The moment Joe had waited for all his life.

CHAPTER THREE

The time had come. Joe stood on his toes to see the dragon eggs revealed.

Duke Vigo stepped forward now. He looked serious and distant. Not the calm, kind man Joe knew from family gatherings. The duke's deep voice carried right to the back of the crowd. 'Citizens of Arcosi, guests from Sartola, I bid you most welcome.'

Everyone turned to look at Isak's partner, Luca, the King of Sartola, who was standing in the front row beside Tarya. Luca smiled and nodded at this welcome, raising one hand to wave at the crowds.

'We are fortunate to be blessed with this clutch,' Duke Vigo went on. 'As you know, this is a sacred ceremony, protected by law.' The duke looked fierce as he spoke the formal warning, and there was total silence for a moment.

Joe wondered if this was aimed at the Brotherhood. He had a quick look round, but he couldn't see anyone wearing black.

Then the duke smiled, like the sun coming out from behind a cloud, and his face changed entirely: 'Let the ceremony begin!'

Isak lifted the protective covering from the eggs.

There were five eggs! Joe counted and re-counted to be sure.

The whole marketplace was filled with a soft twittering of anticipation mixed with awe.

Five eggs. Ten Potentials. Half of them would be going to the dragonhall. Half would be going home miserable. Joe held his breath and prayed it wouldn't be him, Conor or Amina.

There was a tawny-cream egg, a blue-green egg, a golden yellow and, unusually, two the same colour: both pale lilac. That was a kind of purple – not the deep purple from his dreams, exactly, but close enough.

I'm coming, he said silently to the eggs, to the dragons waiting inside.

Milla was standing in the front row behind her enormous blue dragon. She leaned round Iggie's neck to smile at Joe and mouth at him, 'Good luck!'

Still no one moved.

What was the delay? Joe rubbed his neck, feeling the sun hot on his skin. He started to itch with impatience. His face was on fire. He studied the crowd to calm himself and his gaze snagged on the only face looking stricken. It was Winter, one of the Dragonless. Her dragon had died two years ago in the Great Loss. Some of the Dragonless had died then too. Most had fled the island, unable to live with the constant reminders of what they'd lost. Only she remained.

There were rumours of a ghost in the ruined north-west quarter of the island – the shadow strip – but Joe's parents always said it was just Winter, in her grey dress and dark cloak, emerging from the shadows and vanishing again.

Her mother still lived in the lower town, but Winter wandered the streets day and night, talking to her dead dragon, Jin. People were kind, steering her home, giving her food, but she was gaunt and ragged as a scarecrow, looking much older than her fourteen years.

Usually her grey eyes looked right through everyone. Today though, Winter's gaze fell on Joe, and what Joe read there was too much to bear. He saw unimaginable pain, fathom-deep. He had to look away.

'Potentials! Come and sit in a circle. Not too near. Give the eggs space.' Isak was calling them forward, finally.

The crowd seemed to hold its breath then. All eyes were on them. Conor led the way.

Joe had forgotten how to walk. His whole body had turned to lead. He could feel the weight of everyone staring at him.

Amina nudged him forwards gently.

He started to move, hot and clumsy. He stepped on Conor's heel, making him swear.

Then he halted abruptly, and Amina slammed into the back of him.

'Joe! Not now,' she whispered.

'Sorry! Sorry!' he muttered to them both, his heart racing.

Finally they were there, at the front. Ravenna growled lightly.

'Spread out, a whole circle, no one any nearer than anyone else!' Isak reminded them, pointing to their places. 'Now sit!'

Joe sank down on legs that shook with excitement. He could feel the sweat trickling down his spine.

Amina sat very straight, solemn for once.

Conor looked lit up from within.

Joe cast a glance round the circle, checking the faces of his competition. They looked serious or eager or nervous. All except Noah, opposite, who was glaring at him.

Joe looked away, focusing on the eggs.

In the silence that followed, there came a distinct, crisp *crack*.

CHAPTER FOUR

The first dragon hatched from the blue-green egg. It poked its head out of the crack, a shiny dark green, and then suddenly it fell out, panting, as the egg broke in two. It looked like a small lizard, with an extra mass on its back, where its wings were folded up. Joe was on his knees, leaning forwards, listening hard. *Come on, dragon, choose me! Here I am!* he willed it, in spite of his dream. He didn't mind what colour his dragon was. At other ceremonies, he'd seen children sing or whistle or call to a hatchling. He tried to tell if there was anything like that bubbling up in him. But he could only hear a dull buzz in his ears.

Then the oldest boy, Tiago, spoke from the other side of the circle. 'Lina!' he called out. 'Li-na!' His round open face was focused entirely on this dragon. He had a patchy beard on his cheeks and chin, and big brown eyes, brimming with tears.

Joe held his breath to see if he was bluffing. But no. The

little green dragon sprang to life at his call and tried to respond in the same rhythm.

Isak made his judgement: 'Tiago, you may go to Lina. Feed her. Keep her warm.'

Joe felt it in his chest, as if he'd been winded.

Four eggs left.

The creamy-brown egg hatched next. A tiny little hole was chipped out of the top. He could see the dragon's egg-tooth – the little bump on the top of its nose – tapping through from inside.

This time, it was the smallest of all of them: Flavia, a tiny Sartolan girl a few places over to Joe's left, who looked barely old enough to be here. She had skinny sparrow legs and enormous eyes, with black hair cropped short to her neck. She sang out to the baby dragon, a surprisingly deep, trilling song. And even before it had fully emerged, this dragon stuck its head out of its eggshell and chirruped back.

They all had to wait painful long minutes, while it slowly fought its way free and the little girl scooped it up. She had to go past Joe, Conor and Amina, and he saw his friends' expressions, as crushed as he felt. At least they were in this together. Just for a moment, he let himself picture the three of them afterwards, talking it over, comforting each other.

Joe didn't look at Noah.

Two young people held two young dragons, cooing and feeding them scraps of chicken from a tray, and letting them drink spring water from little silver bowls. Isak watched everything, his blue eyes unreadable behind his glasses. Almost halfway there. There was a hushed murmur from the crowd: relief still mixed with anticipation. This was a sacred ceremony and no one would move until Isak spoke the closing words.

Joe looked again at the other Potentials, all except Noah. They were huddled in their places in the circle: some looked desperate now; others determined. He couldn't think of them. He fixed his eyes on the final three eggs. He wiped his damp forehead and realised his hands were trembling, so he sat on them.

He could hear something: another one of the eggs was hatching.

With a sharp tap from within, a large zigzag split the yellow shell.

Then, with a *crack*, the egg broke into three pieces. A small damp body was wriggling there among the fragments.

'Oh!' Joe gasped.

Slowly, slowly, the dark yellow dragon pushed itself up onto four legs, and lifted its little head to listen. It turned in Joe's direction.

Through glittering green eyes, it gazed right at him.

What could he do? What could he say? What did this creature need? Joe prayed it would be him. He had so much to give.

Before Joe could do anything, Noah started whistling a three-note tune, and the dragon turned away from Joe to stare at him instead. Noah's face was transformed by concentration, leaning forwards, his honey-coloured hair falling across one eye, his cheeks pulled tight as he whistled.

No, it couldn't be. Not him. Anyone but him.

Surely this dragon wouldn't listen to Noah?

Noah was just pretending. He must be.

Joe tried to remember a tune, any tune, something from music class. His mind went blank. No, not now, when he needed it most.

'Please?' he begged in a whisper.

The world held its breath. Everyone in the whole city watched and waited.

The yellow dragon inhaled.

Joe could see its scaly ribs, glistening with egg sheen.

It chirped the three notes back at Noah.

Noah laughed and opened his hands, as the dragon started crawling towards him. Then he spared a moment to shoot a glance at Joe: full of triumph.

Joe knew he should feel some compassion. Noah had lost his father: didn't he deserve a dragon of his own? He inhaled slowly, trying to smother his envy and kindle some kindness for his classmate.

There were still two eggs.

Joe stared at them. He poured all his thoughts in that direction: all his focus, all his love, all his strength.

The pale purple eggs waited on their cushions.

Come on, eggs. Can you hear me? He willed it, harder than anything he'd ever felt before. Surely one of these was his? His dream had told him so.

Just then, the purple eggs started to move.

It was time for the remaining two dragons to hatch.

CHAPTER FIVE

There was a pause. It lasted years. Joe's heart thumped painfully in his chest.

He stared at the lilac-coloured eggs. They were rocking slightly. He wasn't the only one who noticed. An excited ripple passed through the crowd. The rocking increased. Both eggs were moving rhythmically, back and forth, back and forth.

Joe stole a glance at Isak: even he looked surprised. This hadn't happened before.

Suddenly the pale purple eggs rolled towards each other and collided with a crunch, shattering apart. Joe craned his neck to see.

'Oh!' That was Conor, over to Joe's right, sounding more excited than he'd ever heard him.

'Careful!' That was Amina, sitting to his left, her face more tender and gentle than he'd ever seen before.

From the broken shards, the dragons emerged and this

time they headed for each other. Their bodies became entwined, squirming, damp, palest purple.

As one, Joe's best friends responded, calling out two different names in the same instant.

'*Maric!*' said Amina.

'*Ariel!*' called Conor.

No, no, no. Joe's heart twisted violently, in envy and bitter disappointment.

The dragons listened to his friends. Like mirror images of each other, they lifted their heads and opened their mouths to mew hoarsely in reply.

Isak glanced at Milla, who gave a tiny tilt of her head, then Isak nodded to Amina and Conor in his turn. Joe's brother awarded the purple dragons to his friends.

Amina and Conor scrambled up and lifted the two lilac dragons to their hearts.

And just like that, it was all over.

Joe's dreams were over.

Five children nursed five baby dragons.

Joe sat there, his hands empty, feeling his heart crack. No dragon wanted him.

Lanys threw herself at Ravenna, tears pouring down her face. 'Ravenna, you're back. Oh, well done, well done, you brilliant dragon.'

'Lanys, you were supposed to await my word,' Isak called out, sounding tense. 'Now you may welcome back your dragon.'

Lanys scowled at him mutinously, but then Ravenna pressed her huge black scaly head against her person's chest, to be embraced, praised, thanked, and she was lost in the reunion.

Joe found himself on his feet, swaying slightly.

The others turned to him, puzzled. There was a heartbeat of time when he teetered there on the edge. He could pull back, sit down, apologise, let the ceremony continue.

But he didn't.

It wasn't fair. What about him? What about his dream?

Why didn't any dragon want him?

He would have done anything, given everything. He needed a dragon so badly it hurt. He'd never wanted anything else. He couldn't do anything else, or be anything else. He was born to be a dragonrider. So why did none of the dragons want him?

His future was a slammed door, leaving him bewildered.

He couldn't bear to see Conor and Amina sitting there, their lives secure for ever now. And they didn't even need this! They had other plans, working with their families, all laid out. And most of all, he couldn't look at Noah.

'*Sit down*, Jowan!' Isak ordered.

No one ever used Joe's full name.

'We're not finished.' Isak looked stonily at him.

Joe hardly heard him. He stood there, legs trembling.

Noah sniggered in the silence, and whispered, 'Happy birthday, Joe,' just loud enough for him to hear.

From that spark, Joe's fury and disappointment swelled, then exploded. It burned like wildfire, out of control. He felt rage, fiery and vengeful, boiling up like lava and poisoning all his thoughts.

'I'm going!' The words were out before Joe knew it. He heard all the other Potentials gasp, heard it echo round the wider crowd.

'You must sit down, Joe. Right now,' Isak said tightly.

'I'm FINISHED!' he shouted. 'I've had enough!' Joe saw his parents' faces in a blur: aghast, humiliated, the opposite of proud. Well, they didn't need to worry about him any more: he was leaving.

He started blundering away, blinded by tears of anger.

'No!' a voice squeaked by his feet. It was Flavia, the little Sartolan girl, huddling away from him, clutching the cream-coloured dragon to her chest.

For one awful moment, he imagined stamping on the girl and her dragon, pictured his feet crushing the hatchling's tender limbs. He wanted to make someone hurt the way he was hurting, lost in the white-heat of his rage.

The little girl whimpered in fright, and the tiny dragon tumbled from her arms, right into Joe's path.

Joe snarled in response, standing over the baby dragon. He drew back his right leg.

He heard a deep growl behind him and felt the air grow warm as Ravenna kindled flame in her chest. *No!* How did she know? He hadn't done it. He hadn't done anything. The heat built up, but Joe couldn't move.

'No!' a new voice shrieked. 'Stop her kindling, Lanys! Do it now. Stop her!'

From the corner of his eye, he saw his cousin Milla rushing forwards, putting herself between him and a potential blast of flame from this protective mother dragon.

'*Hold*, Ravenna!' Lanys cried to her dragon. 'Stop it.'

But it was too late: the black dragon had already kindled and her chest was blushing with flame. She opened her mouth and the fire burst out.

Joe was glued to the spot. The flames rushed towards him. At the last moment, he flinched away, bending low, hands over head. He felt the heat bite his skin, smelled the sharp acrid stink of burning hair. He rolled and slapped the flames out before real damage was done.

From the corner of his eye, he saw Milla leaning in and pushing the black dragon's head upwards, so that the jet of flame shot straight up into the air.

'*Aie!*' Milla screamed, ducking down and plunging her fingers into a bowl of spring water. She'd burned herself, touching Ravenna's throat. She'd burned herself saving Joe's life.

The other dragons crowded close, circling Milla, while Iggie sprang to her defence. Iggie growled and bared his teeth, furious with Ravenna for hurting Milla. They faced off: blue dragon and black dragon, wings spread, jaws open.

Ravenna flamed again.

Iggie ducked his huge head, just in time, and the flag behind him caught fire.

The sacred ceremony fell into chaos. Children started crying. People turned to flee, screaming, bunching up so tightly that some got crushed in the stampede.

Isak was gathering all the newly bonded and their hatchlings to him, and his dragon, Belara, joined him now to protect them, golden wings spread wide.

Duke Vigo was bellowing for calm, but the smoke made him cough and his words were lost.

Tarya and Rosa both had their swords drawn. They were shouting orders to their troops, marching in from the sides of the square, but the dragons blocked their way. They couldn't reach those who needed them most.

'Help!' a desperate voice cried. 'My son! He's getting trampled! Get back. Oh, help us!'

But no one listened as the crowd surged away, trying to escape the dragons and the fire.

And suddenly the Brotherhood were there, black-clad men at the back of the marketplace. Some were hauling people up to safety, while others shouted insults at Duke Vigo and Joe's sister.

'Some duke you are!' one called. 'Letting this happen? You're not fit to rule.'

'A general who can't calm her kid brother?' yelled another. 'She can't lead an army, not in her state, not ever!'

One of them stood apart, watching Joe, watching the chaos.

Joe had done this. Shame filled him and fuelled his escape. He pushed through the panicking crowd, moving against the tide, away from the city. People turned from him. Their faces told him he was a monster. Horrified, he shouldered his way through, faster and faster, his breath coming in gasps, his whole body surging with fiery anger and remorse.

His new white jacket ripped. He was glad. These ridiculous clothes marked him out for what he was now: a failure. A *waddler*. He was leaving. He couldn't go home, not now, not after seeing his parents' horror-stricken faces. He couldn't ever follow his friends to the dragonhall, not without a dragon of his own.

Joe rushed away from the ceremony he'd ruined, knowing that what he had done was something he could never take back.

CHAPTER SIX

Joe didn't know where he was going. Driven by anger and guilt, he ran on, on, on, through the deserted docks of Arcosi baking in the hot sun. He'd never seen the city so quiet. The only noise was his clattering footsteps, echoing round the narrow, twisting streets.

He reached the edge of the city, where the houses and shops gave way to warehouses overlooking the harbour. His father still owned some of these. He couldn't think about him now. He pushed on, further west, to where the buildings ended. He crossed the shallow beach where he'd learned to swim, his tired feet slowed by the soft golden sand. He had only good memories of this place – playing in the surf; chasing shoals of little silver fish through clear blue sea; swimming right out to the ancient weathered rocks that edged the beach, their worn arches like a sea serpent's coils turned to stone. But today the beauty of the place only taunted him. It belonged to his past life, and that was gone.

He turned and began to climb up the rocky headland, till he knew he was invisible from the beach. He didn't stop till he was deep in the wildest part of the island. There, perched high on the steep slope, he finally stopped. He had used up all his anger. He felt finished.

He could hear nothing except the cries of distant gulls. He could see nothing but sea and sky, feel only the springy grass and rock beneath him. Then he curled up in a tight ball and covered his head with his injured hands. His skin was on fire, burning with agony, but it felt like a fitting punishment. His hope was crushed. His future was gone. He didn't even know who he was any more. Someone who turned from his friends? Someone who couldn't be glad for them? Someone who thought of killing a baby dragon and caused harm to innocent people? He couldn't forget the look in their eyes as they ran in terror.

Joe lay there for hours, till the sky turned violet and full of shadows, warning of a storm.

Eventually he found the energy to sit up, feeling like a sea-scoured shell; so empty, he was barely there. He swallowed hard. His throat hurt. His lips were cracked and dry. He was hungry and desperately thirsty. He felt through his pockets, but he had nothing to eat.

He looked around him. Further to the north, there were some small, shrubby bushes. He crawled over, and saw with relief the orange clusters of sea-buckthorn berries, clinging to the wind-gnarled branches. He tore them off – bitter sourness bursting in his mouth – till his stomach ached and his burned fingers were bloody from the spikes between the fruit. His head cleared after he'd eaten, just enough to think about the next step. If he was going to survive – and a small stubborn instinct told him he must – he had to find shelter for the night.

Above him there was a rocky overhang with black shadows pooling underneath. Was it a cave? As he looked, a fragment of shadow detached itself and flew in a crazy, skittering loop in the dark blue sky. A bat! So it must be a cave. It would be dry and safe.

Joe clambered up, towards the dark mouth of the cave. The last part was very steep, and he didn't dare look back. With burning arms and wobbling legs, he dragged himself up, till grass became gravel then rock under his fingertips. The cave mouth was larger than he expected, so he stood up and walked in. Eyes wide in the pitch-black, he could see nothing. He felt as if he'd gone blind. But it was dry and cool inside, sandy underfoot. He stopped and listened. He felt the quality of the space change. The air on his face was moving. Beyond the entrance, this cave was large.

'Argh!' Something brushed past his face. His heart was pounding so loud he couldn't think past it. *It's a bat*, he told himself. *Just another bat*. When his heart calmed, he heard them from over to his right, a busy, distant sound. A thousand high-pitched squeaks. There must be a whole colony of bats in there. He didn't mind. He liked birds and animals; he'd always found them easier than people.

Joe had no light and he didn't want to get lost, so he didn't go far. The cave widened and there was a bed of sand to his left. He knelt and patted his way round the curve in

42

the rock. It was just big enough for him. A boy-shaped bed for the night. He let himself collapse on it. Finally the terrible day was over.

When Joe woke, moonlight was streaming in through the entrance to the cave. He groaned, stiff and cold, the burned skin on his neck and hands still flaring painfully. He made himself crawl back outside, then stood and stretched the cramp from his legs and shook himself awake again. It was almost as light as day, the full moon shining down, casting a pearly reflection on the inky-dark sea. This was the perfect chance, he realised numbly. He could go back home without being seen.

He felt like a ghost, slipping through the empty streets. He saw only a cat and, once, a shadow flickering at the corner of his eye, but when he turned there was nothing there. He avoided the main gate by climbing up the back wall, into the garden. He fell on his knees by the kitchen well. He thrust his hands under the pure cold water and kept them there till the burning finally stopped. Then Joe filled a bucket and drank the whole thing greedily, spilling it down himself, till his stomach complained. Afterwards, he stood and looked around.

He could hear the quiet murmur of the night watchman talking to someone at the main gate.

The house was quiet, the lights out. Everyone must be asleep.

He could go to his parents and beg forgiveness.

But then he remembered what he'd done.

And what he'd almost done.

No. He found himself unable to move.

Today, he'd meant to make them proud. Instead, he'd brought shame on them, and on his sister and brother.

After today, his family was better off without him.

He saw it now. He was the odd one out. His parents had Tarya, the island's general. They had Isak, its Head Dragonguard. They had Milla, heir to the ancient bloodline of Arcosi, who'd planned the revolution that brought Duke Vigo to power. They didn't need a disgrace like Joe, a spoiled, angry child. No. Until he had done something worthwhile, something to make up for today, he had to stay away.

He pushed open the kitchen door and sneaked into the storeroom. He grabbed a pastry and shoved it in his mouth, eating so fast he almost choked on it. He took a soft leather backpack and filled it with food: cheese, dried meat, raisins. He found an empty flask and filled it with water from the well. He took one of the storm lanterns and its spare oil.

What else did he need? *The shipwreck kit.* He risked the main door and slipped inside the house, soft moonlight showing him the way up to his room.

Where was it? Joe searched in the gloom till his hands fell on the cylinder. He looped the strap round his shoulders, ready to leave.

His gaze fell on the purple hat and dragonrider gloves, laid out there, waiting for a life that would never happen. He'd dreamed of a future that wasn't his. He didn't deserve it, just like he didn't deserve these white robes. He tugged at the ripped jacket, throwing it off, dressing himself in his warmest old clothes. The gifts from Conor and Amina fell on the floor, and he almost left them. At the last moment, he stuffed them in his pockets, then he headed for the door.

Something stopped him.

He should tell them he was alive, at least. But how?

His fingers went to the chain around his neck where the small silver medal dangled, the birthday gift from Milla. He unfastened it now.

One day, maybe he would earn it back. Till then, he didn't deserve to wear it any more. He was a disgrace to his family. The black sheep, the waddler, the monster.

He laid the chain on top of the purple gloves and left, clutching the shipwreck kit close.

He padded down the main stairs, listening hard. The house creaked in its old familiar way, telling him it was empty. So where were his parents? He heard voices in the garden. He crept through the front doors and hid in the shadows, waiting for his chance to climb down the steep wall behind the practice yard.

'What did he say?' one voice asked. It was Matteo, the cook.

Why was Matteo still awake when he always rose before dawn? It wasn't like him: he'd be too tired to cook tomorrow.

'Ah, still looking – they'll be out all night.' That was the night watchman, Gabriel, who stood sentry duty at the main gates each night. His father kept him on, unable to give up his old habits, even now the island was safe and peaceful again.

Looking for who? For him? Joe's heart beat faster, and he strained to hear over the blood pounding in his ears. He hated to think of his father, tired and disappointed, still out there searching for his disgraced son.

'Bad business.' Gabriel hissed through his teeth.

'Didn't see it, but he's a good lad, Joe. He wouldn't mean any harm,' Matteo defended him.

'Huh,' Gabriel tutted. 'Mean it or not, he caused it. Plenty were harmed today. The healers don't know if the crushed boy will live. No, Joe will have to answer for it.'

'I heard the Brotherhood made the most of it.'

'Aye, and maybe they should. Maybe they've got a point.'

'That's serious trouble for his sister and the duke.' Their voices faded as they turned away from Joe.

He wanted the ground to open up and gobble him down. Had he caused the death of a child? The idea was unbearable. The whole island must hate him now, and who could blame them?

He couldn't hear the next mumbled words as the men moved away, but he heard the final part all right.

'He'd be dead if it weren't for the Lady Milla. Maybe it'd be better for his folks if he were.' Gabriel spoke Joe's worst fears out loud.

He stopped breathing.

Is that what people thought?

Hearing it in someone else's voice made it true and real

in a way that sliced right through him. *It would be better if he were dead.*

In one day, his whole life had burned away, leaving nothing but ash and disappointment behind. Not caring who saw him now, Joe fled from his parents' home, knowing he'd never be able to return.

CHAPTER SEVEN

J oe was never quite sure what happened next. If he'd been burning with anger at the ceremony, now he was left frozen and numb with shock, blundering through a nightmare. Strong winds brought sheeting rain. Later, he'd see the bruises and scrapes, his clothes ripped and soaked in mud, so he must have run, climbed, fallen. He vaguely recalled his hellish tour of the harbour in the pouring rain, begging each captain in turn for passage off the island. Two things made that impossible: he had no money, and each sailor took one glance at him and knew he was Nestan's son. They told him to go home and tell his parents he was safe. Their voices weren't angry, but their eyes told another story: distant and disappointed, they wanted nothing to do with him.

He was trapped.

His life on the island was over, but he couldn't leave.

Again, he ran.

As dawn broke, he came to himself, like waking from a

bad dream. He was standing on a grassy ledge on the north-west clifftops of Arcosi, alone.

A gusty wind blew, spattering his face with raindrops in a way that felt personal. The sky was mottled grey and full of moisture. He looked down: far, far below him, the jagged rocks gave way to deep water. From here it appeared blackish-blue, and very cold.

He stared down again and imagined a way out. He was already so overwhelmed by his shame that the idea of being free of it, even like this, seemed appealing.

He'd have to leap out, to be sure. He wanted it to be quick. He tried to imagine the pain, but he found it was impossible.

He shivered. He didn't really want to die – he just wanted to start again, be someone else. Someone better.

What took more courage? To live or to die? He couldn't tell any more. He was so tired.

He closed his eyes, gathering himself.

Just then, the sun heaved itself over the horizon into a narrow gap between clouds. Joe felt the light change. Behind his eyelids, the world turned deep purple, the purple of his dreams.

The purple of the dragon he didn't have.

It wasn't painful. It was comforting.

Joe stood there trembling, eyes closed, basking in the purple glow. And he felt the first tiny twist of hope. There was something out there, waiting for him. It might be an illusion, caused by lack of sleep, but he clung to it. Maybe even monsters were allowed to dream.

He *could* start again, but he would have to do it the hard way. If he wanted to be someone better, that was up to him. And if he started now, maybe one day he'd be able to hold his head high again.

Maybe one day he'd be able to go home.

Slowly, slowly, he opened his eyes, sticky with tears and salt. He fell to his knees, feeling the sodden grass, cool under his scorched fingertips. He pushed back from the edge of the cliff and let himself cry at last. Deep, racking sobs shook his whole body, spread-eagled on the earth.

He wept for the strange and dangerous person he'd been today.

He wept out his anger and disappointment.

He wept out his jealousy and arrogance.

He wept out his shame and his sorrow.

He wept until there was nothing left.

He felt like a blank sheet of parchment, and it was a relief. Time to begin a new story.

Then he stumbled back to his hiding place in the cave. Somehow he still had his shipwreck kit and the lantern looped over his shoulders, but he had lost the bag of food.

Back at the cave mouth, he took a moment to light the storm lantern, noticing distantly that his burned fingers were shaking. He ignored that and lifted it high to cast a trembling golden pool of light. Now he could see the entrance to the cave clearly, with the little rounded curve at the side where he'd slept last night, and a larger cavern to the right that was full of roosting bats. He wrinkled his nose at the strong, distinctive smell. A few paces past both, there was a kind of doorway facing him. He went through and saw a wide flight of worn steps.

Steps?

Steps were made by someone. Steps led somewhere.

Hadn't he wanted a new path? Well, here it was. Not caring where it took him, Joe lifted the storm lantern and started down the stone stairs. The darkness didn't scare him. He put one hand to the inner wall: it felt cool and coarse. The air smelled of salt and damp and dust. The yellow circle of light held him safe as he walked down, down, down.

Joe came to the bottom step. The passage led away into the gloom. It was wide enough for him to walk with his arms outstretched, tall enough so he wouldn't bang his head. The walls had a gentle curve to them, as if carved by wind or rain, but it was too deep down here for either. The tunnel turned and Joe carried on, taking it slow and steady. He climbed, twisted, turned and turned, travelling up the tunnel like a rat.

He rounded a corner and halted, stunned.

He stood in a massive cavern reaching away in every direction, bigger than the great dining hall at the palace. He couldn't even see the roof, but it must have a hole in it, high above him, because a shaft of light fell down, piercing the darkness. He could hear rushing water too. A stream ran through the cavern, bubbling into a pool on the far eastern side before surging away out of sight. Joe went over and dipped one finger into the water. He sniffed, then licked it. The water tasted clean, with its usual metallic tang and a slight taste of sulphur. He cupped his hand and drank a mouthful, so cold that it hurt his teeth.

He took his time exploring the cave, finding it dry and roomy, dappled with light filtering down from far above. It was like a dragonhall underground, he realised with a painful wrench. He took a wavering breath in, accepting all he'd lost – and what he'd found. This secret place would be his alone. A home for a monster. A hidden kingdom beneath Arcosi. He could live here while he rebuilt his life. He could live down here for ever.

CHAPTER EIGHT

Joe slept in the huge underground cavern for the rest of that day. When he woke, he was freezing cold and utterly alone, and both those things took his breath away. For a moment he couldn't move. His clothes were wet. His knees and shins were covered in bruises, and now his burned fingertips were also bloodied and bashed, throbbing in a way that worried him.

He climbed awkwardly back through the tunnel and peered outside. Heavy rain blurred the beach into a grey smudge. Joe needed salt water to keep his wounds clean: Milla had taught him that years ago. Ignoring the stiffness in his legs, he threw himself outside, blinking hard, slipping down the steep hillside and onto the beach, heading for the sea. He took his shoes off, rolled up his trouser legs and shirt sleeves and walked right in, plunging his arms into the waves.

He gasped at the deeper cold and the sting of the salt

water. Soon his burns were entirely numb – along with the rest of his arms and both feet. His teeth started chattering. His wet clothes clung to him and the rain plastered his hair in his eyes.

He was ravenously hungry. Maybe one day he'd be able to catch fish or snare a rabbit, but not today, not in this state. He had no choice: he'd have to go back into the city to find food.

He waited until it was dark. The storm seemed to have passed, or at least the rain had finally paused for breath. Joe retraced his steps over the western beach, past the ware-houses and into the shadowy streets of Arcosi, looking for signs of life and the chance to steal some food. He followed the smell of woodsmoke and roasting meat until he came to a tall building that sounded full of people. If there was a party going on, they might not notice an uninvited guest.

Joe crept across the street, listening hard. He stared between a crack in the shutters, but saw only a jumble of bodies, nothing clear. He looked up, searching for some-thing to climb to get a better view, but the wall was smooth and high. Above him, a few stars were caught in a net of white cloud.

He strained to hear. There was loud cheering. There must be dozens of people in there.

'You look hungry. Drowned rat ain't the half of it.'

Joe spun round, finding himself face to face with a short burly man. He was standing like a soldier on the balls of his feet, holding a sword as if it weighed no more than a spoon.

'Yes, I mean, no, I mean . . . what do you mean?' Joe

babbled. He swayed, suddenly light-headed, shaking hard with cold.

'Steady on, lad,' the man said, holding him up with his free hand, smiling now. 'No need to panic.' He had receding white hair in two stripes either side of his scalp, making him look like a kindly badger. 'Anyone can see you need hot food and somewhere to dry off. Come on, with me.' He sheathed his sword and gestured for Joe to follow.

'Why? What is this place?' Joe remembered stories of young men being drugged, then forced onto ships to work as sailors. Hadn't he wanted that, to leave the island? Suddenly he wasn't so sure.

Before the man could answer him, someone stuck his head out of the window next to them, calling, 'Any stragglers, Yannic? Come on in, we're about to start.' This man's face loomed over them. He had short hair, silver in the moon-light, hollow stubbled cheeks, and a curving boat-shaped scar under one eye.

'Coming, Asa!' Yannic replied, steering Joe towards the double doors of the building. 'Come eat with us, and welcome. Our doors are always open to friends . . .'

He went to the door and knocked, three times, in a slow-quick-quick rhythm. With a squeak of rusty hinges, it opened up, letting out a warm flood of lamplight and the delicious savoury aroma of hot food. The man vanished inside.

The door started to close. Joe had to decide before it slammed in his face. His stomach grumbled painfully, making his decision for him. 'Wait!' he called. 'I'm coming too.' He'd worry about everything else when he'd eaten.

He went through the doors, finding himself in a small lobby with bare wooden boards and a staircase winding up to the left. There were two strangers studying him suspiciously, standing guard in front of large doors with ornate brass handles.

'Armed?' one demanded, patting Joe down roughly.

'Just this.' Joe took out the dragon-handled knife that Conor had given him on his birthday. He felt a sudden pang for everything he'd lost since yesterday morning.

The shorter man took it, adding it to the deep shelves under the stairs, which were filled with an alarming assortment of weapons.

'Don't look so worried, lad.' The other guard clapped him on the back, hard. 'We don't bite.' He pushed him towards the double doors. 'Not yet, anyway.'

With their laughter in his ears, Joe fumbled nervously with the door handle. He couldn't even get that right! Finally it opened, and he slipped through into the large, overcrowded room beyond.

The first thing he noticed was the heat: damp, sweaty and sour. There must have been a hundred or more men, and a few women, tightly packed, all facing forwards. He shuffled in and found himself wedged tightly between a tall ginger-bearded stranger, and a short bald man he vaguely recognised from Amina's neighbourhood. All were Norlanders, every single one.

He stood on tiptoe: he could just make out the man called Asa standing at the front of the room. There were a few benches and trestle tables at one side, laden with three large barrels that must contain ale, he guessed, by the strong yeasty smell in the air.

'Hey, hungry boy?' Yannic appeared, holding a wooden plate in one hand, piled with slices of sausage and dense dark bread, and a bowl of soup in the other.

Joe took the food, wobbly with relief. 'Thank you.'

'Sit there. Eat. I'll be back soon.' Yannic pointed to a bench at the back of the room and then vanished into the crowd.

Joe pushed his way to the bench, only spilling a bit of soup, and wolfed down the food, no longer caring if it was laced with something to make him sleep. If he woke and found himself on the deck of a strange ship, he'd consider it a fair trade right now.

Asa's voice carried, loud and clear. 'Now, let's begin our evening in the usual way.'

There was a smattering of applause, grunts of approval. Then, to Joe's surprise, everyone started singing. It was a traditional Norlander song about the sea, and Joe half remembered it.

The nearest man seemed to be glaring down at him, so Joe mumbled along, trying not to stand out.

'Hey, you,' the man said, leaning over and nudging his shoulder hard.

'What?' Joe asked, eating faster. If he was going to get thrown out, he wanted to get as much food down him as possible.

'You can't sing without a drink – take this!' And he passed Joe a slopping cup of something frothy.

'Er, thanks!' Joe took it and gulped a mouthful. He'd

stolen a taste of ale from his father's mug before, and recognised the strong bitter flavour. He found himself slowly
relaxing, warmed by the ale and the food and the company.
Maybe he wasn't alone after all. Maybe there was a place for
him here, with these people. They seemed open and kind.
He sang louder.

When the song finished, everyone started moving around,
looking for friends in the crowd. Joe was deafened by the
yelling of names, cries of greeting.

He looked around as he chewed his bread, trying to work
out what this meeting was for. People were now huddled in
small groups, talking intently.

Yannic reappeared, holding an old blanket which he threw
around Joe's shoulders. 'Feeling better?' he asked, coming to
stand in front of him. He smiled again in a friendly enough
way, but Joe got the feeling he was trying to block his view.

'Uh-huh, thank you,' he mumbled through a mouthful of
sausage spiced with pepper. 'What is this?' he dared to ask
next, finding that the ale had loosened his tongue. 'I mean,
what's happening here?'

'Just friends, catching up,' Yannic said.

Joe was unconvinced; he had always been good at noticing
things, and this felt too organised to be a social gathering.
Each of the groups now had exactly twelve people in it and
there were at least ten different groups. 'You've got lots of
friends,' he said. 'And they're all Norlanders.' That was un-
usual on an island that was full of people from all over their
corner of the world and beyond.

'That's right,' Yannic chuckled. 'Curious little jackdaw,

aren't you?' He edged even closer, so all Joe could see was Yannic's generous stomach and the buckles on his leather belt. He'd kept his sword, he saw, while everyone else had had to leave theirs outside. So maybe he was in charge. 'What about you? What's your story?'

'No one cares about that now,' Joe told him gloomily, chasing the last crumbs on his plate. He hated the self-pity that crept into his voice.

'What if we do?' Asa suddenly reappeared, at Yannic's elbow. 'You are a Norlander, after all. Those blue eyes don't lie.'

They obviously didn't know who he was or what he'd done. They wouldn't be so friendly once they found out. 'What does that matter?' Joe asked clumsily. 'What's so great about Norlanders?'

They laughed as if he'd said something funny.

'We celebrate our heritage here,' Asa told him. 'We sing Norlander songs, eat Norlander food, tell the folk tales of our homelands.'

That sounded harmless enough. Joe nodded, but he hadn't finished.

'We are keeping the old ways alive, that's all.' Asa's face took on a flinty look now. 'So they don't get lost, with everything else . . .'

Now Joe had eaten, he felt more alert. With a jolt, he noticed something he should have seen immediately: Yannic and Asa and about half the people in the room were wearing tattered black clothes. Some had cloaks or jackets over the top, so he hadn't noticed before.

They were wearing the old army uniform, the one from *before*. The one from the old duke's reign. Suddenly he knew exactly who these people were and what he'd stumbled into – they all belonged to the Brotherhood! He cursed himself for his woolly-headedness earlier. He tried to keep his face steady.

'What's been lost?' he asked, hoping he sounded curious, not suspicious.

'Ah, we've all lost something, Jowan Thornsen,' Yannic said slowly. 'Time's coming for us to take it back.'

So they did know who he was! Joe flushed with shame. He knew the Brotherhood wanted to cause trouble for his sister and the duke. Would they hurt him to get to her? He focused with difficulty on what the men were saying.

'We were in the last duke's army, in the old days, when this island was properly run, with Norlanders in charge,' Yannic said, puffing up his chest.

And just like that, the warm friendly atmosphere vanished.

Joe didn't answer. Milla had told him how hard it used to be, for anyone who *wasn't* Norlander. She'd said the old days had been unfair and unequal.

'Not this shambles we all saw yesterday,' Yannic went on. 'A woman can't be a general – we all saw her fail to restore calm.'

'That was my fault, not my sister's!' Joe felt hot and squirmed uncomfortably on the hard bench. Everything took on a sinister light now he knew he didn't belong. Exactly what were they doing here? What were they planning?

'Not so,' Asa growled.

Joe waited. What would they do, now they knew who he was, now they knew he was only a – what had Noah said? – a *halfie*? Now Joe thought of him, Noah did sound a bit like the Brotherhood, always going on about the old days and how important Norlanders were.

'You had the courage to speak up,' Asa said to Joe. 'Then and now.' He paused a beat. 'We value that skill.'

Hardly listening any more, Joe looked around the room, trying to work out how he could escape. The back window would be his best route. He'd only have to get past more than a hundred people who had reason to resent him, first.

Asa was watching him, his blue eyes glittering in the lamplight. 'Right, that's enough for your first visit.'

Joe felt trapped in that gaze. What were they going to do with him?

'We'll only bore you, with our reminiscing,' Asa said smoothly. 'You don't want to hear old men talking about better days.'

Joe shivered. Better days? Better for whom? He hoped he looked less alarmed than he felt.

'Leave us now.' Asa's tone changed, turned commanding. 'But think about what we've said. We could use a lad like you in the Brotherhood.'

Joe's head shot up, surprised. Use him how? Against his sister? How could they even think he might want to join them? Then he recalled how they'd watched him yesterday, at the ceremony.

They'd seen him at his worst and seen someone they wanted to work with.

While he was having these thoughts, he found himself hustled to the door. He half heard their muttered comments as he passed:

'*Why they letting him go?*'

'*Better use if he's willing.*'

'*You sure that's the one?*'

Then the guards returned his knife and bundled him into the street.

Joe tripped and fell hard, grazing the burns on his hands so they seeped blood and a pale ooze which he wiped on his half-dried clothes. Alone again. He didn't belong here. He didn't belong anywhere. He was a fool to have thought anything else, lulled by good food and strong ale.

He was engulfed by a wave of exhaustion, and it was hard to think through the pain in his hands.

There was only one place he could go now.

Joe got up and limped through the streets, till he found one he recognised. He took a long route to be sure he wasn't followed and slowly wobbled his way back towards the cave.

Crossing the west beach nearly finished him: the sand seemed to suck at his feet, and he almost sank down into it, but he didn't know if he'd have the strength to rise again. His legs felt leaden now, but he forced them to keep moving.

He made it to the first cave, where he'd left his lantern. With shaking fingers, he managed to squeeze a spark from the flint and light the wick.

He stumbled in the gloom, heading deeper into the caves.

He came to the steps and realised dimly that he hadn't checked his lantern properly. The flame guttered and went out.

It was the last straw, yet more proof of his stupidity, as if any were needed. Only a fool would have walked into a meeting of the Brotherhood without realising.

He cursed himself and threw down the lamp in fury, listening to it clank down the steps in the near darkness, spilling oil as it went.

'Well done, Joe,' he muttered to himself. 'That really helped.' He sighed and started trudging blindly after it.

Several things happened then, one after the other: Joe's heel slipped on the spilt oil. He went flying down the steps. His head flew back and slammed down hard.

Everything went black.

CHAPTER NINE

Time passed strangely for Joe. He knew two states: pain or sleep. It was dark and he was dreaming. *Dragons were searching for him, soaring low over black water, coming closer, closer, closer.*

Finally he woke with a gasp, clammy and cold. His fingers moved first: he was lying on a bundle of roughspun fabric. It stank of old sweat, oil and grime. He found a flask next to him, and he fumbled for it, tugging the cork free and sucking the water down till his aching throat could take no more.

His head felt as if Iggie had sat on it, and his right shoulder burned when he moved. He twisted round and tried to prop himself up on his left side instead.

He moaned in pain, then bit it down.

Where was he? Who had brought him here? What was going on?

His thoughts cleared a little and he looked around for clues.

Joe was lying on a dusty black cloak in a small rocky cave. On a ledge above his head, an old-fashioned lamp burned low – no more than a little pool of oil in a large clam shell with a crude wick poking out one end. It would soon burn out, so he made the most of the light while he could. The cave was small and dry and otherwise empty.

Joe found that moving his head made him feel dizzy and sick, so he tried to keep as still as possible. Slowly, slowly, he got to his hands and knees. Then he realised this was tricky too, as his right arm wouldn't take his weight. Leaning on the left and shifting very gradually, he shuffled himself to the cave mouth and peered out – it opened into one of the long straight tunnels, with a flight of stone steps leading up to the left.

He struggled to his feet with effort, took one step. Another.

Purple clouds began blotting his vision. Sweat poured down his back. Then Joe was falling through darkness again.

Twice more Joe woke, tried to move and passed out.

The next time, he woke to find a blurry face peering anxiously down at him. 'Hello,' it said.

Joe managed something between a grunt and a moan.

'Hurt badly?'

Grunt.

'Drink this. Should help.' A strong hand tilted his shoulders forwards, and a cup was brought to his lips.

Joe gulped, and then retched at the bitter taste of the

liquid. He wondered if he was being poisoned, but then he found he didn't care because the pain was blotted out by a beautiful blanket of nothingness.

When he woke again, his mouth tasted like a rat had died in it, but the pain was less and he could think straight.

He opened his eyes and struggled up onto his left elbow, and found himself staring at Winter, the Dragonless, the girl he'd seen at the ceremony. The ghost who haunted the island.

Winter was even taller than him and desperately thin, with very straight black hair which fell down one side of her face like a curtain. She had large grey eyes and her mouth was wide, twisted now into a kind of smile.

'You're back,' she said. 'Better?'

'A bit,' Joe managed. 'Did you . . . ?'

'Drag you here? Yes. Bring you water? Medicine? Yes. Yes.'

She must be stronger than she looked.

'Thanks. What happened?' he asked.

'Hit your head. Wasn't sure if you'd make it. Tried to clean it.'

Joe reached up and winced as his fingers explored the back of his head, finding matted hair and dried blood. Pain exploded again.

'Bad idea. Going to be sick?'

But Joe swallowed down the nausea and concentrated on breathing: in, out, in, out. He was broken. But not alone.

'Thank you,' he said again. 'I'm Joe.' He knew that much, but other things were still hazy. He had a strange sense of dread, as if something awful was going to happen, if he could just recall what it was.

'Winter,' she replied.

Joe didn't say that he knew. How must it feel to be Winter and have everyone always knowing who you were and why?

'Do you live down here?' he asked instead.

'Sometimes. Like to keep moving. These tunnels let me do that.'

So that must be why people mistook her for a ghost. The tunnels must have other exits, Joe thought. 'How long have you known about the tunnels?' he asked her.

'*Since* . . .' One word was enough. Her sorrow seemed to fill the air like mist.

Since her dragon, Jin, had died in the Great Loss two years ago. Joe didn't know what to say to that.

A memory was dislodged: seeing Winter on Hatching Day. And, with a horrible rush, all the events of the last few days came flooding back and Joe remembered everything. He sank back down and closed his eyes, breathing through the pain. He put one arm over his face as if he could blot it all out: what his anger had done. His parents' shame. What everyone knew.

They stayed like that for a while, till Joe's stomach gave a loud growl. How many days since he'd eaten properly?

'You must eat,' Winter said, holding something out to him. 'It's been three days since I found you.'

'Three days!' Joe took it and shoved it in his mouth – some kind of fried meat in a dusty flour wrap – and gulped the food down. 'Thanks.' He felt stronger almost immediately, his thoughts flowing more clearly.

Four days then since he'd seen his parents. He'd never been away from home for so long before. Missing them felt like a pain in his chest, taking his breath away. He slumped forwards.

'What is it?' Winter asked.

'My family. I miss them.' He'd have to get better at managing that, in this new life he'd chosen. 'But I can't go back . . . not till I've done something, something good,' he finished clumsily.

Pity flickered across her face. 'There's a rumour.'

'What rumour?' What else did people think he'd done?

'Ship went down. In the storm.' She spoke in strange short bursts. 'With you aboard, they think.'

'People think I'm dead?' Joe began shivering hard.

Winter nodded. 'You were seen. At the harbour.'

'But no one would take me!' he cried. Then he realised: perhaps it was better this way. He couldn't go back and hurt them again. He couldn't make it worse. He couldn't shame them any more. He rubbed his face with his hands and winced at the pain in his shoulder and in his burns.

'How are you?' Winter reached over and touched his forehead. 'Just cold and shock. Not fever.' She seemed satisfied.

'Why are you helping me?' Joe asked, sitting up again and wiping his face. 'I mean, I'm grateful, I am – thank you!' But what was in it for her?

'I found you.' Winter's eyes gleamed brightly in the wavering lamplight.

Joe studied her. In her dark cloak, she reminded him of

a blackbird maybe, or a starling: hopping, peering intently, ready to fly away.

'Why should you die? If I can help?' Winter said. Under his gaze she suddenly grew agitated, as if she'd used up the day's supply of words and needed to be gone to find more. Tilting her head in that birdlike way, she said, 'I must go. Find a blanket, find more food.'

'Wait!' Joe called. 'Please. Did the boy live, the one who was crushed on Hatching Day?'

She was already backing away, muttering as she went down the corridor. 'Yes. He lived. Now you must.'

The lamp went out. Joe lay there in complete darkness, full of relief at that news. There was nothing else he could do now – he was stuck, suspended in the dark. His old life was over. He'd messed it up spectacularly, but it was finished. He couldn't hurt his parents any more. This was the new start he'd been looking for. He would begin again, and he would learn to tame his anger, so he didn't hurt anyone else.

It was like the night watchman Gabriel had said: Joe's parents would be better off if he were dead. And now he was. That would be his gift to them. Until he had become someone his parents could be proud of, he would stay dead.

CHAPTER TEN

Joe and Winter fell into a kind of rhythm. Winter would bring food: simple, but good – cheese, bread, sardines, pears. Joe ate and slept, recovering slowly. When he woke, sometimes Winter was there, changing the bandages on his burned hands, keeping his head injury clean. More often, he was alone. He had no idea how many days passed: night and day were the same in this cave. He lost great swathes of time to strange unquiet sleep. Sometimes he woke up screaming and beating at himself, thinking he was on fire. Slowly, slowly, he let his old life slip away, grieving for it in dreams and nightmares.

Finally, one day, he found he could stand without swaying. His shoulder would take longer to heal. In the end, Winter tied his arm in a sling, and Joe tried to forget about it, focusing on walking further down the corridor each day, determined to get better, till he could even tackle the steps: one by one. The top still seemed very far away.

Even when she was there, Winter didn't like to talk for long, Joe realised. She could manage a short sentence or three before she got that hunted look and she'd need to fly away.

Joe's questions multiplied in the hours of solitude. He planned his words carefully in the spaces when he was alone, polishing them into small shiny nuggets to be ready for Winter's return.

'Do you know all the tunnels?' he asked.

'Not yet. Exploring slowly,' she explained. 'Didn't want to get lost.'

'How far do they go?'

'Far.'

'What are they for?'

She shrugged. 'Escaping.'

Did she mean them, or someone else? Joe wanted to ask more, but she was already eyeing the passageway and getting up to leave.

One day, he was very bored, and his head was itching terribly. He decided to explore, but his legs collapsed half-way up the nearest flight of stone steps. Joe crawled back to the cave just as Winter arrived. He was ready to scream with pain and frustration. He heaved himself into the cave, slumped against a wall and put both hands over his mouth so he couldn't let out his anger. It was like fire. And like fire, he had to control it, or contain it. Otherwise it would destroy him and damage others. This was his new start and he would not wreck it. He breathed in and out till he was sure he could speak without raging against the pain.

Winter just stood there looking at him in her quiet way.

Suddenly he needed to know more about her too. What did she want? What did she do? She'd seen his worst moment, on his birthday, and yet she'd still helped him.

'You know when I saw you before,' Joe said, 'at the hatching ceremony?' It burst out before he could stop it.

He waited for Winter to pull away, to show her disapproval of what Joe had done.

'Yes?' Winter said, holding his gaze. One of her feet was drumming on the floor as she spoke.

'Well, I'm not like that. Usually. I just lost my temper.' He braced himself for her next words. For her dismissal. 'I didn't mean for all that to happen.'

Nothing came. Again.

'Look at us, both without a dragon.' As soon as the words were out, he regretted them. How could he think of comparing them? She'd had a dragon, but he had died.

A shadow passed over her face, but she didn't react.

'Sorry! Sorry, I don't mean we're the same. It's just . . . I was wondering. Most of the Dragonless left. Except you . . . Why did you stay?' he asked, as gently as he could.

She only looked at him, unblinking.

It was Joe who looked away first, cheeks burning at his awkward attempts to get to know her. He shouldn't have pushed her. She'd tell him when she was ready.

Winter laid down her parcels of food and left.

Joe wondered if she would come back. Long dark hours followed. He took out his knife and started hacking at the cave wall, taking his frustration out on it.

If Winter didn't return – and why should she? – he'd have the choice of starving alone down here or crawling the long tunnels to daylight, which might be the same thing in the end.

He kept chipping away at the wall, keeping his hands busy while his thoughts chased themselves in circles.

Why had he said that? He knew she grieved for her dragon. He could see Winter was fragile. But she was also his lifeline.

He peered at the hole he'd gouged out of the cave wall. It was roughly the shape of the huge cavern, the one he'd called the dragonhall underground. That gave him an idea. He added a new line, leading to it, and carved the little curved space where he'd slept that first night.

When he heard footsteps a few hours later, he rolled on his back and basked in the rush of relief.

'You're back! Thank you. I thought you might not . . .' Joe realised he was babbling again. With an effort, he fell silent. This time, he didn't ask anything. He smiled but stayed quiet and waited for her to speak.

This worked better. When she took her time, the words almost flowed freely. Maybe she was just out of practice at speaking, Joe thought. He even managed to make her smile.

'Go on, then,' Winter said, after a while. 'Ask me.'

'Ask you what?' Joe said.

'About my dragon. You wanted to ask. So, you get one question today.'

'What did it feel like, when he first hatched?' It was like pressing a bruise, but he needed to know. 'What does it feel like to bond?'

'Huge but natural. Like catching a wave. Also, my life depended on it. Like breathing,' Winter answered and then she left.

And the next day, Joe got another question.

'Did you know, before he climbed out of his egg?' That one hurt him to ask, and it obviously hurt Winter to answer.

'Yes,' she said, taking it slow. Her eyes were huge and glittering. 'I only cared about Jin's egg, not the others.'

Unexpectedly, that made Joe feel better. He was never going to have bonded with any of those eggs at the ceremony: he should have guessed. He felt calmer now, remembering it, and from then on he stopped going over and over what he'd done on Hatching Day.

The days slipped past. Joe looked forward to Winter's arrival, and each time she came, she stayed longer and talked more. As gradual as the change of the seasons, they turned from strangers into friends.

'Soon you'll be well,' Winter said one day, after they'd been giggling over Joe's imitation of the baker. 'You can walk up the tunnels and into the city again.'

'No.' He shook his head. 'I won't go back.'

'You have a home up there.'

'Not any more. Can't I stay here?' Joe added quietly. 'There's room for both of us. There's room for the whole city.'

'It's my home. It's safe. It's secret.' She shook her curtain of black hair so it covered her face.

She hid.

That's what she did, Joe realised. Hiding had kept her safe these past two years and let her mourn in peace.

'I know, I know! I won't change that. I'm not going to tell anyone else, I promise!' He tried to explain. 'I can't go home, not till I've changed, till I've done something to be proud of.'

She seemed frozen and he didn't know if she was listening.

He took a deep breath and all his stored-up thoughts came tumbling out now. 'But I need to start on that. I need to find a new path, something to work at.' He fumbled around, lifted the lamp and showed her where he'd used his knife to chip away at the wall. 'I've made this – look.'

She peered up through her curtains of hair.

'This is where I came in, and this is the largest cavern, the one as big as a dragonhall. I don't know where we are now – but you do, don't you?'

'It's part of a map,' she said slowly, reaching up and touching it with one finger. 'I never thought of that. I've been sticking to a few main routes, so I didn't get lost . . .' She sat very still in the warm circle of lamplight, shadows trembling and dancing all around her as she thought it through. 'If we copy this – and other passages – down onto parchment and bring it with us, we could go anywhere!' Her eyes sparkled now, catching his excitement.

'Yes! We can explore it all. These tunnels were used once, so there must be something worth finding down here. Something ancient! Maybe there's buried treasure. I could trade with it or buy passage off the island: make my new start. Who knows what we might find?'

'All right, we'll do it.' Winter shook her hair back, no

longer hiding. 'I'll get some parchment. We'll start as soon as you're strong enough.'

'Thank you.' Joe grinned. She trusted him! He felt it like a warm glow in his chest, all his frustration gone. He would focus on recovering his strength, eager to turn the next page in his new story and start exploring the secret kingdom underground.

CHAPTER ELEVEN

One day, a month now after Joe's fall, Winter produced some wrinkled parchment and a stub of charcoal. 'We can make a map of the tunnels. But' – she took a breath – 'promise me, Joe Thornsen, you will never share this? This is just for us.'

'I promise,' he said solemnly.

She drew a rough map to show Joe the tunnels she already knew by heart. 'Look,' she said, pointing at the scrawling lines. 'That is where you fell, and here is the passage back to this cave we are in. Now this one *here* goes up to the palace. This one, down to the docks.' She'd been using the main passageways, the wide ones, but there were so many side tunnels she hadn't been in yet, for fear of getting lost.

'That one to the docks must be an escape route,' Joe said, eagerness building. 'Maybe the old kings of Arcosi used it for sneaking away!'

'Or smuggling things in?' she suggested, matching his

enthusiasm. 'We are *here*.' She showed him a small marked cave. 'This is the way I get to market. I haven't been down there yet' – she pointed to another area on the parchment – 'further west.'

'Let's start there!' Joe was impatient to begin. Every day he had more energy, and it felt good to have a new purpose after this strange in-between time of healing and darkness.

They worked together to explore the unknown tunnels. They secured the fishing line from the shipwreck kit he had left in the huge cavern, then reeled it out as they walked deeper and deeper into the rocky heart of the mountain that made up Arcosi, marking the tunnel walls at each turn to show their way back. They found evidence of the old days: fragments of broken pottery, shreds of half-rotten fabric, tantalising clues to the people who'd used these tunnels. Every day they added new lines to their map. Every night, they carved a copy painstakingly into the rocky wall of the largest cavern – Joe's 'dragonhall' – which they used as a base now.

They were a good team: Winter was steady and methodical, while Joe was eager and creative, and his energy carried them on when they were both tired. He was still reliant on her for food, and her knowledge of the main tunnels, but soon he knew them almost as well as she did.

'Where shall we head tomorrow?' Winter asked one night as they gnawed on some stale bread rolls.

Joe held up the clam-shell light, carefully so he didn't spill the oil. He studied the master map carved into the cave wall. The cavern where they stood looked like the heart of the island, and these tunnels were its veins.

'Let's go west,' he suggested. 'This branch here.' He pointed, tracing the groove with his fingertips. The burns were all healed up now, though his shoulder still ached where he'd fallen, and he could feel his hair growing back in curly tufts where it had been scorched. 'I feel like there's more to find over here. See this tunnel above it? That goes right to the shadow strip.' He pointed to the ruined neighbourhood in the far north-west of the island. 'So maybe this one has an interesting end too. Do we have enough parchment?'

'Sure,' Winter said. 'I can draw on the back of this.' She smoothed out the section they'd used the day before.

'Why do the tunnels only cover the west side of the island, not the east?' Joe asked, without looking round, fingers tracing the whole network now. He'd discovered that they had secret entrances in many different neighbourhoods, including one near the Yellow House, his old home. His heart lurched as ever at the thought of his parents, but he focused on the lines in the rock, determined to stay strong. It was better for everyone this way.

'Everyone forgot the tunnels,' she shrugged. 'They forgot the reason for them too.'

'I wonder if they knew about them in my great-grandmother's day, when the dragons almost died out? They had to abandon the island. Maybe the knowledge of the tunnels went with them too?' Joe's great-grandparents Karys Stormrider and Gallus Dorato had fled the violence of mad Duke Rufus, along with the only remaining dragons, Cato and Aelia. Aelia laid four dragon eggs, the ones Iggie and his nest-mates had hatched from more than fifty years later.

'I did go to school too, you know,' Winter teased him. 'If I recall, we never stopped hearing about your brother Isak who set the school up.'

'I know! Imagine what it's like being his little brother,' Joe said dryly, gesturing for her to carry on and trying to ignore the pang he felt at the thought of Isak, who would now believe he was dead.

'So when the Norlanders came, they didn't know about the tunnels,' Winter continued. 'That knowledge had gone with Karys's people and the dragons.'

Joe nodded thoughtfully. His father's people had arrived, fleeing famine and hardship in their homelands. 'The Norlanders moved in, with no idea what was under their feet,' he said slowly. 'And as sea-people, perhaps their focus was on the shores, on the seas, not under the ground. None of us knew, all this time . . .'

'Till now,' Winter said.

'Till us.' Joe smiled at her. There must be secrets down here! Something worth finding. He felt it like a little flame inside, keeping him going.

Later that night, while Winter's breathing turned deep and soft in sleep, Joe lay awake thinking about the lost past. Maybe the tunnels had helped Karys escape the island, back then. He liked the idea of retracing his ancestor's steps. He might be cut off from his living family, but it comforted him to feel connected to Karys Stormrider, so long ago. She was a survivor, and he would be too.

A horrible voice in his mind taunted him then – what if he was more like mad Rufus, the one who'd ruined everything? He pushed the thought aside, and kept it at bay by testing his knowledge of the tunnels, trying to memorise every twist and turn, till sleep finally arrived.

By the time he woke next morning, Winter had already been out, bringing back two hot pastries from the kind baker who always took pity on her. They ate them and drank deeply from the stream flowing through the underground cavern, filling water flasks to take along on their day's travels. Joe felt like they were explorers preparing for an expedition: they had map-making tools, a wrapper of dried fruit and the compass from his shipwreck kit. Holding it now, he realised it wasn't just any sailor's compass, but the one that had always belonged to his father. He looked down at the circular worn metal case that just fitted in the palm of his hand, watching the needle spin and shiver, seeking north.

Another memory rose up, like a tentacle, pulling him under:

His father had found him playing with his compass one day, years ago. Joe didn't know what the shiny thing was. He just liked the way the pointer moved. He laughed as he shook it, turning it over and over in his hands.

'Hey, Joe.' His father took it gently from him. 'It's not a toy.'

'Why not?' Joe asked, disappointed.

'Look, let me show you.' His father's eyes twinkled blue

like the sea, telling Joe he wasn't in trouble. 'This little needle always points north,' he said. 'So you line it up like this.'

Joe watched.

'Over there, where the sun rises?' Nestan pointed. 'That's east – see? – the compass knows it too. That's south, where the sun is now . . .' He pointed again, shading his eyes from the strong sunshine. He showed Joe all the cardinal points in turn. 'So this little compass is your friend. It won't let you get lost, even when you can't see the sun.'

But I did get lost, Joe thought, swallowing a lump at the back of his throat. He missed his parents so much, it hurt. It was a physical pain in his chest, making it hard to breathe. All his life, his father had taught him patiently, given him everything he needed. Even now, with this shipwreck kit, Nestan was still providing all the tools he needed. And how had Joe repaid him?

He'd repay him by staying hidden, he reminded himself. He'd stay hidden until he'd tamed his anger, till he was sure he was nothing like his ancestor Rufus, till he'd done something to earn back his parents' broken trust.

'Joe?' Winter's voice broke into his thoughts. 'Are you all right?'

'Yeah,' he muttered. 'Just remembering. You know?'

She did seem to know. She understood these tidal waves of loss that could sweep in and leave you gasping. She put one hand on his arm and squeezed gently. 'Come on, let's go,' she said, leading the way with her lamp.

The tunnels seemed very long and very narrow today, with the slender thread of knotted fishing lines trailing after them into the dark. Joe paused, and tried not to think about the huge expanse of rock and earth above them, which suddenly seemed to be pressing down and taking his air.

'Tell me something,' he said, when he could breathe and speak normally again. 'Where did you grow up? What was it like?' He wanted to hear her memories, so he didn't drown in his own.

'Lower town, Seawall Street,' Winter called over her shoulder as she spooled out the line. 'It was fine, for a while. Good neighbours. Us kids all played together. Dad was a carpenter. Mum's a craftswoman. Leatherwork. She made this – look.' Winter showed him her soft leather satchel. She told him next how her father got sick when she was small, and died soon after. 'Don't remember him much. Mum did her best for me, and she was so proud when Jin chose me.' She talked on and on, more than Joe had ever heard.

He stayed quiet, listening as they went up and up through the unexplored tunnels. He felt like she was giving him something very rare and very valuable, word by word, a thread for him to follow, like this fishing line.

It was the longest he'd walked since his fall. Joe's legs started shuddering from the climb. Soon he was freezing cold and drenched in sweat. His head ached badly and his right shoulder was throbbing. 'Can we stop?' he panted finally.

'What's wrong?' Winter peered down at him from the next step, raising her lantern so its golden circle of light fell full on his face.

He leaned against the wall and closed his eyes, teeth chattering. 'I don't know.'

'There's a cave up ahead.' She looked worried. 'Maybe we can rest there awhile.'

He started to trudge forwards again, following her. The tunnel widened, and there was a small circular chamber opening off it.

'Joe, look!' Winter sounded awestruck.

He peered in. There was a raised oval platform in the centre of the cave – like a table, but carved from the rock of the cave itself.

He went in: one step, two. Something was different in here. The air was charged. It felt warmer.

As soon as he entered, he felt better and his headache eased.

They put their lanterns on the floor and their light cast strange shadows that flickered on the walls as they approached the table.

'Joe, you were right,' Winter said. 'They did leave something down here.' She moved to the side, so he could see.

He felt the hairs on the back of his neck stand on end.

The table had two large boxes on it.

CHAPTER TWELVE

There were two chests of carved wood side by side. Joe ran his fingers over the beautiful textures. The first chest had patterns of waves, fish and dragon heads, all woven together in a complex design. It was fastened with a dull brass clasp.

'Let's see what's inside?' He reached out and it flipped open with a satisfying click. With both hands, he eased up the carved lid. It yawned open on its hinges to reveal a pile of coins, glittering darkly.

Here was the hidden treasure he'd dreamed of!

Joe laughed out loud and thrust his hands deep into the pile of coins. 'Gold! Winter, I think it's gold!' Here were riches enough to pave any new path he might dream of! Futures opened up in his mind, shimmering with possibility.

Winter blurted in astonishment. 'B-b-but that's a fortune!'

Joe picked up one of the coins. The face carved on one

side was not one he'd seen before. He made out the name *Forlano* in old-fashioned runic lettering. It must be one of the old kings of Arcosi, but he'd never heard this name. It must be ancient!

'Let's just take a couple of coins for now,' he checked. 'Enough to live on? We can come back for more.'

She nodded.

He took three gold coins from the top of the pile and slipped them into his pocket where they clinked against each other as he moved.

Winter did the same.

Joe looked at the other box, feeling pulled towards it, like his compass needle seeking north. 'Shall we?' he whispered.

'Yes!' Winter said, eyes wide.

Joe moved crabwise and stood in front of the second box. He put his hands on it, feeling the softness of the polished wood. The other clasp was thicker and more ornate. The polished carvings on the box were different too: moon, sun, crashing waves and something that looked like flames. He took a deep breath, then slowly undid the catch and eased the lid open.

At first he could see only darkness within.

Then he saw the eggs.

Winter picked up her lantern. Her hand shook, causing the light to flicker.

Two scaly eggs lay nestled against folds of dark blue velvet, glowing slightly in the near darkness. One had a pattern of purple spots; the other was green, with stripes like a brindled hunting hound.

For a moment, Joe could barely breathe. He blinked and checked again. It was real. Two eggs lay shimmering in the gloom.

His eyes jumped straight to the purple spotted one. It was a deep dark violet. This was the purple from his dreams. He leaned forwards and ran his hand lightly over its ridges. Something sparked against his fingers, and he gasped.

'What?' Winter asked. 'Did it hurt?'

'I don't know,' he said, pulling back and studying his hand. 'It felt like . . . like pins and needles.' He reached out again gingerly, but this time nothing happened.

Winter joined him, staring down at the green striped egg with wonder and longing.

Two of them. Two eggs.

For a heartbeat, Joe dared to dream of a future where this purple egg hatched and whatever was inside it belonged to him. They weren't dragon eggs, though: they were too small, and ridged all over, not smooth.

He didn't care if it wasn't a dragon. He would love it anyway.

A smile spread across his face. It was true, he realised. He cared desperately about this egg, in a way that hadn't happened at the hatching ceremony.

He memorised its pattern, its strange glittering luminescence. He'd seen this kind of light before, out at sea one evening on a trip beyond Sartola with his father. At night the ocean had been full of lights, as if the stars had fallen into the water. It was the same kind of glow, a moonlike night-time brightness that had nothing to do with the sun.

He wriggled his fingers deeper, round the egg, and carefully lifted it up.

He was vaguely aware of Winter doing the same with the other egg, and gasping when she must've felt that tingle under her fingertips.

'Hello, you,' he said. It was heavier than it looked. It felt charged with potential. It wasn't alive exactly, not yet, but it could be, Joe felt sure.

He stared down at it.

This egg was his.

Suddenly everything made sense. Of course he'd failed at the ceremony! If he hadn't, he wouldn't be here now. He felt calm. He felt happy, for the first time in weeks.

They stayed there for a long time.

When they'd placed the eggs safely back in the casket, Winter and Joe turned to each other.

'What do you think?' he asked, gripping both her arms, giddy with excitement. 'What are they?'

'Not like any dragon eggs I've ever seen. Not like Jin's egg – that was smoother and larger.' Winter grimaced with pain then, her eyes full of shadows.

'We need to find out. We need to know what they are, what they need, how to look after them.' Joe's head was spinning with new energy and ideas. He dropped Winter's arms and started pacing up and down.

She was nodding. 'The city library, at the palace.' Her voice was soft and faint. 'We should try there.'

Joe was about to agree with her. Then he remembered. 'I can't. I'm supposed to be dead, remember?' But in the next moment, a new sense of purpose washed over him, and it was stronger than fear. For this egg, he could do it. He could do anything. 'Wait. The tunnels go that far, don't they? Could they get us into the palace grounds?'

'Of course,' Winter said, retreating and huddling against the wall as if she were cold. 'You know the maps.'

'Then we'll find a way. Even if we have to break in. We'll—' He stopped dead, suddenly noticing she didn't share his mood. 'What's wrong?' He paused, taming his excitement. He took in her fearful expression, her hunched posture.

From the moment she'd compared this egg to that of her lost dragon, Jin, Winter had seemed to slip away from him, battling against the shadows in her past.

He should have realised. This was different for her. She'd lost one dragon. It was natural she would be anxious as well as protective of another egg.

'It's all right,' he told her quietly. 'They're safe here, aren't they? Let's go home to our cave and make a plan.' That's how he thought of it now. As home.

'Can you walk?' Winter said, sounding worried.

Joe stretched up in the warm damp air, surprised at how well his injured shoulder moved. He turned his head, this way and that. Nothing hurt any more. He felt better than ever.

'Yes,' he said. 'I can. I don't know how, but I can.'

PART TWO - EARTH

AIR

FIRE

WATER

EARTH

CHAPTER THIRTEEN

They were too excited to sleep much, talking all night about the eggs and dozing lightly. Winter slipped out again in the early morning and returned a while later with a mismatched set of clothes for Joe. 'Bought from four different stalls!' she said, eyes wide and cheeks pink. 'Will they fit?'

'Let me try them on,' Joe said, and, when she didn't move, 'on my own?' He had to spell it out, feeling his face grow warmer.

Winter shrugged and left the cave, returning when he called. She burst out laughing.

'That bad?' he said ruefully. 'I'm tall, but not that tall.' The fisherman's trousers were baggy and faded blue, sagging softly over his feet, while the shirt came down almost to his knees. The large jacket was grey linen, finely tailored, though it swamped him, hiding his hands completely. His hair always curled up at the front like a duck's tail – he'd never been able to tame it – but now he squashed it flat and tugged the navy cap low. That fit perfectly, at least. He didn't mind; he was just glad to have something clean to wear.

Winter hid her smile behind one hand. 'I've got an old belt you can have. If we trim the trouser legs, fold back the sleeves, you'll be fine. Mostly.'

He couldn't help laughing too, as he looked down. It felt good to be out of his old clothes, now piled in a stained heap in one corner.

Winter held up her lantern and gave him a long glance, head to toe. 'I can't say no one will notice you, but – eyes down, walk slowly – they will never recognise you as Jowan Thornsen. Here, have some breakfast.' She sat and unwrapped fresh cheese, crusty bread and dried apricots. 'I changed one gold coin for coppers.' She spoke with her mouth full and patted the bulging leather purse at her belt. 'It'll last for ages! We're going to be eating much better now.'

Joe sat down to join her, tucking the dragon-handled knife from Conor and the woven silk from Amina into the pockets of the jacket. They felt like good-luck charms: a connection to his past, even if he could never see his friends again. At the thought of them, his stomach churned, but he made himself think of the eggs and focus on their plan.

Soon they were ready to head up to the library. They chose to go early in the day, to make the most of the daylight and spend as long as possible reading.

They walked through the tunnels for what felt like hours. Winter led the way with her lamp, and Joe was pleased to note he'd learned the route by heart too, from memorising their maps.

'We're here!' she said finally. She bent to unlatch a small iron door, only waist-high, and light streamed in. 'When we go through, we'll be in the palace grounds, near the stables.' She put out the lanterns and placed them on the ground.

'You do mean right inside? Beyond the walls?' Joe had to double-check.

'Joe, you know this, you carved the map,' Winter said. She tapped the wall impatiently. 'Are you ready?'

His heart was beating fast. 'Ready.'

But he wasn't. The daylight was dazzling as he stumbled out; after all those weeks underground, it hurt his eyes and sent tears streaming down his cheeks. He tripped and fell to his knees.

'Quickly, before anyone sees us,' Winter hissed, pulling him upright. 'Just walk, can't you?'

Somehow Joe made his feet obey. His shirt stuck to his back, damply. His legs were wobbling. He squinted against the sunshine, shading his face with his hand.

'I can't . . . I can't. It's too much.' His chest felt tight, like a water flask about to burst. He gripped Winter's arm, as if he were drowning, sucking in cool air.

'It's all right,' she said. Her voice was steady and warm, as if she were calming a spooked horse. 'Not far now. One more step. And another.'

Slowly, the panic receded. Joe stood a little taller and looked around them for the first time. They were walk-ing through the palace gardens, past the dragonhalls – the ancient one from the olden days, and the newer ones that made up Arcosi's dragonschool. The gardens were full of city folk taking a break in the shade. People were sitting on benches, or strolling through the gardens, past the fountains splashing cool water and the late-blooming roses that filled the air with their rich sweet scent.

Normal life was happening, to other people. Joe felt like a ghost, watching the living. His old life was gone, and he felt miles away from all the ordinary people of Arcosi.

The dragonhalls were built in a horseshoe shape with the oldest one in the middle. Its door was open, and Joe could see his sister Tarya's red dragon, Heral, dozing there. The newer halls had their doors closed and Joe heard Isak's voice in the middle of a lesson.

Isak! His brother was right there. Where Joe had longed to be for so long.

He remembered how angry Isak had been on Hatching Day. Joe had shamed him in the worst possible way. He'd ruined the sacred ceremony that Isak had so carefully organised, people had been injured, Milla had been burned. Any of the hatchlings might have been hurt, or killed in the stampede, all because of him. And since the Great Loss, every baby dragon was more precious than ever.

He stood still, fighting the urge to run to Isak and beg forgiveness.

No, Joe had to stay dead. He had to keep up this sacrifice, for his family's sake.

'Come on, Joe,' Winter whispered. 'Let's keep moving. Remember why we're here.'

She was right. He was on a different path now, and it had led him to his purple egg. He held his head a little higher and started walking.

The library was in one of the turrets of the palace itself – that ancient stone castle with four towers, the palace of the four winds. Even though he'd been coming here all his life, it still took Joe's breath away: the curving stone buttresses that braced the main building like ribs; all the stone carvings of stars and dragons, fishes and flames; and then, as he headed for the steps, he crossed the famous black dragon mosaic that dated back to the time of the old kings.

They slipped inside, walking softly across the polished floors.

Going into the library felt like coming home. Joe had always loved it here. He'd spent hours as a small boy leafing through the old books that Isak let him touch – the ones with the vivid paintings of other lands, of high seas or frozen mountains, tangled forests and stalking tigers. He loved its curved walls lined with books, the way light slanted down from the high windows. He loved the odd stepladders built on two wheels, to be moved from shelf to shelf, so he could reach even the highest books, and he'd tested those ladders to their limits. Why had he stopped coming? He couldn't remember. Only that in recent years, there had been other things to do.

There was a large grey-haired woman in flowing robes reading at the librarian's desk. She smiled a warm greeting. 'Come in, come in.'

'Hello, Susanna,' Winter said.

'Morning, Winter, we haven't seen you in a few weeks.'

'Been busy,' Winter mumbled and shuffled off inside.

Then Susanna turned to Joe and asked brightly, 'First visit?'

Face burning, throat dry, Joe gulped. 'Er, hello. Yes, yes, it's my first visit,' he lied.

'Let me know if I can help with anything,' Susanna said, peering over her eyeglasses.

'Thank you!' Fizzy with relief, he said, 'Please can you help me? I'm, er . . .' What could he say? 'I'm researching . . . rare animals!'

Susanna looked quizzical. 'Can you narrow it down?'

'I mean, myths! Or maybe a mixture of animals and myths? Things that hatch from eggs, but not typical dragons.' He was babbling again.

She pointed towards the back of the library and Joe scuttled away in that direction. People of all ages were dotted around the room, poring over books. It had that special, intense kind of quiet: a mixture of calmness and concentration.

In the old days, Duke Olvar had kept the library a secret, hoarding the books for his own use. Now every person in Arcosi was welcome to visit here and read anything they liked. Joe's brother, Isak, had added to the old duke's collection, buying more books and scrolls from around the world, travelling with his golden dragon Belara to trade for rare manuscripts in distant lands.

He'd added an inner circle of smaller shelves, and it was behind one of these that Joe found Winter, lying on the floor reading, concealed in the shadows.

She showed him where she'd just started her research, and he set to work on a different section.

They spent the whole day leafing through old books and papers.

'Have you found anything?' Joe asked after a few hours, daring to lift his hat off and scratch his head, checking no one was looking in their direction.

Winter's head drifted up and her eyes lost their faraway look. 'Maybe.' She put her book down, stretching till her shoulders clicked. 'I've been reading one legend . . . have you heard of shadow dragons before? It says they hatch from eggs, like other dragons, but they're linked somehow to volcanoes.'

'Volcanoes? That doesn't sound good.'

'Where is there a volcano, anyway?' Winter asked. 'Not on the island.'

'Out at sea, maybe?' Joe said vaguely. 'I remember something from school: Mount Bara – isn't that a volcano?'

'Surely a volcano would destroy everything. I don't understand . . .' Winter said. 'Let me ask the librarian for help.'

Joe watched her from the other side of the room, keeping his face low. He could just hear them murmuring.

'Hmm. Shadow dragons. Yes!' Susanna sat taller. 'That's a rare one. Now where have I heard that before? Bear with me. Let me check something, and I'll come and find you in a moment.' The librarian started looking through a huge catalogue behind her desk, intent on her search.

Winter returned, and they read and read until it started to grow dark.

Eventually, Susanna came to find them, holding a book bound in soft honey-coloured leather, with one finger marking a particular page. 'Here! I found it at last. I'll leave it with you. Bring it back to me before you go, please.'

'We will. Thank you.' Joe took it carefully, as Winter's hands were full of books.

'I need to go and light the lamps. We'll be closing soon, all right? Not long now.'

He gazed down at the book in his hands. The spine was stamped in gold, and its pages were thick and yellowed with age. He opened it. The first page was hand-lettered in old script, with gorgeous scarlet flames encircling the words: *Rare Beasts of the Ancient World*.

Joe spoke and read both of his parents' languages: his mother's Sartolan, which was spoken all over the region; and Norlandish, from his father's distant homelands. This book was written in an old-fashioned kind of Sartolan.

He found the page that Susanna had indicated, and traced his fingers over the image. *Finally!*

CHAPTER FOURTEEN

'Look! Look at this picture!' Joe whispered to Winter.

The page was quartered, and each of the four parts was vividly illustrated. One was full of fiery flames, with its sunset-tinted sky giving way to clearer blue in the other top quarter. The lower left had surging waves, leading to a rocky shore with deep caves in the last quarter. The long-dead scribe who'd created this page had painstakingly lettered a little banner on each section.

Joe read out: '*Fire. Air. Water. Earth.*'

In the watery section, the ocean was finely coloured in blue, green and grey, teeming with underwater life: fish, a huge whale and a dragon.

A dragon, underwater? An indigo dragon, dark purplish blue, swimming with its wings folded on its back.

'Look, there's an egg.' It was Winter who saw it, in the rocky cave section.

They studied it hungrily, passing it between them and holding it close to focus in the dim light.

Joe peered closer. 'It looks like our eggs. We're on the right path!' He could clearly see a pattern on its surface, a zigzag, in orange this time, and the ancient artist had managed to convey the strange luminous colour. 'Do you think . . . our eggs might be . . . shadow dragons?'

'*Shadow dragons!*' Winter breathed. Their eyes met. Hers were dancing with excitement. 'Is there more?' she asked, and he turned another page.

Joe stared, running one finger along the lines.

'What does it say? Read it out,' Winter urged him. 'We need to know everything!'

Joe whispered it slowly, puzzling out the old-fashioned language:

'In the island's secret heart,
From liquid flame, there comes a spark.

With fire and water, earth and air,
Forged in the ocean's hidden lair,

A broken heart will dare it all,
Take the leap and risk the fall.

From ash and bone, new life will rise,
Shadow dragons roam the skies!'

'What does it mean?' she asked.

'I don't know . . .' Joe read it again. He didn't like the sound of ash and bone – it sounded too much like dead things. He muttered the words again, trying to carve them on his memory. Then he recalled a half-forgotten lesson from school, wishing he'd paid more attention. 'These are the four elements. Didn't the ancients believe everything was made up of them?'

He looked at Winter. She'd gone to the city school once too, like all the children of Arcosi. He guessed that Winter was about eleven when she bonded with her dragon, Jin, and moved into the dragonschool. So she'd had a whole year at the dragonschool before Jin and the other dragons got sick and died.

She wouldn't want to talk about it. But he had to ask.

'When you were at the dragonschool, you must have learned things like this. What do you remember – about other kinds of dragons?'

Winter's face was illuminated by one of the ornate metal lanterns hanging in the window: half was lit by soft orange light; the other half was lost in shadow. 'Don't. I can't speak of *then*.'

Joe felt his excitement turn to frustration. She'd been one of the lucky ones, one of the dragonbonded. Why couldn't she share those secrets, for the sake of these eggs?

Winter's eyes filled with tears. She looked at him, pleading, as tears overspilled and ran down one cheek, like molten gold.

Joe remembered the egg, waiting for him. He already knew he would do anything for it. His mind made a leap, daring to dream of a future with a dragon. How would he feel if that dragon died? He couldn't even imagine. It was too much. Darkness and dust. Would he be strong enough to keep living? He wasn't sure. 'I'm sorry.' He let out a long slow sigh, feeling his anger subside. He looked at Winter, not sure what to say. If it had been Amina or Conor, he'd have tried a joke, but this was Winter – a mysterious girl, cloaked in shadows.

Winter's face crumpled, and she jumped to her feet and fled, leaving Joe to curse himself yet again.

Joe ran after her – earning a glare from Susanna as he thrust the precious book at her, mouthing *thank you* – but Winter was faster than him.

Outside, in the cool night air, he watched her disappear into the shadows, heading for the stables and the secret door to the tunnels.

Should he follow or not? He decided that Winter probably needed to be alone, without his clumsy attempts to apologise.

Instead, he used the cover of darkness to go somewhere he knew he shouldn't. He began sneaking through the palace gardens, listening out for the guards' footsteps.

Three times he heard the guards approaching; three times he hid. It wasn't hard to avoid them. His sister was usually more strict with her patrols than that. Was the island's army growing careless? Today it suited him, but Joe worried what it meant for Tarya. Was her pregnancy stopping her from working, or had Rosa taken over already? Either way, things were different.

Without admitting to himself where he was going, Joe tiptoed closer and closer towards the dragonschool of Arcosi, its tall wooden buildings looming in the darkness. Each was home to a clutch of dragons. Each clutch and their people shared a special bond, like a family. He wondered which one Winter and her dragon Jin had lived in.

The nearest dragonhall had its doors ajar and Joe peeked inside. A large brick stove burned in the centre of the room, casting a blaze of heat. A metal perch curved round the stove and Joe counted five small dragons basking there. He almost missed one, because Maric and Ariel were so tightly coiled together, a bundle of scaly purple limbs and tails. There was the green one, the creamy one, and finally, Noah's dragon. It raised its yellow head and growled in Joe's direction.

Typical.

'What's wrong, Della?' Noah asked.

Joe flattened himself against the outside of the dragon-hall and held his breath, blood pulsing in his ears.

CHAPTER FIFTEEN

No one came out of the dragonhall to see what the disturbance was, and soon Joe dared to peep back in. He needed to see what he was missing. It was like picking at a scab – he knew it would be painful, but he couldn't resist.

The five new dragonbonded children were finishing their meal at a table behind the stove. Then they pushed their chairs back and went to collect their dragons, greeting them tenderly.

Noah's yellow dragon nuzzled herself against his hand, and hissed, showing tiny sharp teeth.

They all settled down on large cushions near the stove, speaking sometimes to the dragons, sometimes to each other.

Joe listened, without moving. They were discussing a lesson from Isak earlier that day.

'Why is he working us so hard?' Noah was grumbling.

'There's a lot to learn,' Conor said mildly.

What were they learning? Joe wished he knew. How hard he would've worked, if he'd been given this chance.

'He's just doing his job, I guess.' That was Tiago, with the little green hatchling called Lina. 'Anyway, he's leaving for Sartola in the morning, and we'll get one of the other teachers.'

'Isak blames us for Joe's death,' Noah said now. 'I bet that's why he's leaving. It's nothing to do with us!' He bent down and cooed to his hatchling. 'It's not our fault none of you wanted his brother, is it, Della? Turns out you chose right in the end, eh? You're mine, aren't you?'

That stung, like salt in a wound, but Joe couldn't seem to drag himself away. He pressed his face against the gap between the door and its frame, a little crack of light that he could see through.

'Noah! That's not true,' Conor was saying. 'Course he doesn't blame us.'

'Just cos you're Isak's favourite,' Noah snapped. 'And I wonder why that is? Only cos you were friends with his brother.'

Without speaking, Amina went to Conor's side. They both wore pale lilac clothes now to match their hatchlings: trousers, shirts and loose jackets.

Amina shook her head, telling Conor not to react. Their dragons touched noses.

'Isak is grieving,' Tiago said. 'That's why he's been distracted lately.'

Tiago seemed to be the peacemaker in this grouping, Joe saw.

'We're all grieving!' Amina cried, her voice catching. 'Or would be, if you even cared.' Then, catching a frown from the youngest girl, she broke down, near tears. 'You didn't know him like we did, Flavia.'

The little girl only looked down and cuddled her dragon.

'Oh, so now *you've* lost someone, the world has to stop and listen?' Noah muttered.

Conor and Amina stood side by side. Conor rubbed his eyes with one hand, as if he fought back tears, too.

Joe was about to step out and run to his friends – *I'm alive! It's all right!* But he stopped himself just in time. Going to them now would be selfish. They were better off without him. His anger made him a danger to them. Hadn't he just got frustrated with Winter? So much for his new start.

'What he did on Hatching Day wasn't like him at all,' Conor said. 'Joe wasn't like that. He was kind.'

A horrible mixture of guilt and relief rushed through Joe, hearing his friends defend him. He wanted to be the person they thought he was, the person they mourned. Maybe, one distant day, he could be.

'I only know what I saw.' Flavia shrugged dismissively. 'He was about to hurt me and Elias. Ravenna knew, didn't she? She flamed him.'

Joe stood there, burning with shame. That was true: he'd been so close to hurting Flavia's hatchling. That was why he had to stay away. So he didn't endanger anyone. He could do it: he could let them live their new lives without him. They had their dragons to comfort them now.

He stayed still. He stayed silent. It was better that Amina

and Conor should remember him well, than live with him and come to fear him.

'Joe's our best friend,' Conor cried then. 'He wouldn't—'

'*Was*,' Noah interrupted. '*Was* your best friend.'

Joe bit his lip to stop from crying out.

'It's all right, Della,' Noah crooned to his dragon. 'Joe's gone, and he won't be able to hurt anyone any more.'

The words landed like blows. Joe staggered backwards across the grass, towards the palace stables, not caring who saw him now. With tear-blurred vision, somehow he found the small iron gate, yanked it open and threw himself into the tunnels. They'd left a couple of makeshift lamps to use on the return journey: Winter's was gone already.

He stumbled through the tunnels, his thoughts spinning faster and faster, like a whirlpool.

Because of what he'd done, Joe was dead to everyone who'd loved him. He'd caused them terrible pain. He'd hurt them, shamed them, risked their dragons' lives on Hatching Day. Noah was right; that was why it hurt so much. To protect them, he had to stay away from his friends and their dragons.

Even the thought of his egg didn't soothe him now. Of course he was drawn to some weird egg that no one had ever heard of, a strange egg that belonged underground in the shadows, just like him. Maybe the creature that hatched would be angry and dangerous, just like him, while his friends lived in the light with the proper dragons.

He felt hot and breathless, desperate for air. He lurched forwards, one hand holding the lantern, the other patting along the rough tunnel walls, until finally he found himself in the huge cave with the underground pool. Stopping to catch his breath, he dipped his free hand in to take a drink.

He spat it out immediately.

The water tasted strange – acrid and sour.

But there was another difference, which changed everything: today the water was warm.

CHAPTER SIXTEEN

Joe slept in the large cavern. He woke when the shaft of sunlight from above reached his face. He heard footsteps and realised he wasn't alone.

'Morning,' Winter mumbled.

'Morning.' Today, Joe felt like a snail without its shell, raw and exposed. He hid his face under one arm and wished he could just disappear. He took a deep breath, as if he could breathe in strength along with the muggy air. He had to start doing better. He had to start now. He dragged himself into a sitting position and blurted: 'I'm sorry about last night.'

At exactly the same moment, Winter said, 'Sorry I ran off.'

They exchanged small, hopeful, slightly shaky smiles.

'Joe?' Winter said.

'Yes?'

'Food.'

'Thanks.' He reached over and took the lump of bread Winter was offering. He nibbled it, trying not to think how much he missed his mother's cooking, or Matteo's fresh cinnamon rolls. He was too thirsty to swallow the dry crumbs, and suddenly he remembered why.

'Winter!' he burst out. 'I tried to drink from the stream last night, but it's gone hot, and it tastes weird.' Grabbing the flask of spring water, he drank deeply.

Then he stumbled back to the stream and dabbled his fingers in the rushing water. Still hot. 'Come over. Feel this!'

Winter looked at him as if he'd lost his mind entirely, but she picked her way across the rocky floor of the cave and scooped up a little water. She sniffed it and touched the end of her tongue to it, before wrinkling her nose and scattering the drops on the floor. 'Urgh! What's wrong with it? It's never done that before. Not in two years.'

'It's coming from underground. It's hot. And smelly. Do you think it could be . . . ?' Joe knew it sounded unlikely.

'What?' Winter looked wary, half-hidden behind her shining black hair.

'Something to do with volcanoes?'

'They have lava, not water,' she said.

'Maybe it's the lava heating the water, down below, and then it bubbles up . . .'

'You just want it to be true' – she spoke quite gently – 'because we read about shadow dragons and volcanoes yesterday.'

Joe felt slapped down. Even her mild disagreement was

112

too much, today. To his horror, he felt his fury rising in response. Not again! He had to defeat his anger. This was supposed to be his new start!

He couldn't, he mustn't. Not with Winter. Never with her.

If he couldn't control it, at least he'd contain it. He ran out of the cavern, blindly stumbling the route he'd memorised, till he found himself back at the egg cave.

He walked straight into the rocky platform, banging his shins, but when he opened the casket, a faint glimmering light filled the cave. He picked up his egg, cradling it carefully, and slid down to lie on the floor, curled around it. There was still this. He might not have anything else, or anyone else, but he had this egg.

It was warm in there again, and without meaning to, he let his eyes close and drifted off to sleep. In his dreams, he held a dragon, not an egg.

When he woke up, Winter was sitting next to him, cradling the green egg. Her black hair fell over her face as she whispered quietly to it.

Joe felt better. His head was clearer. He sat up, being careful not to jolt the purple egg. 'Winter, I'm sorry,' he said again.

'Yeah?' She made him wait.

'For acting like a selfish kid. I mean it. I'm really sorry.'

'S'all right.' She put one hand on his arm.

'Thank you.' He realised it was the first time she'd done something like that. 'Why are you so kind to me?' he asked.

'You've lost your life, from before,' she said softly. 'It's going to hurt.'

His loss was nothing, compared to hers. He didn't dare say anything else.

'And my life has been better since you crashed your way into it.'

'Same,' Joe whispered gratefully. And then he almost dropped his egg in shock. 'Oh!' He stared down at it. He waited, listening. 'No, I must still be dreaming. For a moment, I thought I felt something move, inside.' He spread his fingers over the egg, sensing hard, but it didn't happen again. After a while, he carefully carried his egg over to the casket.

'So,' he asked, when Winter had done the same, 'are you coming?'

'Where?'

'Back to the library.' Joe felt utterly determined now. 'We need to find out about the hot water and volcanoes and what these eggs need.'

'Joe, you slept all day. It's dark now. The library's closed.'

'So?' he said, 'I'm not quite as useless as I look: I can get us in. If we bring lamps, we can still read. It'll be harder, but it will work.'

They retraced their steps from the day before, bringing the storm lantern along, taking extra care when they un-latched the secret iron door into the palace grounds.

There was a little light from the fingernail moon, and Joe's breath shone white like dragonsmoke in the cold air. It was the first hard frost of the autumn.

A patrol was just returning to the barracks that lay to the

east of the palace on a plateau like the palm of a hand. He heard the call and reply of the sentries.

They waited, keeping the storm lantern dark, and stole across the grass, avoiding the paths, circling round to the library in the northernmost turret.

This wasn't just the palace to Joe. It was his sister's home, and Tarya had let him explore every inch of it since he could walk. Now he crept underneath the library windows, in case there was a guard patrolling inside too.

There was a delivery entrance just beyond the rounded curve of the turret leading to the body of the main building. He remembered Isak excitedly pacing just inside, one warm summer day last year, waiting for a shipment of new books to arrive. Joe reached up and tried the handle, just in case, but as he had expected, it was locked. He took out the dragon-handled knife and studied its slender point – slightly too large, but it might do.

His mother had taught him some useful skills from the days before the revolution. She always said he needed to be able to defend himself, needed to be able to escape. He used to think she was over-protective, but now he was grateful to her.

'What are you doing? Don't break it!' Winter whispered, sounding scared.

'Shh. I won't!' Joe tilted his head, holding his breath, feeling for the subtle mechanisms of the lock. The blade slipped, but he started again, patiently wiggling the metal point to push back each point of the lock inside. With a tiny click, it opened.

He breathed out, satisfied.

Carefully, carefully, he pressed the handle down, easing the door open without a sound. They crept inside, onto thick, dark carpet in a wood-panelled corridor. It was dark, but Joe opened the storm lantern a crack, casting a soft golden light on the polished wood. He headed confidently down the corridor, found the library door and opened it.

Inside the northern turret library, they both relaxed a little. Moonlight was filtering faintly from the high windows.

Winter crossed the floor and pointed at a brass label. 'If there's any more information, it'll be here: *Animals, Real and Mythological.* Last time we reached as far as there.'

So that narrowed it down, Joe thought, eyeing the broad section of shelves she was indicating.

'Start at the bottom, work up?' he asked Winter in a whisper.

'Top down. We'll be tired later.' She went to wheel over one of the stepladders and climbed up to reach the highest shelf.

They spent the night scampering up and down the ladders, pausing to read – hunched over the lantern – waving each other over if they needed a second opinion. It was much more awkward, sharing the light, squinting at the page in the dim glow of the lantern.

As time went on, and they still had no new facts, Joe grew more anxious. He read till his eyes hurt. He read about animals he'd never heard of, and some he wasn't sure were real. He read about the sphinx, the lion, the centaur, the cheetah, the phoenix and the elephant. He read about long-dead giant lizards, snakes, frogs, newts. But not a word about shadow dragons.

He was ready to give up. He sat there, wriggling the stiffness from his shoulders and blinking the dryness from his eyes, when he saw the moment that Winter found something.

She was sitting on the floor in her usual tatty grey dress, her cloak pooling around her in dark folds.

It was as if she had scented prey. She sat taller, reading quickly, her lips moving as she did.

'What?' Joe called, forgetting to be quiet.

'I've found something. This is it!' She clasped the book to her chest, eyes glistening. 'It says: *the life cycle of dragons and others of the genus.*'

'What's a genus?'

'I don't know, maybe a grouping of animals? But listen: *eggs are laid by mature dragons. In their dormant state they may survive decades – even up to one hundred years in the case of the rare shadow dragon.*'

'So they're alive!' Joe felt a warm rush of relief pass through him. 'I mean, they could be. They're not dead.' He remembered that spark against his finger. He'd known it, deep down, but this was proof.

'Wait there's more: *For hatching to occur, optimal conditions must prevail, that is, the presence of heat and moisture.*'

'What's *optim* . . . and *prevail*?' That all sounded complicated.

'Let me finish! I'm just getting to the important part,'

Winter said. '*For the rarer shadow dragon, to survive the long dormant years the egg is thick and hard. It hatches at the time of volcanic hot water flows. It may only succeed in the presence of the hatching agent silverblue, common to the region of Sartola. However, if no silverblue is present, the eggshells cannot thin and break, and the shadow dragons will die within.*'

'Winter!' Joe said urgently. 'That's them! That means ours – with the thick eggshells. They might die!'

'They mustn't die! They can't!'

'It's happening, don't you see?' He thought fast. 'It's like it's all coming together – us finding the tunnels and the eggs, the water running hot in the caves last night. It's connected! It's got to be.'

'Joe, are you dreaming? If there's a volcano heating up, it won't matter about the eggs. We'll all be dead.'

'So why does it say the eggs need silverblue to hatch? And what is it? We have to find some. It's important.'

'I don't know.' She sounded tired and full of despair. 'I've read so much I can't see straight. And it's nearly light. We have to go now before we get caught.'

'T-t-there is someone who will know. I mean, there might be.' Joe paused, getting used to the idea. 'Yes. We have to. I know who we can ask,' he said. 'Come on, there's no time to lose.'

They hurriedly replaced the books, with one final glance to check they'd left no sign of their presence. They left the palace through the same door and crept back into the gardens, where the night was fading to ashy dawn.

Joe kept returning to the horrible idea that his dragon might die before it could hatch.

To save its life, he was going to have to come back from the dead . . .

CHAPTER SEVENTEEN

Joe and Winter were more careful now, sneaking first through the tunnels and then out into the empty city as it grew light. Joe led Winter, knowing exactly where to find the person he needed: his cousin Milla.

Milla ran the island's healing centre, bought with her inheritance from their grandmother. With her team of healers, she continued the work done by Vigo's mother, the duchess who'd been killed in the revolution. It was a huge airy building right in the centre of Arcosi. It had a large square garden for dragons to land in, and sandy spaces for them to bask. Milla believed that the dragons speeded healing and that being with the city's people nurtured the dragons in return. Most days you could see people walking slowly or sitting quietly there, one hand on a dragon's scaly flank.

'She's usually here,' Joe whispered to Winter, trying to see between the railings that fenced the square.

To his relief, he saw his cousin sitting on a bench with

her friend Thom Windlass, both drinking coffee, while their dragons – Iggie and Ruby – basked in the cool yellow sunshine. Milla was yawning. Thom sprawled next to her, long legs stretched out in front of him.

Joe had always liked Thom. He looked like Joe's image of a pirate: tall, with a broad handsome face, a neat trimmed beard and long brown hair tied back in a ponytail. He was the son of a fisherman, and he was now in charge of mapping the whole area around Arcosi. He and his dragon, Rubina, Ruby for short, would be gone for days, even weeks, surveying the whole region, and then instructing the cartographers back on Arcosi how to update the ancient maps.

How would they react when they saw him? Would Milla be relieved, or furious? For a moment Joe was paralysed.

Then he thought of the eggs. They had shadow dragons inside. Perhaps even now they were almost ready, preparing to hatch? If they couldn't find some silverblue, these rare creatures would die before they even had a chance to live.

He pushed the gate open and hurried through, his words spilling out like a waterfall. 'Milla, I'm so sorry, for everything. For the ceremony, for disappearing. I fell, down in the tunnels. I hurt my head. This is Winter, who rescued me. And I found some eggs and we think they're shadow dragons and they're going to hatch: the water's gone hot. But we have to find silverblue, or else they'll die. And what about the volcano – is it dangerous?' He ran out of breath and stood there gaping like a landed fish.

'Joe?' Milla whispered, then clapped one hand over her mouth, shocked.

Thom looked equally stunned. 'Joe? Oh my stars,' he said. Milla stood slowly, shakily. Then she collapsed back down. 'No! We thought . . . we thought you were dead!' The colour drained from her face.

'I'm so sorry!' He rushed to her, arms outstretched, and then Milla was hugging him so hard it squeezed all the air from his chest. 'Thank you – for what you did. Your hands . . . The burns . . . Are they . . . ?' he mumbled incoherently into her hair.

'My hands?' Milla's voice was tight with tears. 'They're fine now.'

Iggie bent over them, breathing hot gusts down Joe's neck and making strange high-pitched squeaks that Joe had never heard before.

His cousin pulled back finally, but kept tight hold of Joe's hand and stared at him searchingly from head to toe, apparently satisfied he was well and whole.

'Joe, Joe, Joe. I can't believe it. Oh! Wait.' She spun on her heel and stared at Iggie. For one intense moment, they looked at each other in silence.

Something was passing between them; Joe could almost see it in the air, like a heat haze. Iggie blinked his green eyes, once, twice. Then he stepped away and launched himself into the air, stirring up dust and dried leaves in his wake.

'I've sent him for Josi and Nestan. They need to see you – now. Oh, Joe, I can't believe you didn't tell them . . .' she reproached him softly. 'Have you any idea . . . ?' She saw his expression and broke off.

He looked down, his face flaming with embarrassment.

'I thought they were better off without me. I shamed them. Shamed everyone.'

'Joe, you listen to me: you made a mistake. Everyone does that. That's nothing compared to how much they love you. All this time . . .' Her voice broke, but she struggled on. 'All this time, we've all been blaming ourselves, your parents worst of all. That we didn't prepare you right. That we didn't teach you about disappointment. Or how to manage that temper.'

'Why?' Joe was bewildered. 'It was my fault, no one else's.'

'And that Noah!' Milla swore. 'Amina told me, after-wards, how he teased you.' She shook her head, so her black curls escaped their blue band.

'Milla, please – did you hear what I said about these eggs? It's urgent.' Everything else faded in comparison with them, burning brightly in his mind.

'But Joe, your parents! You've can't just walk in and expect us to f—'

'I know! I don't expect anything. But please, *please* will you help us find some silverblue?'

Thom had been listening, hanging back to give them space. Now he came up and greeted Joe with a hearty slap on the back. 'Hey, Joe. Good to see you're still with us,' he said. 'I know silverblue. What do you need?'

Milla finally released Joe's other hand, accepting that her cousin wasn't about to disappear along with the morning mist. 'Go on, then. Tell us everything.'

So Joe and Winter joined Milla and Thom on their bench,

and he began the story again, more slowly. He told them all about the new eggs, with Winter chipping in to add clarity.

Thom said afterwards, 'The water, the sudden heat – it all matches what I've seen, flying east these past months. There is a volcano, Mount Bara, out at sea, several hours from here. There's smoke and steam, underwater jets bubbling up in the ocean.'

'Isn't it dangerous?' Winter asked.

'Maybe. I don't know,' Thom said. 'I didn't think so – it hasn't erupted for a very long time – but I've been meaning to go back, to speak to the people living near there. Just to make sure.'

'Joe, we've got so much to talk about, I don't even know where to start.' Milla sighed, shaking her head. 'Are you sure this can't wait?'

'I'm sure! We found the eggs. We did the research. We need to act now.' How could he convince her? 'It's important. As important as Iggie's egg was to you.'

'But everyone thinks you're dead. We had a ceremony and everything.'

Joe felt sick. He pictured his parents at his graveside. 'What will happen, if I come back?' he made himself ask. 'Will they punish me?'

'I think you've been punished enough, don't you? And Lanys has answered for Ravenna's lack of control. But we need to see these eggs – will they need a Hatching Day soon?'

Joe gulped. He hadn't thought of that. He'd been so sure the purple egg was his. He imagined having to give it up, having to watch the dragon bond with someone else.

He shook his head. 'We don't have time. We need to get the silverblue first. Please, Milla!' He swallowed his pride and begged her. 'We can't let everyone sit around deciding what's best. We can't let the shadow dragons die, trapped in their shells. Please!' He would risk everything, let them take his egg to a hatching ceremony. But he had to be sure they would live, before anything.

Milla frowned. 'And if we do succeed, what then? If we find the silverblue and we hold a ceremony, the dragon might not choose you.'

'I'll face that if I have to. I'll give up this dragon, if I have to. I'll do *anything*. But we have to find some silverblue quickly. We have to save these eggs.' Joe realised that he meant it: the dragons' lives were more important than his dreams.

Milla nodded, as if that was the answer she'd been waiting for. 'All right, we'll keep your secret for now. I hear you – if these eggs are to hatch while the water runs warm, you'll need to find some silverblue, fast,' she said. 'The volcano could stop rumbling any day.'

'Or it could erupt,' Thom said, earning a glare from Milla. 'Sorry!' he said, holding up his hands. 'It is possible . . .'

'Tell us about silverblue, Thom,' Joe turned to him.

'It's a mineral, a kind of precious stone.'

'Where can we get some?' Winter said. 'The book said it's common across the region.'

'Not any more.' Thom's handsome face clouded. 'Those books you were reading must be old. It used to be found here, but it was mined too deeply. There's none left on Arcosi.'

Joe felt that like a slap. 'None? What are we going to do?' Panic crept into his voice.

'There's an archipelago south of here where I've seen it,' Thom told them. 'You'll have to go there, near the Spice Islands.'

'Then that's what we'll do,' Joe said, his mouth suddenly dry.

'We can't leave the eggs!' Winter said.

'Do you want them to hatch?'

'Of course,' she said.

Joe tried not to think of the alternative: his dragon, inside its egg, struggling vainly to get out. 'I'll do it. I'll do anything.'

'I'll go for you,' Thom offered.

'It's too dangerous!' Milla sounded stern. 'I can't believe you've been going there alone; there are all kinds of wild beasts on the islands. No, if we need to find silverblue, then we all go together.'

'Thank you,' Joe said to his cousin.

Winter looked torn at the idea of leaving the eggs. 'How do we find a boat?' she asked. 'How long will it take?'

'Don't worry,' Thom said, smiling. 'We don't need a boat. We've got two dragons.'

'You'll really help us?' Winter had been hiding under her hair, as usual, but now she smiled at Thom, looking like another person entirely.

Milla put a steadying hand on Thom's arm. 'We will. We can *all* go search for silverblue tomorrow. I'll need the rest of today to prepare. But first things first – you'd better show us these eggs.'

'Now?' Joe asked, hardly daring to believe it.

Just then, Milla looked up, tilting her face to the pale rays of the rising sun. 'Actually, Winter can show us the eggs. Right now, you have something more important to do. Look!'

Iggie was circling overhead, with someone clinging awkwardly to his back. Someone who wasn't used to flying on dragonback.

'Dad!' Joe whispered. Then he shouted, 'Dad!'

Iggie landed in the open garden, flapping hard to keep his balance.

Joe stumbled towards the blue dragon as his vision smeared and blurred.

Nestan was slipping off Iggie's back. Without his cane, he limped towards Joe with an incredulous look of joy and pain that scalded and soothed him all at once.

'Dad. I'm so sorry, I'm—' Joe's words were silenced by that gaze, then he was caught up in Nestan's strong arms. With horror and relief, he felt his father's shoulders shaking with sobs. He'd never even seen him cry before. 'I'm sorry, I'm sorry, I'm sorry,' he mumbled, feeling his own tears begin.

'Jowan. You're alive,' his father managed to say, pulling back and wiping his eyes with one forearm. 'How? I can't believe it . . .' Nestan patted Joe's face and neck, as if trying to convince himself this was his son and no mirage. 'My boy . . .'

'Dad!' he said. 'I'm sorry for everything. What I did—'

'That doesn't matter now.' His father's eyes were

127

bloodshot and tired, but they burned intensely. 'Nothing else matters,' he whispered, 'now you're back.'

Over his father's shoulder, Joe saw the iron gate fly open, and his mother ran through it, breathless, red-faced, tears streaming down her cheeks. 'Joe!' she bellowed. 'Is it really my Joe?'

'Oh, Mum,' Joe's voice sounded strangled and strange. He didn't know if he was laughing or crying. He didn't know what he was saying or doing. All he knew was that he needed this. He'd missed this: his family, together again, weeping and talking and laughing and breathing, warm and real and *his*.

CHAPTER EIGHTEEN

Milla let Joe and his parents use her room in the healing house, so that Joe's return could be kept as quiet as possible, though Milla promised to get the good news to Tarya via their dragons. Thom slipped away briefly to ask his father to visit Sartola on his next fishing trip, so Isak – who had just left Arcosi – wouldn't mourn his brother any longer. Then Winter took Milla and Thom down underground to see the eggs and show them the warm, acrid water.

Meanwhile, Joe, Nestan and Josi spent the day talking, with frequent breaks to eat the food Josi fetched from home.

'Oh, Joe, you really thought we could live without you?' Josi said, her face tracked with tears.

'I thought you were angry . . .'

'We may sometimes be angry, but we will always forgive anything you do.' Joe's father's voice sounded hoarse and choked with emotion.

'I heard someone say—' Joe stopped. 'That . . . that it

would be better if I were dead,' he finished, with difficulty. 'Someone almost died that day. So I believed it. I thought I should stay away. So I couldn't make it worse.'

'Well, that took courage. And surviving like you did . . .' The rest of his mother's words were lost in more sobbing.

'I didn't want to come back till I'd made you proud.'

'We've always been so proud of you,' Nestan hugged Joe to him.

'I'm sorry you thought I was . . .' Joe couldn't finish.

'There was just one sighting of you after the storm . . . it gave us hope for a while,' his father said, speaking into Joe's hair, as he held him close. 'We thought they'd been mistaken. But you did survive, you did!'

It took a few hours to persuade them to let him out of their sight again. But by the time it grew dark, he had their blessing, and Joe felt lighter than he had in weeks. He left his parents with a warm farewell, promising to visit them as soon as he returned from finding the silverblue. Then he hurried through the tunnels and up again to join the others in Milla's dragonhall, where she and Thom, with Winter, were getting ready for the trip.

Milla had hung a sign on the huge double doors, ordering them not to be disturbed, and it seemed to win them some privacy as they packed and planned for the journey. 'Those eggs, Joe! They're beautiful.'

'Shadow dragons? Do you agree?'

'Yes, there's no doubt. You were right.'

Joe needed to hear that. He smiled at Milla and started helping to sort through their supplies.

'And there's something else,' Milla said.

Joe looked up: she sounded awkward, as if there were something she wasn't sure how to say.

'Ah, er, it's too late for these eggs to be given a hatching ceremony,' she said quickly. 'They've already bonded with you and Winter.'

Joe paused, hardly able to believe it. He remembered the spark under his fingertips, how strong the pull to his egg had always been. 'I thought they had! I knew it! I always wanted the purple egg. Oh, Milla!'

He looked over to Winter. She'd obviously heard this already, and her smile was dazzling – soon, she would no longer be Dragonless . . .

'Wait,' Joe said. 'How do you know?'

'I just do,' Milla mumbled.

'Oh, tell him!' Thom said.

'Tell me what?' Joe looked at his cousin uneasily. He'd always trusted her. Why was she keeping something from him now?

'I can see it, that's all,' she said quickly. 'The bond between people and dragons – I see it like a glow.'

'That's amazing!' Joe said. 'What does it look like?'

'The colour of the dragon, usually. So the link between me and Iggie is blue; Thom and Ruby have a red one.'

'Yes, we learned about this in dragonschool,' Winter said. 'About the bond between dragon and their person, and the ways to block it, using a barrier like yew wood, or a herb like lavender . . . But I never knew before that anyone could see it.'

131

Joe could dream now of attending the dragonschool one day. He might finally get to learn everything he'd craved. 'Can everyone do it? Do you learn how to see it at dragonschool?'

Milla looked embarrassed. 'Er, no. I think it's just me. I've never found anyone else who can do it. But Isak always checks with me in a hatching ceremony that I've seen the connection begin, before he confirms the bond.'

'Oh! That's what it was.' He remembered Milla's nod to Isak, back on Hatching Day. He could think of it now without the same awful pain. He was quiet for a while as he went back to his task, absorbing all the new information, still glowing with joy that his bond to his egg would never be challenged now.

Thom was surprisingly strict, swift and highly organised, piling a heap of dried meat for the dragons to eat, and filling huge flasks of water. Joe watched him pack a leather backpack with maps, compass, knife, snare, tinderbox, ropes, water flask and bandages.

'Are you expecting trouble?' Joe said, only part-joking, seeing Milla also packing healing supplies.

'You have to take the right equipment,' Thom said. 'The dragons' lives might depend on it, and ours. If I got injured, Ruby wouldn't leave me. I need to make sure I can get us back safely, whatever happens.'

Thom's enormous scarlet dragon was dozing near the stove, alongside Iggie. Hearing her name, she lifted her huge head and sighed a long smoky breath.

'Hey, Joe, come over here, get to know Ruby a bit more.

It's a long flight tomorrow and everything will be easier if you're used to each other before we start.'

'Good idea, Thom,' Milla said. 'Winter, same to you. You'll be flying with me and Iggie so come and have a sit on his back now while he's basking. He'll get used to the flavour of your thoughts.'

Joe had been worrying about Winter: would she be able to handle being so close to two dragons? Would it bring back memories of Jin? He watched her with concern now, but her curiosity seemed to be winning as she went to greet Iggie.

'What do you mean, *her thoughts*?' Joe asked Milla. 'Do they have a flavour?'

Winter didn't seem surprised – maybe she'd learned this during her training too.

'Of course.' Milla looked up and grinned at him, her hands busy rolling a cloak so it would fit in a small side pocket. 'Dragons can sense more than anyone used to realise: moods, thoughts, feelings, or if you're about to do something.'

'How?' he asked.

'I don't know exactly,' Milla replied. 'It could be a mixture of scent, or if they're sensitive to every movement we make – even ones we aren't aware of. But it's been proved time and again. You saw me tell Iggie to bring your parents today. And when I had to leave him and flee the island during the revolution, your sister's dragon sensed my arrival on the mainland.'

Joe would look forward to sharing all his thoughts with

his purple shadow dragon. For now, he focused on approaching Ruby with nothing but calm and welcoming feelings uppermost in his mind. 'Hello, Ruby,' he said, stopping an arm's-length from her massive head, which was still resting on the floor, her scales glittering in the sunshine.

She opened one eye, full of swirling lights and keen intelligence. It had a massive green iris slashed with a vertical black pupil. She grunted, and Joe wasn't sure what that meant: the sharing of thoughts obviously only went one way. Maybe it would be different with his own dragon.

'Go on,' Thom urged him. 'She's saying you can approach. Just talk to her. Don't worry – if she didn't like you, we'd all know by now.'

'Can I touch her?' Joe called.

'I'm not the boss of her, Joe. Why don't you ask Ruby?'

He focused on the purple-red dragon, trying not to think about how easily she could squash him if she wanted to. He pictured the journey they were about to make. 'Er, hello, Ruby?' he tried again. 'Uh, uh, thank you for letting me ride with you tomorrow. I hope I won't be too heavy.'

Did that sound disrespectful, like he was doubting her strength?

Ruby twitched her ear and let out a whoosh of hot air that smelled of smoke and charred meat.

'I've never ridden a dragon before,' Joe told her, 'so thank you for taking me along.'

Ruby was watching him now with both eyes open. She raised her head slightly and leaned out to sniff him. Her head was the size of Joe's whole torso, and her jaws could snap his arm as easily as he'd take a bite from an apple.

He held his arm steady. *Be calm, Joe*, he told himself, *she's just finding out about you*. He thought then about his hopes for their journey, how he really wanted to find the silverblue so he could take it straight to the hidden eggs. His mind turned to the eggs: his excitement at finding them; his concern for them; his love for the purple one.

Ruby growled gently and then nudged him with her nose, tucking him closer to her massive body.

'See!' Thom shouted over. 'She likes you. Told you.'

Hardly able to believe it, Joe spent some time whispering to Ruby, passing his hands gently over her scaly sides, getting to know her, telling her what was on his mind.

When he looked over her broad back, he could see Winter doing the same with Iggie.

'Right!' Milla called finally. 'That's all our bags packed. You two can sleep here tonight so we can leave at dawn.'

Winter looked at Joe. He knew she wanted to say something. When he'd finished talking to Ruby, he sidled over to join Winter. 'What's wrong?' he asked.

Winter's face showed conflict and concern, but she couldn't speak.

'Do you want to check on the eggs?' he guessed. 'It feels wrong to leave without telling them, doesn't it?'

Winter's smile was brief and bright as a flash of lightning. She nodded.

CHAPTER NINETEEN

Later that night, Joe and Winter slipped out and went back to the hidden eggs. They chose the fastest route: running through the deserted streets of the shadow strip.

'Wait,' Winter said, stopping so suddenly that Joe bumped into her shoulder. 'What's that noise?'

A high-pitched cry floated on the still night air.

'A cat?' Joe guessed.

But then a loud jeering blotted out the cry. It came from a few streets away.

'Oh no.' He recognised a voice. 'The Brotherhood.' He started sprinting towards the sound.

'Joe, no!' Winter shouted after him. 'Wait! Not tonight!'

But he had a horrible feeling about that noise. He sped round the last corner, and halted.

There were only a handful of men, but they were making so much noise, echoing from the walls of the ruined shadow strip, that it seemed like more. They were standing round something huddled on the floor. One held a lantern high, casting a pool of greasy yellow light.

Joe tried to peer through their legs.

It was a person. A young man, Joe saw. He was curled up, with his hands protectively over his head. They were taking it in turns to kick him.

Joe was filled with that boiling rush of anger again – just like on Hatching Day – but this time he welcomed it. He let it fill him – burning, powerful – and without a second thought he pushed through the men.

'Stop!' Joe roared. 'What are you doing?'

They paused, surprised to be interrupted.

His anger won him a few moments. With his heart racing, he glared round the circle. Only then, standing there, facing the men, did he realise how foolish he'd been.

He became their new target.

One of them pushed him hard from behind, and he stumbled into a black-clad man who looked familiar.

Yannic!

'Hey, look, Asa. Look, lads: it's our new friend, Joe Thornsen. The *waddler*!' Yannic shoved his face close to Joe's.

Backing away, Joe almost tripped over the young man on the floor. He glanced around the circle of faces – three new ones, and the tall man, Asa, their leader.

'We meet again. It must be a sign,' Asa said with a slow smile.

'What do you think you're doing?' Joe clung to his anger, because the alternative was helpless fear.

The man on the floor groaned.

'Let me get rid of him, Asa. We were nearly there with the other one. Quick, before someone comes,' Yannic said.

'We've got to get help – he needs a healer now.' Joe looked over his shoulder, and by the wavering lantern-light, caught a glimpse of the injured boy's round face, patched with the beginnings of a beard. He spat blood-streaked saliva. With horror, Joe realised it was Tiago, from Conor and Amina's dragonhall. 'I don't understand. Why would you hurt him?' He searched their faces for some clue. Last time these men had offered him food, ale, warmth. He'd *sung* with them.

There was silence.

Five men stood there. Tiago was barely conscious. Joe was unarmed. He prayed that Winter had run to fetch some-one. He had to make this last long enough for help to arrive.

It took all his strength to ignore the fears that clouded his mind. If they'd welcomed him once before, maybe he could use that now? He forced his shoulders back and looked Asa in the eye. 'So,' he said, 'last time, you said I could join you.'

'Oh no,' Asa said. 'Not so fast . . .'

Joe guessed that they wouldn't be fooled for long, but he tried to sound interested. 'Why don't you tell me more about your Brotherhood?'

'You should be on our side, after what you did at that ceremony. You have the courage to challenge things,' Asa said. His voice was softer now and his eyes narrowed warily. 'If anyone should understand, it should be you. Your father is a great Norlander. And you were cheated of your dragon, by these, these . . . incomer scum.'

Joe shivered, hearing the hatred in his voice.

'Bloody Sartolans,' another one was saying angrily. 'Or Silk Islanders. Or whatever they are. They're like cockroaches.'

'Yeah, we should burn their boats.'

'Leeches, more like. Coming here, taking our jobs. Taking the dragons.'

Joe's mouth went dry and sour with fear. He didn't want to make them angry. He was totally outnumbered. But he couldn't agree with a word they said. The island was full of different people from all over the world – everyone knew that! His father's people had travelled here, seeking a better life. So how could Norlanders object when others settled here too?

He wanted to yell in Asa's face – *You know nothing: Tiago didn't* steal *my dragon. She chose him! Lina was never going to choose me!* – but he needed to buy more time.

'What do I have to do to join the Brotherhood? I know you were soldiers, from the old duke's army, but do you take new recruits as well?' Joe lied boldly, thinking he could at least learn something before they started beating him too.

'You have to be a Norlander,' Yannic said.

'You know I am. You know my father,' Joe said, feeling disloyal to his mother and praying no one started calling him a *halfie*.

'You have to share our values.' That was Asa, sounding suspicious. 'And I don't think you do. Unless you prove it,

139

right now.' He gestured at Tiago on the floor. 'With him. You can take over the persuasion. Get him to talk.'

'What did he do?' Joe played for more time.

'What does he *know*, more like. Dragonschool schedules, patrol routes . . .' Yannic said before Asa shushed him.

'Too many questions,' Asa said quietly. 'I think it's time you chose sides, Joe Thornsen. Are you with us, or against us?'

Joe met his gaze, thinking fast. There was no way he could join them in hurting Tiago – but he needed a distraction.

'If you don't choose, we'll take it badly,' Asa purred. 'We'll take that as a *no*.'

Just then, a hail of rocks started raining down on the narrow street. One hit Yannic hard on the temple. Joe saw his eyes roll back in his head and he slumped down on the cobbles.

Joe put his hands over his head and crouched low, trying to avoid the rocks and half cover Tiago at the same time.

Asa backed away, sword raised, looking all around for the hidden assailants.

Stones came whizzing down – now from this broken window, now from that rotting balcony. But there was no one to be seen.

'It's the ghosts!' one man yelled. 'I told you we shouldn't come here.'

'Don't be a fool—' Asa ordered. But then a stone hit him on the back of his head, and he spun round, looking furious.

Above them, a pair of shutters burst open and a stream of bats came pouring out, a mass of fluttering shadows, flying in all directions.

'Argh! There's a bat in my hair!' one man cried, dropping his sword to brush the bats away.

Meanwhile, the stones kept coming, sometimes hitting the men, sometimes the bats, but never hitting Joe or Tiago, though one bounced off the cobbles right by Joe's foot.

It was too much. The men fled in terror, leaving Yannic unconscious on the floor, while Asa stood there, still searching for his hidden enemy, his vision clouded by the swooping swirling bats.

Joe saw his chance. He bent and grabbed Tiago under the arms and dragged him to his feet. Struggling under his weight, he managed to wrap his right arm round his shoulders, and stumble away down a side street. He ignored the bats – he was used to them now from the cave.

'Walk! Come on, Tiago,' he hissed in his ear. 'Use your feet. We've got to get away.'

With his eyes still closed, and blood dribbling from his nose, Tiago managed to stay upright and help Joe a little as they fled the scene.

They struggled through the streets back to the healing house, always choosing the narrowest ones.

'Joe! Wait for me.'

He gently lowered Tiago to sit down, and peered round, as a patch of shadow detached itself from the walls.

Winter emerged, breathing hard, dangling a catapult from one hand. She held a stone in the other.

'It was you!' Joe could hardly believe it. 'Where did you learn to do that?'

'A girl alone has to be able to defend herself,' she said.

'You were amazing! Thank you!'

'Not really. They're superstitious fools. Scared of harmless bats! Is he all right?'

Tiago was folded forwards on his knees, holding his head in both hands. One eye was so swollen he could barely see, and his face was dappled with bruising.

'He will be, once the healers have him.' He asked, 'Did you hear those men? What they said?'

'Once I thought they were drunken fools,' Winter said tightly. 'But the Brotherhood are getting bolder. I've seen them – meeting at night. They're not going to go away.'

'My sister and the duke will have a plan to deal with them. I'm sure they will.' But Joe shivered, remembering the meeting he'd been to, and he hoped he was right.

CHAPTER TWENTY

Joe and Winter got barely any sleep after running around the city all night. They managed a brief visit to the eggs after they'd left Tiago at the healing house, making him promise never to say who had helped him. It seemed to Joe that he had only just closed his eyes when Thom was there, shaking him awake in the dim warmth of the old dragonhall.

'Come on, today's the day.' Thom sounded painfully cheerful.

Joe struggled into his warmest clothes, clumsy with fatigue, yawning constantly. Milla had found the fur-lined hat and long leather gloves his mother had given him on his birthday, which he had left behind that awful day, and he pulled them on gratefully now. He was going to ride on a dragon!

Milla lent Winter a set of her dragonrider blues, insisting she needed to be well wrapped up for the heights they'd reach on their flight. 'The winds go right through you up there,' she said, making her put on a hat, scarf and gloves. 'And, Joe? I've got something else that belongs to you. Come here.'

She stood on her tiptoes and reached up to fasten something round Joe's neck. He felt the cool metal disc settle into place at his throat, where it belonged, and he knew it was the medal she'd given him on his birthday. 'I haven't earned it yet,' he whispered.

'You never had to. We are family, Joe. Nothing will change that.'

'Thank you,' he mumbled, praying that he would be worthy of it one day soon.

'What's wrong with you two today?' Milla asked next, peering at them more closely.

Joe met Winter's glance. Milla was right: she looked awful, with purple shadows under her eyes. Winter shook her head slightly. They'd agreed not to talk about the attack last night. Tiago was safe and cared for. If they told Milla now, she would want to investigate, the trip would be delayed, and their eggs might miss their chance at hatching. They didn't know how long the cave stream would run warm.

Time was running out.

'Didn't sleep much,' Joe said, 'from excitement.' That part was almost true.

While the dragons ate huge quantities of roast goat, Joe forced himself to eat a bread roll, even though it seemed tasteless and claggy in his throat.

The dragons took themselves for a short warm-up flight

before their long journey, and Joe, Winter, Milla and Thom walked in a strange procession, laden with supplies, to meet them on the highest point of the island. The hill behind the palace was the easiest place to launch from, Milla told them.

'You all right, Joe?' Thom called as he led the way. 'Ready?'

Joe let out a strange laugh. No. He wasn't *all right*. He was something else entirely. 'Fine,' he managed to say. He was shivering hard, and he had no idea if it was from cold, nerves or excitement. One thing was clear: he felt as though his real life had begun. At last. It had begun the day he met the purple egg. Here he was, setting out to achieve something, finally.

They reached the hill and clambered up over the rocks, pushing past bushes.

Winter looked different today in the new clothes, taller, stronger: like a dragonrider. Her black hair was plaited tightly against her head. Joe realised there was a practical reason for the style all the dragonriders wore – so your hair didn't blow in your face and blind you while flying. Winter's movements seemed more confident and practised today, reminding Joe that she'd done all this before. But her face was closed in concentration, giving nothing away.

Finally, the four of them stood on the rocky outcrop on the highest point of the island – even the palace lay below them now. Away to the north, grey-blue sea glittered in a wide sweep to the horizon.

'Right, let's go,' Milla said. She held her arms up and called, 'Iggie? Down!' and gestured for him to land.

Iggie circled, lower and lower, and then with a rushing of air and a beating of blue wings, he landed and roared his greeting.

Milla embraced him, running her hands over his neck. 'Yes, he's ready. Let's go, Winter, before he gets cold.'

Milla climbed on first, her backpack bulging. Thom helped her to sling the heavy water flasks round Iggie's neck in a kind of leather pannier, and then Winter clambered up and sat in front of Milla. They looked like sisters today in their matching blue clothes and black plaits.

Joe grinned and shouted, 'Safe flight! See you at the half-way island!' They'd pored over Thom's maps and realised there was only one place they could rest, half a day's flight away. *If they navigated wrong and missed it, what would happen?* he wondered. The dragons would fly till they could fly no more. He pushed the fear of a watery death from his mind. Thom knew the way; he did this all the time. But not with a passenger – that was extra weight that Ruby wasn't used to.

The red dragon's landing jolted him from his worries.

'Stop dreaming and get on the dragon,' Thom shouted, climbing up on her back.

And then it was all happening.

Ruby's green eyes. Her vastness, filling his vision. Her red scales beneath Joe's fingers. Thom behind him, his strong arm round his waist – 'Just till we're in the air, mate' – and the feeling of Ruby's strength. Her wings opening. The massive reach of them in the corner of Joe's eye. The flapping, the lurch and the jump – *surely they weren't going to make it?* – the sea, the rocks, the rocks – *and, oh! They were flying.* The sea was falling away below them; the air was rushing past his face. The sun rising, dazzle-bright. They flew south, with Arcosi to the west, looking like Joe'd never seen it before, a jumble of rooftops, trees and towers.

The world was transformed into air and wind. The horizon vanished in a veil of cloud. The speed of it made Joe's heart race. He wanted this; oh, how he wanted this! One day, with his dragon, would he do this? The wind pulled tears from his eyes and the world blurred into brightness.

'Wow!' he shouted.

'You've got that right,' Thom said, laughing in his ear. 'It never gets dull, I promise you. We are lucky men, thank you, Ruby!'

Joe felt the dragon's rumbling growl in response, actually felt it, in her body beneath him. 'It feels like a miracle!'

And for the next few hours, it seemed true, as they flew steadily over the sea.

Joe heard the map flapping in the wind behind him several times as Thom pulled it out to check their position. Joe had brought along his father's compass, and he called out readings as they flew. Thom and Ruby seemed to be communicating – he felt Thom moving his heels and hands on her sides, and told himself to sit very still and let them do their job.

Thom finally yelled, 'There!' and pointed ahead at a tiny speck of gold in the vastness of the blue sea.

Joe felt giddy with relief. The island grew bigger and

bigger as they approached. It turned out to be a tiny lump of rock and sand, with no trees and no water.

By the time they landed, it was clear the dragons were tired and the people were numb with cold. Joe went tumbling over Ruby's shoulders as she landed awkwardly. Clambering up, stiff with cramp and very hungry, for the first time, Joe doubted if they would make it.

'How long to go?' he asked Thom, as he poured out some fresh water into a depression in the rock for the dragons to drink.

'Three hours at least,' Thom said, checking the sun. 'Don't worry, it's all going according to plan. We'll need to fly a survey of the first island we come to, make a safe camp, and then go dig out the silverblue.'

It sounded so easy.

'So how will we find it?' Winter said. She was pacing in small circles, spinning her arms around after hours of sitting still. 'We don't even know what we're looking for.'

Joe was glad she'd said it. So far, they'd been carried along with Thom and Milla's planning.

'I do,' Thom said. 'When it's polished and worked, it looks a bit like opal, a bit like pearl.' He gestured in the direction they were headed. 'And flying over those islands, I have seen the seams of raw silverblue in the cliffs.'

'It sounds beautiful!' Winter said. 'Is that why there's none left on Arcosi?'

'Yes. Beautiful and rare – that's a combination some people will pay anything for.'

'But the dragons need it!' Joe said.

'How long have you known it was there?' Winter asked.

'A year, or so.' Thom looked embarrassed. 'I, er, I might have taken some.'

'Why didn't you say?' Joe asked. 'Where is it?'

'I don't have it now! I'm sorry. I didn't know it was important, before. No one knew about the shadow dragon eggs.' He paused. 'I've got to make a living. I trade things from my trips.'

'So you've been selling silverblue secretly all year! I thought you were flashing your gold around a bit freely, Thomsen Windlass!' Milla teased him. 'How much did you take?'

'A bagful. Maybe two. I wish I'd kept it!'

'What did you do with it?' Joe couldn't help asking.

'I sold it, after I'd had it made into jewellery. I'm sorry, Joe: if I'd known, I never would've. But the coin was welcome, and there's a silversmith in Sartola who owes me a favour,' Thom finished, apologetically.

'Oh, I'm sure he does,' Milla replied. 'Why didn't you tell me if you needed money?'

'I've got to keep up with my fancy friends, don't I?' Thom's eyes were alive with mischief now. 'Some of them are even related to ancient royalty.'

'Oh, stop it,' Milla scolded, but she was laughing too. 'I guess there was no harm in taking some of the silverblue before you knew what it was for.'

'Thank you!' Thom retorted, 'I didn't realise I needed your permission . . .'

They carried on teasing each other, as Joe laid himself

down in the warm sand and closed his eyes, giving in to the tiredness.

In his dream, Joe was trapped underground and water was rising all around him, bubbling, boiling. It was getting higher and higher. It covered his feet, then his legs, then his torso. It rose over his neck and he started to panic. He felt the water covering his mouth his nose, his eyes. All he could see was water, and bubbles, filling his thoughts until—

'Joe!'

He woke, gasping, and jerked up to a sitting position.

'All right, Joe?' Winter was there, still looking unfamiliar in Milla's borrowed jacket and clothes.

'Bad dream.'

'I was about to wake you anyway. It's time to go.'

Joe couldn't shake off the feeling that the dream was a warning. He wanted to fly straight back to the eggs, but he couldn't return empty-handed. Last night, he had made a promise to his egg. *Next time I come*, he'd whispered to the purple egg, *I'll bring silverblue, and you can hatch!*

He got wearily to his feet, ready for the last part of the journey, hoping he would be able to keep his promise.

CHAPTER TWENTY-ONE

The rest of the journey passed in a hazy blur for Joe. He felt so befuddled with tiredness it was all he could do to cling to Ruby's back and not tumble over her neck into the sea far below. His joy at flying was now numbed by exhaustion. He kept his eyes on Winter and Milla on Iggie's back, their black plaits down their backs, the dragon's blue wings wide open with the wind beneath.

'Wake up, Joe,' Thom said, 'We're there. You can see the Spice Islands, in the far distance . . .'

Joe peered ahead and, sure enough, there was a scattering of small islands like pebbles in the sea. 'Does anyone live there?'

'Not on the first three,' Thom answered. 'People prefer the southern ones. You can't grow much on these steep hills.'

Ruby started losing height, getting ready to land.

The first island, Joe could see, had sheer cliffs. It was topped with a rocky hill of loose scree and slate, with a fringe of green trees, shrubs and tangled vines. 'Where's the silverblue?' he asked. He needed to stay focused, and fight the tiredness. They had one job: get the silverblue, then they could get some sleep, and get home to the eggs.

'There!' Thom pointed, his arm stretching over Joe's shoulder.

They swooped down suddenly. Joe's stomach lurched and he bit his lip, tasting blood. He gripped Ruby as hard as he could with his legs, clutching backwards at Thom with both hands, and praying they didn't all slip off and get smashed on the rocks.

Thom laughed, but it wasn't unkind.

When Ruby levelled out, they were flying alongside the cliffs, the sea foaming below. The cliff face was dark grey, but it had veins of glittering blue-white threaded through it. *Silverblue!*

'How do we get it out?' Joe yelled into the wind.

'You'll see.'

The dragons circled the island, till Thom decided it was safe to land.

It wasn't any easier the second time, and Joe went flying over Ruby's head again to land in a heap at his cousin's feet, his bag a few strides beyond him.

Winter helped him up, as the dragons greeted each other and set to preening while the sun was still warm.

Milla was frowning and looking behind them. They stood on a narrow strip of grass on the clifftop, obviously cropped short by rabbits or goats. 'I don't like it, Thom,' she said.

'Why?'

'There's the forest at our backs. There's the sea in front. Not an ideal camping spot. Nowhere to run.'

'We don't need to run. We can fly,' Thom said. 'The dragons are right here. We don't need long. I've done this before, remember? Just enough time to tie a good knot and lower myself down and chip away some of the blue stuff.'

'You're going down?' Joe asked. He should have guessed someone would have to.

'Just watch me,' Thom said, unbuckling his backpack and taking out a coil of rope.

'What do we do?' Winter asked Milla.

'Stay alert,' Milla said. 'Iggie's usually the first to scent trouble, from people or predators, so we should be fine, but we need to post a lookout . . .'

But before she could finish, Thom started walking towards the first trees, the rope slung over one shoulder. He bent to tie it round the trunk of a sturdy evergreen. He tugged it hard to check the knot, and shouted, 'Let's go!'

It all happened so fast then, Joe could hardly believe it afterwards.

A bulky shadow rushed out from the shade of the trees. Ruby bellowed, but she was too late. The creature leaped at Thom and he was on the floor, being pawed and mauled by – what was it? A boar? A rhino? It was moving so fast Joe couldn't tell.

Milla shrieked and sped towards Thom, drawing a dagger from her boot, and sprinting fast.

Thom was fighting off the animal, his hands up to protect his face, but it was biting and slashing, and they rolled over and over as they fought. It had the thick armour of a rhino, the head of a boar, horns and huge teeth, and the sturdy muscular legs of a wolf.

Ruby launched herself towards them, but she couldn't attack, not without risking injury to Thom too. Milla struck, sharp and swift, managing to plunge her knife between two armoured plates, into the creature's ribs. She withdrew the blade and it dropped to the ground.

Then there was another snarling beast streaking across the grass towards them.

'Winter!' Joe yelled. 'Look out!' He pulled his dragon-handled knife out and crouched, blade up, ready to fight.

This time Iggie reached the attacker first. With his powerful hind legs, he squashed the animal entirely. He twisted down and gripped it in his powerful jaws, shaking it to and fro and finally flinging it away, right over the cliff.

Joe and Winter stood back to back, so they could see in both directions.

'They're senglars, I think,' she cried. 'I read about them in one of those library books. Dangerous predators, native to these islands.'

'Did you also read about the best way to kill them?' Joe shouted hopefully.

Iggie kept guard, roaring his fury at this strange animal who had dared to attack the people under his protection.

Milla was dragging Thom back towards them under Ruby's watchful eye. His arms were slashed and bleeding, and there was a gash across his forehead, but he was conscious enough to look utterly embarrassed.

'Thom!' Joe cried. 'Are you all right?'

'He's an idiot,' Milla snapped. 'He should have waited till we'd posted a lookout. Iggie? Ruby? Guard us, while I clean him up.'

The dragons seemed to understand. Ruby took up a defensive stance next to them, while Milla laid Thom down on the cliff edge, and started rummaging through her bags for bandages and healing supplies. Meanwhile, Iggie paced closer to the trees, ready to pounce if anything else should emerge.

'Right,' Joe said, putting his knife away. 'I'll get that rope. If Thom can't get the silverblue, I'll do it.'

'No!' Winter said. 'You have no idea what to do.'

'It's our best chance,' Joe told her. 'Listen, my dad's a sailor too, as well as a merchant.'

'What has that got to do with it?' Winter looked bewildered.

'He taught me knots and ropes. I can do this,' he said, making himself sound more confident than he felt.

Before he could change his mind, he went and picked up the rope Thom had managed to knot around the tree before he was attacked, and he set to work.

CHAPTER TWENTY-TWO

Tiredness and fear rolled through Joe, and then left, leaving him calm and clear, like the sky after a storm. *Either I'm going to get the silverblue*, he thought, *or I'm going to die trying.* It seemed very simple.

Thom looked over, groaning, but able to instruct him. 'That line's too tight,' he said through gritted teeth. 'It needs to flow as you move. Let me—' he tried.

'No, Thom,' Milla scolded him. 'You're still losing blood.'

Joe went over to him. Thom dragged himself into a kneeling position to help him adjust the rope: it went in a kind of zigzag from his right hand, then between his legs, through his belt buckle, then over his shoulder to be payed out through his other hand.

Winter was darting around, collecting Thom's tools and bringing them to Joe – a fabric sling that he wore round his chest to collect the silverblue, and a small iron chisel to chip it out of the rock face.

He tucked the chisel in the sling for safekeeping.

Then it was time.

He looked at the others: at Thom lying on the grass, looking ashen and sick with pain. At Milla bending low over him, working fast to clean and cover the deep scratches on his face and arms. At Winter in her blue clothes – at her face, so full of anxiety.

He looked away. He had to focus.

He leaned on the rope, testing it. It was fine quality and very strong – Thom was a fisherman's son, all right – and Joe trusted the knot he'd tied round the tree. He pulled the rope taut and let it flow through his fingers, slowly, slowly, edging towards the cliff edge.

He peered over his shoulder, seeing it approach, and then he was there, his feet on the final fringe of grass, peering over, to the dark blue frothing sea so far below. One foot slipped, and he caught himself, but his heart was trying to leap right out of his chest now, and his fingers were hot and damp on the rope's coarse fibres.

He breathed slowly in the salty breeze that flowed up from the sea. *Come on, Joe, do it for your egg.*

And even though every part of him was screaming danger, he leaned back into the wind, letting the rope take his weight, holding himself in the strange, fragile harness he'd created with his body and the line, and he made his feet step over the edge of the cliff.

He'd seen people do this to take birds' eggs from a cliff face. The trick was to lean right back and trust the rope, keeping your feet steady on the cliff and walk backwards, as if it was a perfectly normal thing to do.

The other trick was not to look down.

Too late – he caught a glimpse of slick black rocks far below and the waves surging over them.

He forced his chin up, holding himself steady with the rope in both hands, and took another step down, and another.

He stared hard at the cliff face and, just below him, there sparkled something that looked like silverblue. Was it? Excited now, he peered down and caught sight of a wider seam, pearly pale in the dark grey rock. This was what he needed. Another few steps.

Now came the hardest part. He had to knot the lower part of the rope to the upper, passing it round his chest slowly, so he didn't tumble out entirely. His hands were shaking, clumsy, damp with sweat. Painstakingly, he pushed the rope into a knot and tugged it tight. Now he was dangling in the loop he'd made, so he could free one hand and use it to dig out the silverblue.

Carefully, he bent his knees, coming closer to the cliff. Not taking his eyes from the silverblue, he wiggled his left hand into the folds of the sling and felt for the chisel. It fell from the sling – he cursed! – but it landed on his bent knees and he snatched it up before it could tumble into the sea.

Sweat was trickling down his neck. His right arm strained on the rope. His heart was racing. He took a deep breath, brought the chisel up and chipped at the blue-white rock. A little piece fell away, right down into the sea, but more chunks landed on his lap, caught in the fabric of his trousers.

Joe transferred the chisel to his teeth, gripping it tight,

while his fingers roamed blindly and found each precious crumb of silverblue, tucking it away safely in his pockets and sling.

Next time he pushed back a little further, creating momentum to force the chisel in harder. Once it was stuck fast, he levered out a larger lump, and to his relief, it fell on him, not past him and down into the sea.

Again, he rammed the chisel in his jaws for a moment, grabbed the silverblue and went back in for another swipe.

It was hot and painstaking work, chipping away, sometimes losing the bits of silverblue, sometimes catching them, but he kept on, and on, until he knew his arms could take no more.

Just then, Winter's head appeared over the edge of the cliff above him – she must be lying on her stomach – and she shouted down, 'Joe! Are you all right? Is it working?'

'Yes!' he called back, trying not to think about how he'd climb back up again. His right arm started to shake with the strain. 'I've got some. Not sure how much we need!'

Just then, there was a distant scream. Winter vanished from view.

'Winter!' Joe yelled, dropping the chisel and hearing it skitter down the cliff and clang onto the rocks. What was happening? He dangled there, helpless. He tried to listen for more clues, but he could hear only the endless crashing of the waves and the pounding of the blood in his ears.

He pictured terrible things: Winter hurt; Milla bleeding; Thom dead. He fumbled with the line, tightening the loop so he held the upper rope in both hands again, with its snaking shape round his body. He slipped, crushing one arm against the cliff, trying to get some purchase on the rock again, so he could start climbing up, an inch at time.

He was gripping the rope tightly, and even that seemed impossible now he was so tired. Somehow, he had to let go with one hand, and grab the next section, just a little higher, then repeat it, fist over fist, climbing up and up and up, grimly determined.

His palms were already raw and his arms were soon burning with agony. He counted in his head each time he reached up another fistful of rope, rewarding himself for every single tiny movement in the right direction. One . . . two . . . three . . . Somehow it helped him focus.

He'd just reached nine, when something huge flew overhead. Clinging to the rope, twisting his head round, he saw it was Milla and Thom on Ruby.

Joe felt as if he'd turned to ice, his mind frozen in shock and fear.

Where was Iggie? Where was Winter?

His mind felt numb and disbelieving. It made it impossible to go on.

He hung there, arms screaming to let go.

And then, in a blur of blue wings, another dragon blotted out the sky and flew overhead: Iggie, with Winter clinging to his back.

They were leaving.

For a horrible, heart-stopping moment, Joe thought they were abandoning him. Then Iggie circled round and returned to hover, near enough for Winter to yell across to him.

'Joe! There are more senglars up there. Too many to fight off.'

So what could Joe do? He couldn't go up, and he couldn't last long here. He gulped, desperate, looking down and wondering if he'd survive the fall.

If only he could leap across to Iggie – but he had nowhere to jump from. 'Can you come nearer, Iggie?' he shouted.

Iggie's wings beat fast, but it was an impossible manoeuvre, so close to the cliffs – he risked injuring his wings, and then they'd all be lost.

'Trust Iggie!' Winter was screaming. 'That's what Milla said. You have to trust him.'

'To do what?' he cried. Clinging to the rope, his arms were near their limits, hot and painful, he couldn't hold on much longer. With his eyes squeezed tight against the sun, he caught a glimpse of the blue dragon.

Iggie was battling to hold position in the air, fixing him with his fierce green glare.

Help me, Joe thought. *I can't hold on.*

His fingers started slipping on the rope, his mind a whirl of desperate fear. He was going to fall. The rope whipped through his belt. It rushed through his hands, burning his fingers. He caught the last section, hanging there by one hand. He had only moments left.

What had Winter said? *Trust Iggie?*

So he did. He screwed his eyes tight and let go, praying the blue dragon could reach him in time.

Iggie!

He was falling!

And then he wasn't.

'Argh!' he cried out, gripped by sharp claws.

The rope dangled uselessly against the cliff.

Joe was lifted by Iggie's powerful talons. He was carried up, up, up, into the air, his palms ablaze, and his arms as stiff and solid as if they'd turned to stone. Iggie carried him right over the heads of the pack of grunting, snapping senglars, tiny eyes narrowed, furious at losing their prey.

Joe's vision began to swim. In one final glimpse, he saw that Iggie was heading for the other side of the island. Distantly, he realised he was being dropped onto a rocky slope. He felt the pain as he sliced his skin on stony scree. Finally, he couldn't see anything. As he slipped into unconsciousness, he heard Winter's voice and her strong arms dragging him onto Iggie's back.

'You did it, Joe! You got the silverblue!'

He let himself loll there, exhausted, unable to move or speak, but he felt one arm around his waist, the dragon's leap into flight and the beat of wings, and he knew Iggie and Winter would never let him fall.

CHAPTER TWENTY-THREE

This was not the plan. They were supposed to camp on the island and return the next day, refreshed by sleep and food. Instead, the exhausted dragons carried their injured people home to Arcosi, flying through the dusk. The sea was a vast darkness stretching out beneath them. There was a streak of orange light in the western skies, and the stars appeared one by one as the sky faded to inky black.

Joe slipped in and out of consciousness, sure that Winter's iron grip round his waist kept him safe. Every time he jolted awake, his rope-blistered hands went to the sling round his chest, checking the silverblue was still there. At first, he could still see Ruby, carrying Milla and Thom, but soon they vanished in the night.

Finally Winter spoke into his ear, rousing him from a strange fitful slumber. 'Joe! Wake up. We're home. Careful now.'

He jerked into wakefulness. His shoulders were throbbing

where Iggie had grabbed him; and even the slightest movement of his arms caused agony. He hissed at the pain, and tried to keep still, using his legs to hold on as Iggie started soaring down, towards the lights of Arcosi.

Iggie let the winds carry them past the island, and then they circled back, losing height fast. Joe clung on and prayed they'd land somewhere near a tunnel entrance. He wasn't sure how far he could walk.

To his relief, it worked: perhaps Iggie felt his desperation. The blue dragon landed, clumsily this time, only just missing some apple trees in the overgrown gardens of the shadow strip. Dragons' night vision must be better than mine, Joe thought. Flares burned on the palace garden walls high above them, lending a faint orange tinge to the darkness, just enough to see by.

Wincing, careful of every move, he managed to swing his leg over Iggie's ears and dismount. 'Thank you. Oh, thank you, Iggie.' He bowed his head in deep respect. 'You saved my life.'

Milla's dragon rumbled a response, deep in his vast ribcage, and his wings folded down at last.

'Here, there's a well.' Winter tumbled off and showed Iggie where he could drink. They heard the gulp and hiss as the blue dragon sucked down huge amounts of spring water. Winter ran her hands over his back, deep midnight-blue in the near-dark, whispering her thanks too.

'Will he be all right?' Joe mumbled. He felt ready to collapse, and it seemed impossible that Iggie could launch again, after such a long gruelling day.

'Ig, can you find Milla? Do you know where she is?' Winter asked. 'Did she take Thom to the healing house?'

Iggie finished drinking and raised his head, scenting the air. He started lumbering to the edge of the gardens. He seemed restless suddenly, and eager to leave.

'What's wrong?' Joe asked. 'What if something's happened to Milla, and Iggie knows?'

'It's all right – he just needs to find his person,' Winter said. 'And we need to find our eggs.'

Joe's hand fell on the sling and he pulled his mind back to the task they'd risked everything to achieve. They had to get the silverblue to the eggs, and fast. It began to sink in finally: the eggs had a chance, right now, a real chance of hatching.

Iggie perched on the wall at the edge of the gardens and used the drop to help him launch. Joe listened to the wingbeats disappearing, then turned to Winter. 'All right. I'm ready.' He gritted his teeth against the pain. He could do this.

'Wait, let me fetch a light. You can refill the water flasks and wash your scratches in the well.' Winter vanished into the nearest ruined villa and Joe did as he was told, grateful not to have to make any more decisions. She reappeared holding a lit candle moments later. 'All these houses in the shadow strip were abandoned. Some were taken, along the lower street, but people think these ones are haunted. It means they haven't been looted, so they're full of useful things.'

By the flickering golden light, she found a cellar door

she'd used before, and they descended into the tunnels, cool and damp, with that sulphurous smell.

They reached the egg cave and went in, clumsy suddenly, as they grew near.

Joe fell on his knees, and with trembling, painful hands, he opened the casket. The eggs waited there, but their glow was fainter. There was a new smell rising from them – sour, rank, rotten – like old seaweed at the high-tide line.

'What's wrong with them?' Winter cried. 'Are they dying?'

'Quickly! There's no time to lose.' Joe fumbled in the sling for the pieces of silverblue. They fell in a pale scatter and he dotted them around the eggs, on the velvet. 'Should they it touching, or just near them?'

Winter shook her head, eyes dark in the candlelight.

'What did it say in the book, do you remember? Something about sparks and liquid fire?' Joe eyed the candle. 'I did feel a spark that time – you felt it too, didn't you?'

Winter recited the words she'd memorised from the ancient book:

'In the island's secret heart,
From liquid flame, there comes a spark.

With fire and water, earth and air,
Forged in the ocean's hidden lair,

A broken heart will dare it all,
Take the leap and risk the fall.

From ash and bone, new life will rise,
Shadow dragons roam the skies!'

'But what does it mean?' he cried anxiously. They had risked it all, hadn't they? He'd taken the leap when he went over the cliff. What else did they need?

'We've done what we can. We've brought the silverblue. Maybe it takes a while. Let's wait till morning and see what happens?' Winter suggested.

They sat down in the dim fuggy cave, trying to stay awake. The warmth made Joe's head swim and his vision blur. He had to stay awake, he *had* to! What if he missed the hatching? But his eyelids grew heavy. He'd had so little rest the last two nights. *I'll just rest my head for a moment*, he thought, *just a moment*. He lay back and put his head on his aching arms.

He woke, hours later, and immediately knew something was wrong. The candle had burned to a stub, but it still cast a soft yellow light round the cave.

'Winter! Winter! Wake up.' He scrambled to his feet and peered at the eggs.

'What is it?' Winter gasped, rubbing sleep from her eyes. 'Are they dead?'

Joe grabbed for the purple egg: there was no spark today and its glow was dimmer, almost gone. Its ridged surface seemed parched and there was a crack on one side, not a crack as if it was hatching, but a dried-out brokenness.

Winter was right: the eggs were dying.

He held it up, close to his face. 'Please don't die.' His

heart felt like a bruise in his chest, sore and tender. 'What did we do wrong?' This was *his* dragon. His only dragon, his only chance. He'd known it from the first moment he'd seen this egg. Despair threatened to swamp him.

He hardly dared turn to Winter. He'd failed her. Winter, who'd lost so much. What would happen if she lost this as well? It was too much to bear. She seemed so different from that restless brittle girl he'd first met. And now this: it wasn't fair.

She was holding her egg, rocking it, tears pouring down her face. 'Don't go,' she pleaded. 'Don't leave me.'

Joe closed his eyes, wishing there was something he could do, wishing they knew more. He fought not to sink below the crashing waves of grief and fear.

All at once, he recalled his nightmare from the other day: water rising, rising, rising. Maybe it wasn't a warning. Maybe it was an instruction.

He swayed where he stood, stronger than last night. He rolled his shoulders experimentally – yes, they were better. He checked his hands: the scratches were healing. The eggs must still be alive if their strange healing power still worked.

'I've got an idea,' he said, hope growing inside him now. He wedged his egg in the crook of his left arm. *And we have nothing to lose, if they really are dying*, he thought, but didn't say, wanting to protect Winter from that as long as possible. He gathered up the pieces of silverblue. 'Winter? Let's go to the stream in our cavern.'

She looked up blearily, her face slick with tears. 'Joe, it's too late . . .'

'It's not! Please. I have an idea,' he repeated. 'Remember what the book said, about silverblue and heat and moisture? Well, I reckon they actually need to be in the water!' He saw her battling with the decision, as if it was easier to slip into despair than to dare to hope. 'Winter! Don't give up. Not yet. Not till we've tried everything,' he begged her.

She didn't reply, but she too tucked her egg carefully under one arm, then reached out with her other and let Joe help her up.

They left as fast as they dared, back down the steps and through the winding tunnels under Arcosi, all the way back to the large cavern.

They found the stream of water that bubbled and flowed through one side of the large cave. Joe dipped his hand into the pool, fearing it would be as ice-cold as that first day.

No, it was hot now, even hotter than before. What did that say about the volcano if there were hot jets bubbling up all over the region, even this far away from Mount Bara? He couldn't worry about that now.

Joe stood next to the pool with his egg in his hands. Was he really going to do this? He had a strong instinctive sense it was the right thing. 'They're shadow dragons,' he said aloud. 'They're different. They swim, don't they? They belong in the water now.' *I hope!* he added silently.

'Joe, I'm scared,' Winter said.

'Me too, but we have to try. We can't let them die.' He held her gaze steady, wishing with all his heart that he was right. 'Remember what else the book said, all the stuff about the elements? Well, they're all here, all the elements: the silverblue we mined from the island, maybe that's *earth*. There's *air* that we breathe and the bubbles in the water. There's heat from the volcanic flows – that must count as *fire*. And there's *water* right here. Look, I'll go first, to see if it works.'

He brought the egg to his chest and wished it all the luck in the world, and then he lowered it slowly into the pool of hot water.

There was a ledge there, and he released the egg carefully onto the rocky shelf. It stayed in position, the warm water flowing over it. The purple luminescence grew brighter, flaring below the water.

'Look! That's got to be good, right?' Joe said.

Winter gasped, and hurried to do the same thing with her egg.

Joe felt for the silverblue, the little blue-white rocks gleaming like moonlight, and he put them in too, all around the eggs, like a nest.

They started fizzing. Each piece of silverblue sent up a stream of tiny bubbles.

'What's happening?' Winter asked.

'They're reacting – that's what the other book said. It must be part of the hatching process, to thin the eggshell . . .' Joe watched all the silverblue pieces dissolve and vanish.

'What shall we do now?' Winter's face was streaked with tears and dirt, but her eyes were brighter again.

'We wait,' Joe said firmly.

They sat cross-legged on the rocky floor and kept their

eyes on the eggs on their little ledge, glowing brighter and brighter with every passing moment.

'It's working,' Winter whispered hoarsely. 'Thank you, Joe.'

CHAPTER TWENTY-FOUR

Nothing happened immediately, although the increased glow from the eggs gave Joe hope. They sat, watching the eggs, passing the water flask between them and sharing a handful of dusty raisins from the bottom of the backpack. Winter lit another candle from the stub of the last one.

'What time is it?' Winter asked. 'Wait, what day is it, even?'

'I've no idea,' Joe said. He'd lost all sense of time down here in the darkness. 'Does it matter?'

'The other eggs hatched at full moon – do you remember how full the moon was last night?'

He remembered how velvety dark the sky and the sea had been. 'Definitely not full – there was hardly any moonlight, was there?'

'Oh.' She sounded concerned. 'Do you think it's going to take that long – till the moon is full again?'

'Maybe they're the opposite of usual dragon eggs. Maybe

the dark moon is just what shadow dragons need?' He realised again how little they knew, as he watched the eggs glowing under the water. He thought of Milla – it must have been the same for her when Iggie hatched. That made him feel better.

'What if they are already dead? What if they drown because of what we've done?' Winter said. 'Or, what if they actually live under the water?'

'I can swim,' Joe said firmly. 'Can you?'

'Yes, but . . . not just that, also, what do we feed them? What if they need fire? What if . . .'

'Winter,' Joe put a hand on her arm. 'We'll work it out, whatever it is, when they hatch.' He paused. 'When Jin hatched, you said it was natural as breathing, like catching a wave?'

'That's true,' she said, sounding stronger. 'It was scary, sure, but I got carried along with it. There was no choice, no time to worry.'

'So maybe this will be the same,' Joe said, hoping desperately to be right.

It was so hard to sit and wait, not knowing how long it would take or if anything would happen. But when he compared it to the Hatching Day on his birthday, Joe knew this was better. There was no one to see, no one to judge him. Just him and his egg. Just Winter and hers. They could do this.

And then something changed.

The eggs' light started fading.

Joe noticed first. 'No, don't go! Winter, look!' he cried.

The glow dimmed, gradually but undeniably, the way the sun slipped below the horizon, taking the light with it. So the luminescence slowly faded, faded, and went out.

They were left in candlelight. The water looked darker now. Winter leaned over, holding the candle as low as she dared. It was hard to see, with the golden reflection bouncing off the surface. She pulled back and stuck the candle on a ledge, so they both had a clearer view of the eggs, sitting there in the pool.

Joe leaned over, his heart pounding. Was this what he'd dreamed of, or his worst nightmare?

Long moments slipped by in silence.

'Look!' He gave a yelp. 'It's cracking – it really is!'

His egg had a deep split on the surface. Something flickered in the gap, he was sure of it. 'It's moving. It's *alive*!'

Painfully slowly, as if it took huge effort, the purple spotted egg was gradually pushed apart from the inside.

'Come on, little one. Let me see you!' He breathed on the water, leaning right over the pool in his excitement. Nothing else mattered, just this little creature, working its way out.

Finally, the egg cracked into three large pieces, rocking gently in the water, and Joe saw for the first time what had grown inside. There was a small shiny body, a blunt flat head and four skinny limbs, flailing around.

'It needs to breathe!' he gasped, not stopping to question how he knew. He shoved both hands in the hot water and took the wriggling creature in them, lifting it carefully to the surface. It was so slippery he almost dropped it, just managing to cup his hands and lift it up into the air.

The hatchling's head was slick and dark. It took a deep, hoarse breath.

Joe laughed, feeling tears pricking at his eyes. It was so small. Like a baby bird. Like a little wren.

And just like that, he knew who she was.

'Hello, Ren,' he said, bending his head low to see better, to drink in every detail.

The baby dragon was about as big as his hand: her body was slender, with four sleek limbs and a long purple tail that twitched from side to side. Her wings were still folded, lumpen masses of darker plum on her back. She lay there, sides heaving, breathing in-out, in-out.

Joe waited, hope and fear swirling through every part of him. Was she more like a fish? Did she breathe in the air, or the water? Was this the right thing to do?

Then she opened her eyes. He forgot to breathe, lost in her beautiful, golden eyes. They were oval, full of intelligence, full of questions. He felt himself observed, weighed, judged. He waited, hoping, hoping, hoping she would find him worthy.

Finally the hatchling opened her mouth and gave a little croaking mew. She had tiny needle-sharp teeth, white as bone.

'Hey, you.' Joe grinned and let out the breath he'd been holding, as relief flooded through him. 'Hungry yet?' He twisted his head, hissing, 'Winter? What do we have that they might eat?'

'I'll check.'

From the corner of his eye Joe could see her rummaging through the backpack.

'Fish. Dried out, but they should do.'

He knelt back on his heels, bringing the hatchling away from the water and closer to his chest, nestled there on one hand. He took a little dried fish from Winter's outstretched hand and held it near the dragon's mouth.

Ren sniffed, a little haughty, then snapped and swallowed the dried fish in one gulp. Then she stood up properly, strength growing. She stretched her whole body, seeming longer every second – how could she have fitted in that egg? Then she shivered and her wings sprang open: astonishingly wide, smooth and strong, the skin stretched tight between the delicate bones. Joe could see the tiny veins carrying blood to each part of her wing.

Ren flapped a few times, raising a draught, then folded her wings back and mewed for more food. Joe laughed and fetched another fish, glancing over to see he had left enough for Winter's hatchling, when it came.

He peered over. Winter hung over the pool, her face pinched and desperate.

Joe knew better than to ask. There was no sign of life from the green egg.

CHAPTER TWENTY-FIVE

Joe held his hatchling against his neck so Ren could be warmed by his bare skin and he could feel her wriggling body and know she was all right. Inside, his thoughts swished in opposite directions: relief at Ren's arrival; concern for Winter and her egg.

Winter hunched over the pool at the eastern edge of the large cave, tension in every inch of her body. She was still dressed in the dragonrider blues Milla had lent her – a dragonrider with no dragon.

Yet.

But as he watched, something changed. She straightened up, lifted by an invisible string.

'It moved,' she said softly. 'I saw it. It cracked.'

Joe peered down, praying it wasn't just the flowing water nudging the egg. No, there it was, an unmistakeable zigzag fissure across the ridges of the green egg. It was just harder to see because of the stripy markings.

'It's hatching!' Expressions flickered over Winter's face,

hope and fear and grief and love, like a stormy sky split by shafts of sunshine.

Joe could only guess how hard this was for her, with all the echoes of the past. 'It's coming!' he said. 'Your dragon will be here soon. Come on,' he urged it.

He felt Ren notice it too. She lifted her head and chattered encouragement, and he caught sight of her tiny sharp teeth again. Joe cupped his hands and she hopped down onto them, leaning forwards to see what was happening below the water.

Then, all at once, Ren dived off Joe's hands and back into the pool, vanishing under the flowing water.

'Ren!' He swore. Where was she? Would she be swept away by the current? He couldn't see anything in the dark flowing water. 'Ren!' Had he come all this way, only to lose her now? 'Where are you?'

He saw a darting shape under the surface, swimming strongly. He lowered his face, so his chin dipped right in the water. Ren was using her limbs and her folded wings worked like fins, her body undulating, powering through the water. She circled the other egg and then surfaced, taking a deep breath and diving again.

Joe's panic receded a little. She knew what she was doing. He moved his attention back to the other egg, which was taking longer to hatch.

A bigger crack appeared.

'That's it,' Winter encouraged it. 'Come on, nearly there!'

It seemed to get stuck then. There was a long pause with no more movement. Ren swam in agitated circles.

'Maybe it's resting?' Joe said.

'It needs air!' Winter sounded frantic. 'What if it drowns?'

They stared at it, feeling helpless.

'Can't you do something?' he asked.

'They have to do it themselves,' Winter explained quickly. 'They build strength through the hatching process – I remember that from last time. If you help them, they might not survive.'

'But if you don't help it, it might not survive either.'

'Don't you think I know that?' she snapped.

Joe fell silent, flicking his gaze between Ren and the green egg, praying with all his strength that it would hatch safely – and soon.

Then, at last, the egg cracked in two and fell open.

Winter plunged her hands in, and Joe's view was blocked for a time. When he could see again, she was pulling out a shiny dark green hatchling.

Ren surfaced, mewing loudly as she struggled to climb up the slippery sides of the stream.

Joe lifted her out too. He and Winter were both half-soaked now, shivering as the water cooled, holding their hatchlings close.

'Is it alive?' he asked.

Winter held the creature in one hand, stroking it with the other. She breathed warm breath over its body, crooning encouragement.

Joe remembered the fish. He draped Ren on his neck again to free his hands, asking her to be patient. Then he knelt back and rummaged through the backpack till he found more dried fish in a paper wrapper.

When he looked again, the green hatchling was moving. It lifted its head and opened its eyes – that intense gold glare! – and growled lightly, greeting Winter.

She had tears rolling down her face and could barely speak. 'Hello, you. Hello, little one.' She sniffed and coughed, laughing through the tears. 'I know you. I am so glad to know you, Fidell.'

Joe said, 'Fish?' offering one, and watched with satisfaction as Fidell crunched it up and swallowed, looking round for more.

When both hatchlings had eaten enough, they set to preening themselves. Afterwards, Winter held Fidell out in her cupped hands and Joe mirrored her. The hatchlings called to each other, with chattering chirpy noises. They touched noses, and sniffed each other all over. Then Ren wrapped her long neck round Fidell's and curled up to sleep.

'Maybe we should rest too?' Joe said.

Trying not to disturb the hatchlings, they made a nest between their bodies and laid them in it. Joe curved his body in a semicircle on one side; Winter did the same on the other. Then the four of them fell into a deep, exhausted sleep.

PART THREE - FIRE

AIR

FIRE

WATER

EARTH

CHAPTER TWENTY-SIX

Joe woke in total darkness. For a long blank moment, he didn't know where he was, one cheek pressed into a cool sandy floor, an intense ache across both shoulders. Then he remembered: Ren!

His hands fluttered around, feeling for her little body, trying not to squash her.

'Mrrt?' Ren squirmed, nestled against his stomach, telling him he'd disturbed her sleep.

Joe listened carefully, holding his breath, till he was sure he heard Winter's steady breathing and Fidell's answering growl. 'Morning,' he greeted Ren, her claws needling up his arm as she climbed onto his shoulder. His mouth felt sticky and sour, his head pounding. He shook the water bottle and found it almost empty, so he took only a small swig, saving the rest for Winter.

Next, he felt around for the backpack. It took him a few moments to fish out the fire-makings and another candle, longer to squeeze out enough tiny sparks to ignite some kindling and light the taper.

Ren watched it all with great interest, leaning forwards. Her massive eyes reflected the flame: deep gold and so wise. Her head was flatter than a typical dragon, with larger triangular ears, pricked forward now. Her scales were iridescent purple, larger on the top of her head, tiny on her legs. Her neck was elegant and strong; her body neat; her wings unbelievably fine, silken and shiny. She was perfect.

Winter stirred then. Joe saw the moment she came to wakefulness and a wide smile lit up her whole face as she reached for Fidell.

'Morning. We need food – for us and for them. And more water,' he said, passing the flask.

Winter greeted her hatchling tenderly, and then stretched, with a loud yawn.

'I'll go,' she offered. 'You're injured.'

'Take more of the gold coins,' he reminded her, 'so we can get lots of food. Maybe that's why it's there – to provide for them.'

'I'll be quick,' she said. 'I don't want to be away a moment longer than I have to. Will you guard him for me?'

'With my life,' Joe said.

She bent her head to the little green hatchling, talking to Fidell in a soft whisper. His shiny head drooped, showing he'd understood.

Joe held out his hands to him. 'Will you stay with me and Ren?' Still perched on Joe's shoulder, Ren let out a stream of eager *aark aark* noises, welcoming Fidell. The green dragon walked from Winter's hands onto Joe's, climbed up opposite Ren and flopped down heavily. Joe sat very still, hardly daring to move, realising he was responsible for both hatchlings now.

'The quicker I go, the sooner I'll be back,' Winter said. She looked miserable but determined. She lit another candle, hoisted the backpack on her shoulder, and left.

Joe tried to ignore the gnawing ache of hunger in his stomach. He was glad when the shadow dragons jumped down and started to play with each other. They looked something like the sea otters he'd seen on the western beach. They rolled around, growling and play-fighting, then went back to the pool. Ren put her nose in the water, twitched, sneezed, and then dived right in, smooth and sinuous. She swam deep into the pool, rising for air, rolling on her back to see where Fidell had got to, and then diving again.

The green dragon joined her, tumbling in with a splash.

Joe tried to keep an eye on both hatchlings at once. It took all his concentration – and he felt the anxious weight of the responsibility. What could he say to Winter if anything happened to Fidell on his watch? To his relief, the two hatchlings soon got tired of swimming. They climbed out, stronger today, and shook the water off, preening a little and then coming to roost on Joe. They scampered towards him, making little cries of excitement, very pleased with themselves.

'Oh yes, didn't you do well? Fine swimmers! Come on then, come and get warm!' He gestured for them to climb up, laughing at the feel of their tiny claws as they swarmed up his body.

Ren lifted her head up and touched her nose to Joe's, greeting him as her person, telling him she was his. Joe's heart melted. He'd never felt anything like this before. His love for Ren felt vast and limitless: as big as the world.

Ren and Fidell grew sleepy. Ren yawned widely, showing tiny sharp teeth and a dark purple tongue. The shadow dragons curled up, one on each collarbone, and Joe cupped a hand over each of them, blinking hard.

Finally! A dragon had chosen him. He would build his life around her. He wouldn't let her down. He would prove he was worthy of her trust.

Winter returned soon after, with as much water and food as she could carry, dropping it all to scoop up Fidell. He watched them, realising it was the same for Winter and Fidell as it was for him and Ren. They belonged together, and they always would. Winter's face had lost that anxious, pinched look. There was still sadness in her eyes, even now, but it was overlaid with loving attention and delight in her dragon.

So began their winter underground.

Over the next few months, Joe and Winter took it in turns to forage or buy supplies, using the hoard of gold they'd found with the dragons. Joe learned the tunnels by heart till he knew them as well as the streets above ground. He managed to stay unrecognised, always pulling his hat low over his face. He felt like a different person now, walking with pride and purpose – maybe that helped.

He sneaked into the Yellow House to visit his parents

regularly, and his mother always loaded him up with as much food as he could carry. Sometimes Milla was there too. Now his family and friends knew he was safe, he asked them to let him stay down here a little longer, just till Ren was fully grown. The new dragons – and the new Joe – could be introduced to the city another day. For now, Ren filled his mind entirely and he couldn't think about anything else.

The shadow dragons grew sleek and strong, doubling, then tripling in size, again and again, astonishingly fast. They missed the winter storms and Joe and Winter kept warm in the cavern underground, focusing on their young shadow dragons.

Joe was happier than he'd ever imagined he could be.

Somewhere deep down, he knew it couldn't last.

Joe was minding Ren and Fidell in the large cavern one afternoon in spring. 'Hey, Winter, I hope you brought some more rabbits, these two are ravenous after their swim,' he called out, hearing footsteps.

Now large as hunting hounds, the young shadow dragons were always hungry.

Something was wrong. Usually Winter hurried lightly down the stone steps, but these footsteps were slow and uneven, with a strange accompaniment as though something heavy was being dragged along.

Joe sprang up, drawing his dragon-handled knife, which he always wore at his belt now. 'Who's there?'

'It's all right. It's me,' Winter mumbled, not sounding like herself.

Fidell streaked across, with a loud alarm call. Winter struggled down the final few steps, emerging into the circle of candlelight, with Fidell winding himself anxiously round her waist, almost tripping her up.

Joe cried out in horror. Winter's face had a streak of red down one side, clotted blood over her bruised left eye. Her dress was torn at the neck, and stained with something dark and shiny.

'What happened? Are you all right?' He darted over and took her arm. 'Easy now.'

'The city. It's been taken.'

Joe's mind felt slow and stupid. He couldn't make sense of the words. 'What? Taken? Who's taken it?'

'The Brotherhood.'

CHAPTER TWENTY-SEVEN

Joe felt cold. His thoughts flowed sluggishly.

'Let me see, let me help . . .' he tried.

Winter dropped the large sack she'd been dragging and stumbled forwards. Joe caught her, one arm round her waist, and led her across to the stream. He dipped his shirt sleeve in the hot water, bringing it gently to her face. Winter winced, but let him clean the blood from her cheek. Both dragons followed closely, making anxious high-pitched noises in the back of their throats.

'Who did this to you?' Joe asked.

'One of *them*. He tried to stop me. He tried to keep me from you, Fidell,' she muttered, keeping one hand on her dragon's neck all the while.

'Is this blood? Where are you hurt?' Joe demanded, as her dress fell forwards, leaving a crimson smear on his hand.

'Not mine,' Winter said grimly.

Joe gasped, understanding.

'He's not dead – just bleeding. It was his own knife did it. He would've killed me, otherwise.' Winter jutted her chin out defiantly, but he could see her fingers trembling as she stroked Fidell's head. 'They killed others.'

'When?' Joe managed.

'It started yesterday, at dawn. And . . .' She tilted her head, and looked at him. Her eyes were glassy with shock.

He didn't want to hear what she was about to say.

'Joe, they killed a dragon.'

'No. No, they wouldn't! Not even them.' Nausea rose then and Joe had to tip his head forwards, trying not to vomit, breathing fast.

'I saw. They paraded its body through the streets. And its . . . its head.'

'Who? Who was it? What colour?' Joe prayed it wasn't Iggie, or Ruby. It couldn't be.

'Red and yellow, I think. Or the red might have been blood . . .'

'Where's my sister?' Joe burst out, trying to make sense of it all. 'She would never let this happen.' He paused, realising what this meant. 'Oh no! She's not—?' He couldn't bring himself to say it.

'She's not dead,' Winter told him. 'I asked everyone: in the market, at the docks. People said they're prisoners: your sister and the duke.'

'But her baby! It must be coming any day now,' Joe looked down at Ren, full of protective fury. His fear for Tarya came out as anger. 'How could she let this happen?'

'You know how the palace gates are always open now?

It wasn't hard to do. The Brotherhood burned the armoury, surrounded the barracks and the palace.'

'But the dragons! Why didn't they stop them?'

'Rumour says they were dosed or poisoned, or – I don't know. Joe, I'm so sorry, but some of the dragonriders . . . they're on their side. They were there, parading with the Brotherhood.'

'Noah! I bet he is . . . But who else?'

'I can't remember their names,' she mumbled miserably. 'That black dragon, who flamed you.'

'Ravenna!' Joe remembered Hatching Day, how Lanys had looked at the Potentials with such mistrust.

'Your sister's dragon escaped – Heral and Petra, the duke's dragon, were circling the palace all day, trying to fight back. I saw them in the distance. But then they left.' Winter's voice faded out.

'They left? Heral abandoned Tarya? Are you sure?' Joe couldn't believe it. He couldn't believe any of it.

She shrugged, seeming groggy with shock. 'All I know is that they were there, fighting back. And then they weren't.'

'Oh my stars. I've got to go.' He was filled with desperate fear, as her words finally sank in. 'Now! I've got to check on my parents. Find my friends.'

'No!' Winter cried, grabbing his arm. 'Joe, you can't. You didn't see it. They're brutal. You'll be killed, and what will Ren do then?'

Ren's eyes were fixed on him. Joe stared back, finding comfort in her wise golden gaze, as he always did. His heart felt torn in two.

'That's why I brought so much,' Winter was babbling now, pointing at the large sack. 'There's food and water for a week, so we don't have to leave again while it's so dangerous. There's a curfew. There's blood on the streets. We have to stay safe, don't you see?'

Joe gulped. He leaned forward and embraced Ren hard, feeling the beat of her heart, the thrum of life in her scaly throat as she rested her head on his shoulder now. How could he leave her? For a moment he was tempted to stay. He was still a ghost, wasn't he? They weren't part of the city. They could pretend nothing had changed. Their life could carry on, uninterrupted. They'd have to forage at night, but they could survive down here.

But then he thought of his parents, alone. He thought of Conor and Amina – what had happened to their dragons? Where were Milla and Thom? They would fight back, he knew they would. He couldn't let everyone he loved risk their lives, while he kept himself safe.

'Ren, I'm sorry,' he whispered. His heart swelled to breaking point with the conflicting feelings. Her large purple ears twitched at the sound. 'I have to go,' he said, more loudly. 'I need to find my family. If I can get them down here, we can all stay safe. Till we can fight back together.'

'Down here?' Winter's voice turned shrill. 'No, Joe. This is their nest. Fidell and Ren are safe here. The tunnels are our secret: they're *ours*!'

He blinked, staring at her. How could they feel so differently about this? All winter they'd lived together and worked together, and suddenly she felt like a stranger.

'Please, Joe,' Winter begged him. 'I've lost too much. I can't lose Fidell, and I can't lose you.'

'I know. But I can't hide, not now, not any more.' He tried to explain, as softly as he could. 'I might be the only one who can help. I have to find out what's happened to my family and my friends. And if I can bring them down here to safety, I will.'

But she pulled away and wouldn't look at him again. She sat on the rocky lip of the stream, hunched up in her blood-soaked dress, barely able to see through one eye.

Joe felt as if he'd hit her himself. He unpacked the supplies, bringing Winter some fresh water and bread. She ignored him.

Ren and Fidell were making hungry growling noises, so next he found some rabbit carcasses in the sack and set to skinning them. Winter had been setting snares in the overgrown gardens of the shadow strip and they were a good source of fresh meat. He threw the finest parts to the hatchlings, hung some meat to keep for later, and washed his hands in the pool when he was done.

Ren and Fidell snapped the meat up eagerly and then licked themselves clean.

The smell of fresh meat filled the cave, making Joe's stomach roil, and filled his mind with images he wanted to avoid. He fixed his mind determinedly on the plan forming in his head. He knew he needed to stay strong.

Afterwards, he knelt and hugged Ren, leaning on her broad purple chest. Her wings were folded, her scales glinted dully, her ears drooped. *Mraa*, she growled softly, winding her long neck around his.

'I know,' he said. 'I know it's dangerous. I will be as quick as I can. I'll stay in the shadows. I won't take risks, I promise.' It was the best he could do. 'Stay here with Fidell and Winter. Stay safe.' He pressed his lips to her scaly head, wishing she were coming too. If she were smaller, he could hide her. If she were fully grown, she could fight. But she was still at a gangly, awkward, in-between stage – *a bit like me*, he thought – and he couldn't risk her getting hurt.

Walking away from the cavern was one of the hardest things Joe had ever had to do. But having Ren only made it more important to make the right choice. His father would do the same, he was sure. His feet felt heavy as anchors, but he made himself move through the tunnels, clutching Nestan's compass to guide him, to see what was left of the island and the people he loved.

CHAPTER TWENTY-EIGHT

Joe emerged from the tunnels, choosing the door closest to the Yellow House. He pushed it open and peeked out, checking east, west, and back again. The sea mist crept over everything, pale grey and thick as smoke. It took him a moment to recognise the familiar street, its stone cobbles and high walls made strange by the floating white mist clouds.

He climbed out into an alleyway just below the Yellow House. Joe looked back at the wooden door he'd just come through, with its peeling wooden frame. In his old life, he'd passed it hundreds of times, assuming it belonged to the next-door house.

He started creeping down the street, so close to home. If the main road was empty, he was just moments away.

Then he heard footsteps. He flattened himself against the wall, listening hard over the noise of the blood pounding in his ears. Tramping feet and men's voices. It was too late to run back: he'd be seen for sure. But with this mist, and a little luck . . . ?

Joe held his breath, and kept his whole body motionless.

The footsteps grew louder, so loud it seemed impossible they weren't heading this way. They echoed off the high walls of the buildings and the cobbled road, getting louder and louder.

He prayed not to be seen. He had to stay safe for Ren. He had to get back to her: their lives were bound together now.

'Some of them don't even remember – the new ones,' a man's voice was saying loudly. 'We'll show them how it's meant to be!' That earned jeers of approval.

Joe didn't catch the next sentence. They were moving away, down into the city. He was safe, this time. He waited, to be sure the men had gone. He could feel the mist, chill against his face, seeping under his jacket.

He stumbled forwards, out onto the main street, feeling dreadfully exposed. A few steps further and he reached the gate of the Yellow House. He reached out for the iron handle and pushed, hoping it wasn't locked, and to his relief, it opened and let him through.

His relief vanished when he saw the lock: smashed, twisted, hanging open. He tiptoed through, into the courtyard, trying to read what had happened here. His whole body was alert, ready to run or fight. There was a reddish-brown smear on the tiles, broken pots and soil spilling out.

'Dad! Mum!' he yelled now, heedless of his safety.

He ran up the steps to the front door, but it was barricaded from inside: something heavy had been pushed up against it. He hammered hard on the worn wood: 'Is anyone there? It's Joe!'

He cursed himself. He should have been here. Whatever had happened, he should have been here to face it, with his family, where he belonged. Panic gripped him now. His hands were slippery and damp as he tried every window, every handle he could find. He was locked out of his parents' house.

Eventually, he hauled over a bench, tipped it and climbed up, reaching for a first-floor window ledge. He pulled himself up on shaking arms, and slithered through, head-first, landing hard on the floorboards in his old bedroom.

Barely glancing around, he noted it was untouched, still neat and clean, then he was opening the door, listening hard, and padding out into the gloom beyond.

A sharp blade pressed into his chest. He could feel the cold iron bite into his skin. 'Stop right there,' a voice hissed.

'It's Joe! Who's that?' He raised his hands cautiously, peering forwards into the darkness.

The voice swore loudly. 'I nearly killed you, bloody fool!'

'Matteo!' He rubbed his chest where the sword had been, then found himself hugged hard by the old cook he'd known all his life.

'Just in time, lad. You're just in time,' Matteo said hoarsely. 'This way, they're down here.' He led the way down the main stairs. As they passed a gap in the shutters, Joe saw that Matteo looked exhausted. 'Joe, I'm sorry. We tried. We fought back, all of us. But there were too many of them, and we had to retreat. They killed Gabriel, and . . .'

Firelight danced in the largest room, casting shadows on the walls. Matteo gestured to the darkest corner, where a mattress had been piled with blankets, and a familiar shape lay curled amongst them.

Joe dashed over and fell on his knees. His mother was asleep. Her face was in shadow, but he could see clearly where they'd hit her. A bruise bloomed across the whole of her left cheek. He leaned his face close, till he could feel the flutter of her breath, and be sure she was alive.

'Joe?' she mumbled, trying to open her eyes. 'Joe! You came.'

'Of course I came! As soon as I heard.' He hugged her carefully, trying not to hurt her. 'Mum. I'm sorry. I wish I had been here.'

Tears leaked from Josi's eyes and slid down the sides of her face, into her silver-black hair. She'd always been so strong. Invincible. Seeing her like this was a punch to the stomach.

'Where's Dad?'

'Right here,' she croaked, trying to turn.

Joe froze. What he'd thought was a pile of blankets was another person, lying next to his mother.

He clambered over, pulling wildly at the closed drapes to let more light into the room. His father lay on his back, very still, the cold light falling on his face now. His skin looked waxen and grey, apart from the dried blood by one ear and in his white beard.

Joe felt all the air leave his body. He heard a ringing noise, tasted iron. The next thing he knew, he was bending over

Nestan's body, gently patting his face, whispering, 'Dad? Dad, can you hear me?'

His father's breath was barely there; it had dwindled to a feather-light whisper.

'What happened?' Joe lifted the blankets to see how badly he was injured, then wished he hadn't. 'No!' he bawled, shaking his head. 'No. No. No.' His father's shirt was soaked through. The bandages were leaking crimson, low down, round his middle. Joe knew enough to understand you didn't survive a wound like that.

This couldn't be happening.

'It was early this morning,' Matteo was saying. 'They pulled everyone out into the street, giving Norlanders a chance to join them. I think they targeted Nestan. If he'd joined them, a man of his standing, they'd have more authority.'

'Your father refused,' Josi said proudly, shifting her body round so she could face Joe and Nestan, hissing softly at the pain as she did so. 'Of course. Yes, he'd served the old duke, once. But he knows what's right. He would never betray Tarya and Vigo like that. Or me.'

'We fought them off,' Matteo said. 'I'm no soldier, but I have my knives. We tried as hard as we could, but there were more of them.'

'The Brotherhood are cowards!' Joe hated them so much. He hated what they'd done. He hated his powerlessness.

'They think they've won,' his mother said grimly. 'They think they've defeated us. But this isn't over yet.'

'I should have been here,' Joe said, seeing nothing but a blurry haze of firelight now.

'I'm glad you weren't,' his mother told him. 'They'd have hurt you too.' She leaned low over Nestan, stroking his face, checking his forehead, settling the blankets around him.

'Where are the others?' Joe whispered softly, trying not to disturb his father. 'Where's my sister – is her baby here yet? What about Isak?'

His mother told him that Isak was safe in Sartola with Luca; that Milla and Thom were on an expedition far away; and that no one had seen Tarya or Vigo since before the coup.

So none of Nestan's family had been there when he needed them.

'I'm sorry,' Joe said, bending over his father's chest. 'For everything.' He was overwhelmed with remorse then, unable to catch his breath as he wept, gasping and choking.

'Joe.' Nestan's voice was hoarse and low.

'I'm here, Dad,' he sniffed, wiping snot and tears on his jacket sleeve. 'I won't leave you.' There was a flicker of a smile at the corner of Nestan's mouth. Joe fumbled under the blanket, and found his father's hand. It was cold, far too cold. 'Can't we go for a healer?'

'Joe,' Josi said softly. 'I fear we are beyond that. I'm sorry.' His mother shook her head. 'And the island's locked down. You wouldn't make it back again.'

'It won't be long now,' Matteo said quietly. 'But I've given him herbs, for the pain.'

Joe made a space for himself next to his father, keeping hold of his hand, and lay down, as gently as he could.

'Where's your Ren? Is she safe?' Nestan squeezed his fingers lightly.

'Yes,' he said, with a hiccup that was half-laugh, half-sob. 'Ren's with Winter, in the tunnels. I came to take you down there so you'd be safe too.'

'You did it, Joe,' Nestan murmured. 'Did it your way. Always different.' There was something that might have been a laugh. 'Always so proud of you.'

'Oh, Dad,' Joe could barely speak. He wished he'd done more to make him proud, while he could.

'Your mother . . .' Nestan couldn't manage the whole sentence.

'I know,' Joe told him. 'I will take care of her. Promise.'

'Tarya . . . Isak . . .'

'They know,' Joe whispered. 'They know you love them . . .' He turned to the side so his tears didn't drip onto his father's face.

They spent the rest of the day like that, Joe and his mother lying either side of Nestan, Matteo keeping guard in the strange, quiet house. Joe took second watch, pacing by the door, listening to the sounds of violence in the lower city. When it was his turn to sleep, Joe lay down again next to his father and closed his eyes. He thought of Ren and hoped she would understand.

He woke to the sound of his mother weeping. Joe knew what it meant before he opened his eyes. He laid his head on his father's chest, cold and motionless now. 'I'm going to stop them,' he vowed in a whisper. 'I'll stop the Brotherhood before they destroy the whole city.'

CHAPTER TWENTY-NINE

They buried Nestan in the garden, there at the end, by the olive trees, witnessed by just the three of them: Joe, his mother and Matteo the cook. With the city under curfew, they had no other choice. They sat by the freshly turned soil for a while in stunned silence. It was a clear day, the pale lemon sunshine almost warm on Joe's skin. His hands were hot and sore from digging, and he brushed the sandy soil from his fingers. The sea in the distance twinkled light blue. He couldn't believe his father wasn't here to see it. Arcosi was silent, as if it joined them in mourning.

Joe felt as though he were underwater, moving slowly, pressed on all sides by the heavy weight of his grief. 'Come with me, Mum. I promised him I'd keep you safe.'

His mother refused to leave the Yellow House and hide in the tunnels. 'I'm not leaving this house. I'm not leaving Nestan,' she said, keeping her eyes on his grave.

'Well, I'm not leaving you then. Not yet.' The thought of

Ren tugged at Joe's heart, but he knew Winter would take care of her, and her food supplies would be lasting longer without him.

Matteo went to make something for them all to eat: soon the smell of frying garlic snaked out into the cool spring air.

Josi started to speak. In a low murmur she told him more details about everything that had happened on that terrible day. 'They marched the city elders down to the docks and sent them away to Sartola. Your brother – already there – will surely be planning a response: let's hope there's a city still to rescue when Isak gets here.'

Joe felt either dazed and sleepy, or itchily restless. His mind kept jumping around, trying to make plans, but only finding more and more questions. 'And Conor and Amina, all the ones with the newest dragons – do you know what happened to them?'

'No. Also prisoners, I expect, in the dragonhall maybe?' Josi had a blanket over her lap, the sunshine catching the silver in her hair.

Joe felt the beginnings of a new feeling – a stirring of anger, washing away his numbness and disbelief. 'What is everyone doing?' he demanded. 'How can they let this happen?'

'Joe, the Brotherhood used to be soldiers. Then – just before you were born – they lost what they valued most. They lost their place in the army, and with it, their pride. Our mistake was to forget that, and not to realise how much it meant to them. They're ruthless, furious and desperate.' His mother leaned forward, touching Joe's cheek. 'The attack on the city took everyone by surprise. Today, everyone will be hiding, mourning, licking their wounds, as we are. Our neighbours lost people too.'

He saw how fragile she looked, how tired. The bruises were deepening, yellow and plum, and her eyes were bloodshot from crying.

'It's too soon,' she said. 'They're frightened to move while the Brotherhood roam the streets. But they will resist, Joe, you can count on it.'

'I can't just sit here, waiting. I've got to do something.' Joe felt his head clearing a little, as the first shock wore off. It was replaced by more fury. He welcomed the anger, inviting it in. 'Let's strike now, before they get used to being in control.'

'Joe, no. Your father wouldn't want vengeance,' his mother said quickly.

'It's not revenge,' he lied, adding, 'it's what he would have done.' Time was running out. He needed to return to Ren, but he had to take action first. Just the first step. Like lighting the taper on a barrel of firepowder.

'Don't do it because of him. You don't have to prove anything.' Josi's face softened as she stared at her son through tear-filled eyes.

'Don't I?' He sounded bitter, but he didn't care. Of course he had to prove himself! As far as the city knew, he was a brattish, violent child who'd almost hurt a baby dragon and nearly caused a riot. He needed to avenge his father and show everyone he'd changed.

'Of course not,' his mother was saying. 'He loved you,

Joe. Just as you are. You don't have to do anything.' She muttered something that sounded like, 'So hard for you all . . .'

'What do you mean?' He sat very still now, listening.

'He expected a lot from his children. As he did from himself.' Josi sighed, now looking past him, into the far distance, where the city met the sea. 'Nestan had been many things: a sailor, a warrior, a wealthy merchant. He was a lot to live up to.' Tears slid down her cheeks now, but she didn't seem to notice. 'But he never saw that. He was always pushing himself. So kind and generous to others; so hard on himself. But, oh, was he proud of you!'

'Was he?' It was a new thought to Joe, impossible to believe. 'Still? Even after Hatching Day . . . ?'

'*Always*. So don't you go and get yourself killed because you've got something to prove. Promise me, Joe?'

'Mum, I've got to do something,' he insisted. 'Let me try, at least. Before the Brotherhood do any more damage. I'll use the tunnels: I'll be safe.' He kissed her head gently. 'I'm going to do it anyway, but I'd rather have your blessing.'

Josi frowned, wiping away tears with the palm of her hand.

'Anyway, you taught me, didn't you?' He took her hand and tugged it gently, reminding her. 'Sword skills, close combat, lock-picking and codes. You made sure I was ready. What did you do that for if you didn't want me to use it?'

That did it. She smiled ruefully and conceded the point. 'Go, then. I hope I taught you well enough. Know when to retreat, as well as when to fight. Promise me that, instead?'

'Promise.' Joe leaned in and they held each other tightly. He felt his shoulder grow damp with her tears.

Joe left at dawn the next day before his mother or Matteo were awake.

He realised he had to keep moving. If he stopped and let himself think too much, he was finished. He found he could sharpen his grief into a point, like an arrowhead, and use it to keep pushing forwards.

He was wearing old clothes, carrying his father's compass like a talisman now, hoping it would bring him luck. He also carried a storm lantern, a small backpack of supplies and the dragon-handled knife Conor had given him – though he prayed he wouldn't need it. He used the tunnels to enter the palace grounds, using the low door by the stables, and leaving the sack of food that Matteo had prepared for him just inside the entrance.

In the palace gardens it was almost full daylight, though the mist still hung low, making trees loom, eerie and ghostlike.

Joe hid the lantern and backpack, tugged his hat low, then rolled his shoulders, lifted his head, and walked straight towards the dragonhalls as if he did it every day. He reached the first hall without being seen. The doors were ajar. Inside, it was empty, cold and silent.

It didn't mean anything bad, he reasoned; it didn't mean they were dead.

The second was the same. He could taste the fear in his mouth, sour and sharp.

Next he came to the ancient dragonhall, the original one. Armed with a family secret, he slunk round the back, counting his steps, till he found the hidden doorway concealed by ivy. He'd heard the old stories, from Milla and his mother: how this door had helped Milla in the revolution; how it had allowed their grandmother Kara to escape from the old duke. Now it was his turn. The old duke's legacy still haunted this island, but it was time to banish it for good.

Joe unlatched the door, trying not to make a sound. The catch was stiff and rusty, but it opened with a groan after a few moments of pushing. He peered in, eyes struggling to adjust to the dim light inside. There was still a wall hanging concealing the secret door, just as he'd been told.

He squeezed through, leaving the door ajar, hoping the tapestry hid him completely. He stood still, hardly able to breathe. Dust tickled his nose, but he suppressed a sneeze. Listening hard, he could hear subdued voices, and he could swear one of them was Conor.

He edged sideways – one step, two – till he came to the edge of the heavy fabric and peered round it.

The dragonhall was full of people and dragons, and lit by a huge central brick stove. In the dim fuggy warmth, he counted eighteen dragons and fifteen people, including Conor, Amina, Tiago and Flavia. There was no sign of Noah. There were some full-grown dragons from the previous hatching ceremonies, but none of the original dragons of Arcosi, and none of his family.

He had to choose his next move very carefully; he didn't want to scare them in case they attacked, so he decided to use his secret signal. He and Conor had chosen it when they called for each other late on summer evenings. He'd stand below Conor's window and mimic the cry of the herring gull three times, and then Conor would sneak out and they'd run down to the harbour, not willing to waste a minute of daylight.

Joe raised his hands and cupped his mouth. But before he could make a sound, Ariel and Maric let out an excited *aark, aark, aark*, and every person in the room turned to stare.

His mouth went dry. It was just like the hatching ceremony: all those faces glaring at him, thinking the worst.

With a huge effort of will, he stepped out from behind the tapestry, hands up, calling softly, 'I'm a friend! Conor, Amina – tell them!' His voice only wobbled a little.

Neither of them moved.

Did they think he was one of the Brotherhood? The biggest dragons started lumbering to their feet. One of them looked like Ando, the huge orange dragon belonging to Rosa Demarco, Tarya's second-in-command, but she wasn't here, so it couldn't be, could it?

Joe felt exposed and vulnerable, and there was a new absence at his side where Ren should be. The huge dragons towered over him, growling and baring their sharp teeth. He was completely outnumbered.

CHAPTER THIRTY

'Joe?' Conor sounded incredulous, pushing past the large dragons to see.

'But . . . b-but . . .' Amina stuttered. 'What are you doing here? How did you get in?'

'Secret door.' He gestured behind him.

'So it was true, you did survive. You know we thought you were dead?' Her dark brown eyes were hurt and suspicious. 'For a long time.'

'You *let* us think that.' Conor never lost his temper, but he did now. 'And now you dare to walk in here, after everything?' He shook his head in disbelief, one hand pushing back his unruly red hair. 'What?' He tried to make sense of it. 'So you wrecked the ceremony, faked your death, ran away and hid somewhere, while people died and a dragon was killed – and they are *really* dead, Joe, not like you! – and that's the action of a friend? I don't think so.'

Amina went over to stand with him, shooting Joe a fierce

glare. 'It's all right,' she told Conor. 'They probably told us as soon as they could.'

'Not soon enough! I feel like a fool for mourning you, Joe!'

Joe's heart felt like a stone in his chest. All this time, he'd missed his friends; he'd felt bad for deceiving them, but he hadn't really considered what it had been like for them. He started backing away from them, towards the door. This was a mistake. It was too late. He couldn't make up for what he'd done.

'Oh, no you don't. Don't you dare walk away!' Conor roared at him. 'You stay and face us, Jowan Thornsen.'

'You're right,' Joe mumbled. 'I'm sorry. I got badly hurt, and I couldn't come back, not for a while. Then I thought you were all better off without me. Look, I can't explain it all now . . .' He lifted his head and tried to tap into that anger and thirst for revenge once more. 'My father's dead,' he said tightly. 'The Brotherhood killed him, and they must be stopped. So I've come to get you out, so we can fight back together. I'm here to help.'

'Nestan? No!' Amina gasped.

'Don't.' Joe put a hand up to stop her. He couldn't manage any sympathy, not yet. 'Please, don't. You're right to be angry, all of you. Let's just get out of here and I'll explain better afterwards.' He looked at Conor, waiting to see if this would be enough.

Conor looked down at his feet, thinking. Long moments slid past. Joe heard the crackle of a log in the stove; the rustle as a dragon re-settled its wings.

Just then, another person shouldered his way through the circle of people and dragons. 'Joe!' It was Tiago. 'Good to see you. Now I can thank you, finally, for rescuing me last winter.'

Amina and Conor stared open-mouthed at him. 'You'd seen him? Why didn't you say it was Joe who rescued you?'

'I promised.' Tiago came through and shook Joe's hand, clasping his arm in warm greeting. 'I think they'd have killed me, if you hadn't come along just then.'

Joe studied the older boy. He had a slight scar over one eyebrow, and his beard had grown in fully now, otherwise he looked the same as the first time they'd met. 'What else could I do? We had to stop them then, just like we need to stop them now.'

'I'm with Joe,' Tiago said.

'All right,' Conor said finally. 'But this isn't over, Joe.'

Amina nodded slowly. 'You can really get us out? Maric, Ariel, and all the other dragons too?'

'Yes,' he said, meeting their gaze. He hated how they looked at him now, so distantly, when they'd always been so close.

The small pale purple dragons crowded close, sniffing carefully. These two were like twins, almost identical. Maric was a touch larger, while Ariel had a more delicate face and slightly bigger eyes.

'Come on, let's introduce you . . .' Amina said softly. 'Here's my Maric.'

'And this is Ariel,' Conor said stiffly.

Joe bowed and said a polite, 'Hello, good to meet you.' He couldn't help comparing them to Ren: they were both bigger than her, both taller and sturdier. Their wings were thicker, their ears shorter. He felt a sharp homesick pang for Ren, and knew he had to get back to her today.

Maric and Ariel gave him a gentle *aark* of welcome, and the larger dragons finally judged Joe was harmless and allowed him through.

Amina and Conor led him over to the circle of suspicious faces. It was overwhelming to be stared at by so many at once.

'What's *he* doing here?' asked a young man with short black spiky hair.

'I thought he was dead,' said another.

'I thought he was dangerous.' That was Flavia, the young girl whose cream-coloured dragon Joe had almost trampled.

Joe took a deep breath. This wasn't going to be easy, but he had to make them trust him. He looked directly at Flavia. 'I'm sorry, for what I almost did on Hatching Day. I was angry, but that's no excuse, I know.'

She tutted, a loud *pffftt* of disdain, and looked away. He deserved that.

'All I can say is that I've changed, and I want to help. I've come to get you all out of the dragonhall, to freedom. The smaller dragons and their people with me, to hide here in Arcosi – I know where to go. The others will have to use the main doors, and fly to safety.'

Flavia was still glaring in the opposite direction, but Joe thought she was listening.

He peered over everyone's heads at the large double doors. 'They're locked, I take it?'

'Yes – and they've barred the gates with iron so the dragons can't burn their way out,' one of the older dragon-riders answered. 'We were betrayed.' He spat in the sawdust that covered the floor. 'They come past twice a day to throw in food and water. Cowards.'

'That's good.' That was better than he'd hoped. 'When are they due next?'

'Not till tonight,' Amina said. 'They brought food and water at sunrise.'

'Right. Listen to me – this is my plan,' Joe said.

To his surprise, everyone huddled closer. Only Flavia remained apart, glaring at him. 'I don't know why we're listening to him, all of a sudden. It's probably a trap.'

'Are we not trapped now?' Tiago asked pointedly. 'We can trust him. And if I'm wrong, we are no worse off. It's worth the risk.'

'I know a secret way we and the smaller dragons can leave the palace grounds, but it's well hidden,' Joe went on. 'We can get out of here the way I came in, but we'll have to be careful we're not spotted by the Brotherhood. How many guards at the front?'

'Two,' Conor said. 'I've heard them talking. No one wants that job. They're scared of us.'

'Even better. You need to choose your best fighters. They'll leave first, through the hidden door, with me. Two from each direction tackle the front guards, unlock the main doors, and then the dragonriders can escape on their dragons.' He paused and looked at the older dragonriders. 'I can get you out of the hall, but that bit is up to you. We need to do it quickly, so the mist can cover your escape.'

'But they took our blades,' someone said.

'It doesn't matter,' the spiky-haired man said, looking grim. 'We can take them, trust me.' He looked at Joe. 'And then what?'

'Find Isak and Luca on Sartola – they'll welcome you. They'll be planning to fight back, I'm sure. Join them. Then come back and save the island from the Brotherhood. We'll send word if we can.'

'What about Ando? He sounds too big for your hidden way, and he might not leave with us without Rosa. But we don't know where she is,' one woman said grimly. 'Or if she's even alive.'

'Could someone persuade him to follow, communicating through their dragon?' Joe asked.

One of the young men nodded. 'My dragon and I can try. We know Ando well.'

'What about us?' Flavia said. 'Our dragons aren't big enough to ride to Sartola! What's this secret way, and where do we hide?'

So she'd decided to trust him. Her cream-coloured dragon was the smallest in the dragonhall; his back came to her waist, almost ready to ride, but not yet. The dragon was staring at Joe intently, looking ready to scratch his eyes out if he upset Flavia again.

'You'll come with me into the underground tunnels, your dragons too,' he answered her.

'What tunnels?' Flavia scoffed. 'I'm not taking Elias into some hole underground.'

'There's a network of tunnels under the island. I've been living down there. With Winter,' he told them.

'So you've been right here all along?' Flavia burst out accusingly. 'But why—?'

'I had to stay away till I was sure I'd changed. I didn't want to risk hurting anyone, ever again.' He held her gaze, hoping she'd hear the truth in his words. 'But we have to go back now. Winter's guarding our dragons . . .' It was a relief to speak of Ren finally.

So they'd understand what kept him away.

So they'd trust him as one of them.

'What dragons?'

'You can't have. There wasn't another clutch,' one of the riders said.

'They are shadow dragons and we bonded before they hatched,' Joe said. 'I promise I'll share the whole story later. Come on, we need to move.'

Amina sighed. 'It's the best choice we have.'

Around the hall, others nodded in agreement.

More quickly than he could have hoped, they organised themselves into groups. Maybe the bond between the dragons helped, but they moved with smooth shared purpose. Two women and two men declared themselves ready to fight. All the other full-grown dragons and people lined up inside the double doors, ready to fly the moment they were opened.

Conor, Amina, Tiago, Flavia and Joe took up position

beside the secret door. Everyone had grabbed their warmest clothes and a small bag of things they couldn't leave behind. It wasn't much.

Joe felt a flurry of hopeful new sensations flooding through him, thawing the pain of his grief. They were listening to him! He might not be forgiven, but they trusted him. They knew he was one of them.

And then, just as fast, another thought smothered the hope. It meant it would be his fault if they failed.

CHAPTER THIRTY-ONE

Joe went first, through the secret door and out of the dragonhall into the daylight. The sun was burning through the mist, so it swirled, dazzlingly bright, revealing patches of blue sky. He couldn't see any guards.

'Clear!' he mouthed over his shoulder. 'Hurry now.' Time was passing, and he needed to get back to Ren. She and Fidell would need more food, and Winter wouldn't dare leave them alone.

The four dragonrider warriors came next, led by the spiky-haired man. They disappeared silently round the front of the building to ambush the guards and open the double doors.

Without waiting to know if they were successful, Joe called the others through. Amina and Maric came next, Flavia and her dragon Elias, Tiago and Lina, Conor and Ariel. Ariel was shivering and trying to burrow her head under Conor's pale purple jacket.

'Follow me,' Joe said, realising he had to act like a leader now. That meant thinking ahead. 'If anything happens to me, take this map.' He handed over the piece of parchment on which he and Winter had mapped the route through the tunnels. 'You'll have to find the stables, and go through the little iron door into the tunnels, then follow this path.'

He led the way, and the others followed in a shaky line. It felt like a sinister version of one of the games they used to play when they were smaller, like hide-and-seek or back-to-base. They stuck to the outer edge of the curving wall, staying within the shadows at the back of the old hall. But the moment came when they had to dart across to the next building: exposed and vulnerable.

'Just walk,' Joe suggested. 'Try to look confident, not scared, and if anyone sees us, they're less likely to suspect anything. If we run, we look like prey. I'll go first.'

It was harder than he expected, to stroll out onto the wide strip of sunlit grass and cross it slowly, without rushing to shelter. His back itched, expecting an arrow. But he reached the next dragonhall and collapsed against its wall, rubbing the sweat from his forehead and breathing hard.

He watched Amina come next. She was swift and graceful, only her wide brown eyes betraying how hard this was.

She reached Joe and fell against him. 'Maric? Are you all right?' she whispered words of comfort to the dragon who'd followed like her shadow.

Flavia was next. She started walking over to join them, but the pressure was too much, and she bolted, running fast across the grass, her dragon speeding after her.

Amina caught her. 'It's all right, you're safe.' She hugged the little girl until she stopped trembling, saying, 'You did it. Well done!'

Finally Conor and Tiago set out together, tension in every inch of their bodies. They took it slow and steady, while their dragons trotted next to them, noses flaring for the scent of guards.

Nearly there! Joe started to release the breath he'd been holding.

They were almost across, when something shoved Joe, hard, from behind. He sprawled forwards onto the grass.

'Did you really think we'd just let you walk out?' a familiar voice demanded. 'Although you are headed the wrong way. The gate's over there.'

Joe rolled and twisted his head, his heart hammering in his chest. It was Noah, his dragon silhouetted at his side. He kicked Joe hard. Joe doubled up, gasping. This couldn't be happening, not now. He had to escape. He had to get back to Ren.

'News for you, Thornsen.' Noah's voice was calm, and that was almost the worst thing when his words were so full of hate. 'Things have changed. We're in charge now. All of you *incomers*, you *halfies*, we're going to put you in your place. Where you belong.'

It was as if all of Noah's anger and grief and bitterness had been fed and stoked up like a fire. The Brotherhood had used him, fed him lies, kept him hurting, in order to turn him into their weapon.

Well, Joe could match that now. He had his own grief

and desire for vengeance, and he would resist till his last breath. He scrambled up, breathing through the pain, ready to fight. 'Shut it, Noah.'

The words froze on his lips as he realised Noah wasn't alone. Behind him there was a short, heavyset man in a black uniform, a sword in his belt. *Yannic!* He was studying Joe through pale blue eyes, and frowning slightly.

Joe might be able to fight Noah, but he could never defeat Yannic, not with that sword.

Flavia started crying quietly.

'Jowan Thornsen,' Yannic said, 'we'll have to stop bumping into each other like this.'

From the corner of his eye, he saw Tiago stumble backwards, his breathing fast and shallow: he must be recalling his attack.

Joe swore. He felt his anger ready and waiting, like a beacon, ready to blaze. He was trapped and powerless, which made him even angrier.

'Ah, Joe. You never know when to give up, do you?' Noah smirked at him, and his dragon took flight, hissing at Joe. 'You'll always be a loser.'

Just as on Hatching Day, Noah's words ignited Joe's temper. He channelled it deliberately now, drawing energy from his anger. 'I'll never give up, not against you.' He ducked the dragon, launching himself at Noah, and they both slammed hard on the ground. Joe's forehead crashed painfully against Noah's chin.

They rolled on the floor, both cursing and grunting, flailing around, arms tangling so Joe couldn't land a proper punch. Then he was looking up at Noah's lip dripping blood onto him, his hair full of grass and dirt.

Noah glared down and pulled one arm back. 'You'll regret this, Thornsen.'

Joe braced, but nothing came. Instead, the weight lifted from his ribcage; Noah tipped off him sideways and slumped on the grass. Joe pushed himself back onto his feet and stood there swaying, hands raised, still ready to fight on.

Noah's eyes were closed and he didn't move. His dragon, Della, stood over his body, spreading her wings protectively and hissing at the person behind Joe.

Joe glanced round warily. Conor, Tiago, Amina and Flavia all wore the same dazed expression.

He spun round to face Yannic. From its position, Joe guessed he'd just used the rounded pommel of his sword to knock Noah out. 'What did you do that for?'

Yannic slid the sword back into its scabbard. 'To save you,' he said. 'Even if you're an idiot who doesn't know when to stop fighting. Let's go.'

Joe was baffled. 'What? Go where?' Was he being arrested? But why had he hit Noah?

'You tell me,' Yannic said.

'We're not going anywhere with someone from the Brotherhood,' Joe spat.

'Oh, didn't I say . . . ?' Yannic added with a grin. 'Easy mistake to make. I actually work for your sister and the duke.'

CHAPTER THIRTY-TWO

J oe was paralysed, unsure what to believe. Could Yannic really be Tarya's spy? Sure, he'd knocked Noah out of the game, for now, but that could be a ploy. He thought back. Hadn't Yannic tried to take him aside, when they were beating Tiago? Could he have been trying to protect Joe, or let him escape? His mind spun. This was worse than playing chess against his father, he thought. Then he realised, with a stab of loss, he'd never do that again. *Never.* Never was such a long time. The pain of his father's death ambushed him – again.

'How can we trust you?' he demanded, dragging his mind back to the urgent present.

'Good lad,' Yannic said. 'You're not as daft as you look. Look, I have your sister's token to prove it.' From his inside pocket, he took out a gold medal that was stamped with the symbol of the new Arcosi – the dragon in flight below the full moon on one side, then the leaping fish of Sartola on the other. It was supposed to show the unity on the island.

'You could've stolen it! She's your prisoner, after all. I'd be a fool to believe you.' Joe looked to the others for their thoughts.

'Don't trust him!' Tiago gasped. 'He almost killed me.'

'I had a plan, that night,' Yannic insisted. 'I'd've stopped it, only your mate here got there first.'

'He did just help us,' Flavia said, surprising them.

'Also, we need to move quickly before Noah wakes up,' Amina said.

Conor nodded in agreement. 'And Noah won't know who hit him, so Yannic can still pretend to be loyal if they meet up again . . . Let's get out of here – go check for patrols?' He and Amina started checking the paths were clear to the east, while Flavia and Tiago went to check the opposite way.

'Why are you helping us?' Joe asked Yannic, out of earshot of the others. He needed more evidence before he brought a dangerous stranger anywhere near Ren.

'I was in the old duke's army, sure. It was a job: didn't mean I agreed with him. And I don't agree with the Brotherhood now.'

Joe was unconvinced. 'But you were there when they nearly killed Tiago. You've been there all along!'

'Keeping cover,' Yannic retorted. 'When your sister sent for me last year, said she needed someone on the inside to report back . . . I said yes. Also, she pays better. The Brotherhood runs on hot air and revenge.'

'So why didn't you report? Why didn't you warn her what they were planning?'

'I sent the message. I swear to you that I did. But it was coded. Only she and I have the cipher.'

'So, where is my sister? Is she alive?' Joe choked out.

'As I was saying, by the time the message arrived, she was already in labour, and her second, Rosa, was distracted by an explosion in the lower town, just as the Brotherhood wanted. By the time they found my message and decoded it, it was too—'

For a moment, Joe couldn't speak, then the words burst out. 'Shut up! Stop babbling! How is my sister? Did you fetch a midwife?' He found himself hanging on Yannic's collar with both hands. 'Tell me!'

'She's fine. And her daughter.'

'She has a daughter! Oh!' Joe found himself grinning, in spite of everything. 'I have a niece!'

'So that's another reason I'm helping her. You don't lock up pregnant women. Or new mothers and their babies. Not even when they're a general.'

'We've got to get her out!' Joe cried.

'Yes, we do, and we will.' Finally, Yannic turned serious. He leaned in and spoke so quietly that only Joe could hear. 'I'll help you, Joe Thornsen. Do you want to know the real reason why?'

He nodded.

'I was just married, the year before the revolution.' His voice was soft and intense now, and Joe found that more worrying than before. 'My wife, Nova, she was from Sartola originally. She was—' He stopped, unable to carry on. Then he gathered himself, taking a long breath in. 'When the revolution came, we were separated. I heard she'd been imprisoned. I searched. I did.' He finished in a rush, 'But I never saw her again. She was carrying our child.'

Joe started saying, 'I . . . I'm s—'

Yannic looked up and glared so fiercely that Joe froze. 'Those prisons, they were *Asa's* idea – our so-called leader. Remember him from our first meeting? And the attack on your friend? When he was in the army, Duke Olvar listened to him, though who knows why. It's partly why Asa was so vengeful when he lost his position, why he leads the Brotherhood now. But I hate Asa for it. I will see him brought down.'

'You're a good actor,' Joe said drily. 'No one would ever know.'

'What can I say? Lucky for you I missed my calling on the stage. So, I'll help you get your sister out. And the duke. And their child. Now you know why. But we don't speak of this again. And you tell no one my story. Agreed?'

Joe looked at Yannic, seeing a grief in his pale eyes that was even bigger than the one Joe was carrying. 'Agreed,' he said, equally softly.

'There's something else. They're staging a show trial in two days – Duke Vigo and your sister, Tarya.'

'A trial? But she's done nothing wrong!'

'True enough. But if I was a betting man, I'd put all my money on a guilty verdict. And I'm afraid that's not going to end well. Sorry.'

Joe stared at him, horrified. Exactly what did he mean? He feared the worst. 'We've got to get them out.'

'That we do.'

The others were returning, signalling that the paths were clear.

Yannic's mask snapped back into place, his swagger returned, and he was as sour and sarcastic as before. 'Now, move. Before they find us here and decide these dragons don't need their heads either.'

That silenced them all.

Joe watched, dazed, as Yannic bent, lifted Noah and slung him over one shoulder like a sack of flour, ignoring Della who hissed and scratched at his legs.

Yannic laid Noah on the floor inside the dragonhall, barred its door and jogged back over to them. 'They've got food and water – he and his dragon'll be fine in there. Now, tell us your plan, Thornsen.'

Joe was swamped with indecision: how could he leave with Tarya still a prisoner? He felt himself pulled in two different directions. But if the Brotherhood planned a mock trial, Tarya was safe for two more days. Right now, Ren needed him more. The invisible chord between them had tightened with every moment he spent away from her.

'Now! Or we'll be no good to anyone,' Yannic urged.

'Come on, Joe,' Amina urged him. 'This way, wasn't it?'

'Uh-huh,' he mumbled, still not quite ready to trust this soldier. 'Come with us, but if you try anything, I'll make you pay.' He still had his dragon-head knife hidden under his jacket. To protect Ren, he was ready to use it.

Their strange procession made it to the iron gate unchallenged. And to their delight, just as they reached the gate,

226

they heard a low *thrumming* sound as the older dragons and their riders took to the skies and flew to safety. Maric, Ariel, Lina and Elias made small sad *aark*, *aark* noises of farewell, and had to be quickly shushed.

Yannic stood guard while they all crawled into the tunnels. The journey back was hard. Joe only had one lantern, while the others didn't know the tunnels. Yannic's curses were new and interesting, even for Joe. He forced himself to be patient and walk slowly, even though he was seething with frustration and desperate to get back to Ren.

Finally he saw the entrance to the large cavern where he'd left Winter. 'Er, I better go first. Wait here, just a moment.' He left the lantern with Amina, and went forward alone into the darkness.

'Winter? Ren? It's me,' he called. His fears swarmed his mind, as he stumbled forwards, arms outstretched. What if someone had found them? What if Ren had fallen ill without him? 'Winter? Where are you?'

Then he saw it: a trembling glow ahead. She'd stuck candles around the walls, casting a golden light that glinted off the underground stream. Winter was sitting against a rocky wall. The hatchlings flanked her, heads up to sniff the air, eyes aglow, like four little golden suns.

They were safe! He was home! Ren was here!

'Ren!' he cried, running the last stretch to meet his dragon and hold her tightly. Their reunion felt physical to Joe: warm relief spread through his whole body, like basking in front of a hot fire on a cold day.

Ren was wriggling with delight, squeaking loudly and

almost knocking him down. She batted his chest, pressing her head against his cheek, telling him how much she'd missed him.

'I'm sorry, Ren. I'm back now,' he laughed out loud in delight, trying to catch hold of her. They were together again. Everything felt better, more possible, more bearable, when they were together. 'Have you grown? Look at you!'

'Two days!' Winter snapped, interrupting their reunion. 'You left her for two days and two nights. Have you any idea . . . ?'

'You must have known it was something big to keep me away.'

'Something big, yes. Like you being dead!' She looked at him stonily.

'I'm sorry.' He hadn't guessed she might think that. Surely Ren would know if he died? It wasn't the moment to ask. 'Winter, my father was killed,' he said. Ren leaned into him, making a soft crooning noise in the back of her throat.

'Oh, Joe.' Winter's face softened. 'I'm so sorry.'

'There's more,' he said hesitantly. 'I had to bring some people here. They were in danger.'

'Who is here?'

'They're my friends. Or they were, once.' He squirmed under her gaze. 'And Yannic's a spy.'

'I don't believe it!' Winter cried. She stood up and shouted in his face, 'The dragons need to be safe, and you bring danger into the nest?'

'That's not fair.' Joe explained everything that had happened. 'Yannic helped us escape. We need him. You know we have to stop the Brotherhood? You saw it yourself – they've already killed a dragon.'

'Exactly!' she yelled. 'So we need to keep Fidell and Ren hidden from them.'

Joe had never seen her like this. She was like a protective mother dragon, growling and spitting sparks.

'We have to let Yannic in. He's going to help us.' He looked around the candlelit cavern, searching for a way to bridge the gap between them. 'And you think this is dangerous now, bringing Yannic down here? I tell you what will be dangerous: an island controlled by the Brotherhood. They'll lock us up and take our dragons, just like they did to Milla in the last war!'

Winter reached out for Fidell, who was nudging at her waist, rumbling softly.

'But if we use the tunnels to hide and to take messages, we can reach everyone on the island,' Joe hurried on, spotting a chance now. 'We can make a plan, ready to fight back! We don't have long – they're putting my sister on trial in two days.'

'Who's fighting back? I'm not.' Winter grabbed Fidell and clasped him close to her. Both dragons were listening hard, their golden eyes round and solemn as their people debated.

'Fair enough.' He sighed. 'But please let me bring these people into our cave. All of them?'

'Let's just put up a big sign, shall we: *tunnels this way*? This was my home! It felt safe here: you promised me.'

'It will still be safe,' Joe repeated. 'Just shared.' He hated to break his promise, but this was more important.

She didn't reply for a long moment, shoulders hunched miserably. She looked like a cat with its fur fluffed up, hissing and growling.

'Winter, I'm sorry, but this is something we can do to help. Let's do it?'

She didn't reply, but shrugged one shoulder and he decided to interpret that as permission.

'Come in! Amina, Conor, bring everyone in!' Joe shouted.

Amina, Conor, Flavia, Tiago and Yannic came forwards, into the candlelight.

'Winter? Let me introduce my best friends, Amina and Conor. Then this is Flavia, from the last Hatching Day. And Tiago and Yannic – you've seen them once before, when we, er, rescued Tiago. But Yannic works for my sister, really.'

They all stared at each other.

'And this is Winter, who saved my life, and our shadow dragons, Ren and Fidell.'

Amina went forwards to sit next to Winter, crossing her legs and settling down, her dragon by her side. 'My dragon's name is Maric. We're so glad to meet you. Thank you for letting us into your home.'

Fidell leaned forwards with a curious *aark*.

'And is this your shadow dragon?' Amina asked. 'Joe told us about them. He's gorgeous!' She put a hand out to greet Fidell, smiling warmly. 'Hello. I've never met anyone quite like you before.'

Maric reached up to touch noses with Fidell.

Amina and Winter grinned at each other afterwards.

Joe let out a sigh of relief, silently thanking Amina for knowing what to do.

'And here's Ren,' he said proudly, one hand on her back.

'A shadow dragon, you say? Where did you find her then?' Conor said, bringing Ariel over to greet Ren.

Joe met his curious gaze, feeling something thaw and ease between them. He started telling him the story of how they'd found the eggs and their trip to mine the silverblue.

Soon everyone was crowding round to meet Ren and introducing all the dragons to each other.

'Ahem,' Yannic coughed loudly. 'I don't mean to break up your cosy dragon appreciation society, folks. But don't let's forget, there's a battle to fight out there. And we've got two days. So far, we've only got one sword, a few kids and some overgrown lizards on our side.'

Tiago shot a vicious look at him.

Joe was about to snap at Yannic for underestimating them when an idea struck him, fully formed. 'That's it! That's how we'll do it.'

Everyone was looking at him as if he was speaking another language, their faces tinted by candlelight and shadows.

'That's how you see us, right, Yannic?' Joe paced up and down, with Ren following his every move. 'And you're one of them. I mean, you're not, but you were.'

'Slow down, Joe!' Amina said. 'What do you mean?'

'They don't see us as any threat,' he explained. 'We're just kids, to them. And Yannic's one of them. So that'll be our disguise.'

'Go on,' Yannic said. 'Wonderboy might have something.'

231

'The Brotherhood won't see us when we go out into the city. They'll see *children*. With Yannic, they'll see one of their own. That's how we spread the word. We use the tunnels; we go and speak to everyone hiding at home, and we plan our fight. We are going to take Arcosi back. And we are going to start now.'

CHAPTER THIRTY-THREE

They sat in a circle, letting the dragons doze or roam the cavern around them. Joe tried to work through his plan, but his fears and his grief kept getting in the way. They had less than two days to stop the Brotherhood before they killed his sister.

'Right,' he began, looking at the circle of anxious faces. 'So what should we do first?'

Everyone answered at once:

'I need to tell my family I'm safe!'

'Take the dragons off the island.'

'Hide!'

'Fight the Brotherhood.'

Yannic looked at them and sighed. 'Oh my stars, give me strength! Do I have a job on my hands, or what?'

'You *can* go, you know,' Tiago said sharply. 'No one asked you here.'

Joe glanced at Yannic to see how he'd react. They needed

him. He might be irritating, but he was an experienced fighter and their route into the Brotherhood.

'No, no, no, my friend. You see, I'm counting on collecting a juicy reward from Joe's sister, for keeping him alive through this. Been thinking of retiring to Sartola, nice little villa with a view of the sea . . .' Yannic hawked up a gobbet of phlegm and spat it hard.

Joe knew this was all an act. He'd seen what lay behind Yannic's bravado – that bottomless grief – and he also understood why someone might want to hide that behind a mask. He was working hard to keep his own sadness at bay and focus on their plan.

'I know, I know,' Yannic was saying. 'That also requires the general to remain alive. So you see, that's why I'm here. To save Joe's sister, richest woman on the island, and babysit her little brother meanwhile. Don't tell me you couldn't use the help.'

'You want to help?' Joe copied Yannic's tone, arrogant and commanding, to get him to listen. 'You can start by telling us about the Brotherhood. How many are they?'

'That's the thing.' Yannic puffed his chest out importantly now he was the centre of attention. 'They're only five hundred men. They're outnumbered by the actual army who are now locked up in the barracks. They were counting on surprise. And making lots of noise. And when I say noise, I mean, chopping off—'

'Right,' Conor interrupted him, seeing Amina's face. 'So that's the first thing – we need to free the duke's real soldiers.'

'Easier said than done.' Yannic sounded as if he was

enjoying this. 'They've turned the palace back into the fortress it once was. Palace grounds are locked and guarded day and night.'

'We could use the big dragons you freed from the dragonhall,' Flavia said.

'But how do we get word to the others?' Tiago asked. 'If they fled to Sartola? Our dragons aren't big enough to ride on. They chose their moment well.'

Joe put his head in his hands. There were too many elements to consider. It all seemed so daunting. Yannic had it right – they were just children, what did they know? His mother was injured; his father was dead. Isak was on Sartola. No one had seen Milla since she left with Thom. The city was under curfew. They'd never be ready in time. The Brotherhood would put his sister on trial, decide she was guilty, and he didn't want to think about what that meant.

He stopped the spiral of despair before it could take him any further down. Who else was going to stop the Brotherhood? He had to focus on what they had, not what they lacked. They did have two days. He wasn't alone any more. There were seven of them. And they had something no one else knew about: the secret tunnels.

'All right,' he said, looking up again, 'we do it: sunset tomorrow. We free the duke's army and tell everyone to be ready to join the fight.'

The others were nodding.

'How do we tell them,' Flavia asked, 'with this curfew?'

'We take it in turns to go into the city, using the tunnels. I'll draw you all a map!'

Tiago pointed out, 'And if the Brotherhood get hold of a map, we're all finished. They'll come down here and finish us, like rats in a drain.'

'Well, we have to use the tunnels, so we have to risk the maps. Surely this is what the tunnels are for, travelling in secret? They reach all over the western side of the island,' Joe told the others. 'So we can spread the word in each neighbourhood. Some will have to stay here and guard the dragons.'

'There are so few of us.' Conor sounded worried. 'We'll need the duke's army. We can't do it without them.'

'But they're prisoners! We keep going round in circles,' Amina cried. 'How do we reach them? It's no good telling everyone in the city to be ready if we don't have proper fighters.'

'Exactly,' Tiago cried. 'Look, I've felt their anger up close. If I can't defend myself against five of them, what chance do we have against five hundred?'

'Maybe he's right.' Conor's head drooped a little. 'What do we know about fighting? The Brotherhood will kill us all.'

Something occurred to Joe in a flash of inspiration. 'But we don't need to storm the walls, do we?'

The others looked at him, puzzled.

'They might not be trained soldiers, but what if we take back the element of surprise? It worked for them, so it can work for us,' Joe said excitedly.

Yannic was looking blank. 'Nah, you'll have to spell it out,' he said. 'I'm not with you.'

'Rejoin the Brotherhood. Today, before anyone misses you,' Joe said. 'You can hear the gossip, see if anything's changed.'

'Right,' Yannic agreed. 'That makes sense.'

'Then, today we take it in turns to slip out into the city, using the tunnels. I'll copy the maps for you all. Everyone finds their families and friends. Tell them what we plan and when to be ready. But they need to lie low until then.' The plan was forming as Joe spoke.

'My cousins will fight to retake the city!' Flavia said. 'They're bigger than me.' Her cheeks flushed deep red at that. 'I mean, most people are, but they're *really* big.'

Amina smiled at her.

'When do I rejoin the baby rebels?' Yannic asked.

'Come back later,' Joe said decisively. 'Tomorrow we will sneak back into the palace grounds and free the duke's army. They can retake the palace and the people can retake the city. Between us, the Brotherhood will be defeated.'

'How well do you know the barracks, where the army is being held?' Conor asked next. 'How near can we get?'

'They'll be waiting for us.' Tiago wasn't convinced. 'We're all going to die.'

It was Winter who persuaded them, finally. She stood up and cleared her throat, pushing her hair away from her face. 'Look, I'm sorry I wasn't more welcoming to you all, straightaway. I wanted to hide down here and keep Fidell safe.' Her voice was shaky and Joe could see how hard this was for her. She went on, 'But I've seen the Brotherhood in action. Joe's right. We have to stop them. Isn't it better to die trying to save our city and our dragons?'

There was a long silence then. Coming from her – a girl who had been powerless to save her first dragon – the words had more impact.

'It could work,' Yannic said. 'I know the barracks inside and out: they haven't changed since they got rid of us. If we use the tunnels and get really close, then all you'll have to do is break the locks open. But we make our move at night. It won't work by daylight.'

'That works.' Joe repeated, 'We'll move at sunset tomorrow?'

Everyone nodded in agreement, all except Tiago.

Amina was jigging with excitement now. 'Can I go into the city first? Please? We've been cooped up in the dragon-hall for the last couple of days, and I need to tell my family I'm alive. They'll want to fight back, I know they will!'

Joe moved his gaze down to Maric. Would the little dragon stay with him, even though they'd only just met?

'I'm coming too,' Flavia told Amina.

'I need to spend some time with Ren,' Joe said to Conor, 'so why don't we both stay down here with the dragons – they all know one of us at least. We can double up.'

'Right, kids. I'll leave you to sing lullabies to your dragons, or feed them fresh mice, or whatever it is you do . . .' Yannic stood and stretched, scratching his rounded belly through the dusty black fabric of his uniform. 'Wish me luck? See you later. Now, where's my map? Don't fancy getting lost down here . . .'

'Just a moment,' Joe said, searching through his belongings for one of his parchment maps. Then he led Yannic outside the quickest way, using the cave entrance above the western beach.

When he returned, everyone looked urgently at Joe.

'How far do we trust Yannic?' Amina asked.

'I won't ever trust him,' Tiago said. 'But he might be useful.'

Joe looked at their suspicious faces. It was on the tip of his tongue to tell them Yannic's secret, but he resisted, and lied instead. 'We can trust his love of gold. And we have plenty of that.' He explained about the secret hoard. 'We might need to bribe him with it in the end, but for now, don't breathe a word about it, right?'

'What's stopping him bringing the Brotherhood straight down here and killing the lot of us?' Conor was more direct.

'We can sleep in a different cave, and we'd better have another plan in reserve,' Joe said slowly. 'Wait for me here. I'll bring some of the gold – in case we need to persuade anyone.'

Leaving the others, Joe took Ren and went back to the cave where he'd found her egg. As soon as he was alone with his dragon, the sadness came rushing back. *Prrrtt?* Ren asked, sensing his distress. She kept very close to him, her claws clicking on the rocky tunnel as they walked.

As long as he was busy, Joe had managed to keep his grief at a distance, but now it returned, heavier than ever. Tears pricked at his eyes. Even if he was successful and managed to rescue Tarya, his father would never know. If he got his revenge and the Brotherhood were destroyed, his father would never know. For the rest of his life, Joe would do things and Nestan would never know. For a moment, he wanted to lie down right there and never move again. Only Ren's constant presence kept him going.

They reached the egg cave.

'See this? This is where I found you,' he told her, going inside.

She walked in, looking around her with interest, and sniffed the box that had held her egg and Fidell's.

'And see this?' He opened the casket. 'This helps buy our victory.' He filled his pockets with the gold.

Back in the large cavern, Joe divided the gold between them. 'Keep it hidden from Yannic. Use it however you need. I trust you.'

Then Winter, Tiago, Amina and Flavia said goodbye to their dragons and left them behind with Conor and Joe. They set off for the outside world, each with their job to do.

CHAPTER THIRTY-FOUR

Joe and Conor spent a busy day looking after the six dragons. It was awkward at first. They were polite and stiff with each other as they fed the dragons and spoke to them.

'Conor, I am sorry.' Joe realised he had to break the tension. 'Can I try to explain?'

Conor had his back to him, bending over to cut meat for the dragons. He tensed, and paused at his task.

'I know I should've sent a message. My parents . . .' Joe swallowed hard and struggled on. 'They showed me I was wrong, but at the time, I really did think you were all better off without me. What I did on Hatching Day . . .' He took another breath. 'I was out of control. I had to be sure it wouldn't happen again, maybe worse next time. I . . . I hated myself. And I thought you must too.'

'Idiot,' Conor said. He put his knife down, dipped his hands in the stream and turned to Joe, blinking hard. 'As if! We missed you. But I'm glad you told me. Come here!'

They stood up and hugged quickly, while their dragons squeaked and growled in relief.

Conor sat back down and reached out for Ariel, smoothing her scaly neck as he spoke. 'I'm really sorry about your dad. When did it happen?'

Joe told him about his father's death; Conor described their months in the dragonhall, and the awful day the Brotherhood arrived. The terrible news that a dragon had been killed had thrown them all into shock. The day flew past as they tended to all the dragons.

The girls and Tiago arrived back, one by one, bringing news, water and more food for them and the growing dragons.

Flavia was breathless. 'I did it! I found my way home and told everyone the message. They're going to pass it on too. Everyone will know by nightfall. They'll be ready to take the city back as soon as we've freed the duke's soldiers.' Her expression was a strange mixture of pride and worry. 'It worked, just like you said, Joe!' Now she grinned at him for the first time since they'd met. 'I walked under the noses of the Brotherhood a dozen times today. Not one of them noticed me. I might as well be invisible.'

Winter came in behind her. 'I've told my mother and her neighbours.'

'Thank you, Winter.' Joe slumped in relief.

Conor said, smiling, 'There you are, Joe, it looks like your plan will work. Shame we needed a city under siege for your hidden talents to emerge.'

Amina came in last, buzzing with triumph. 'Done!' she

cried. 'And I have spare black clothes for us all if we're to move at night. The craftspeople are ready to act and retake their neighbourhood. I really think it could work, whatever Yannic thinks.'

'You talking about me?' Yannic bellowed in Joe's ear, making him jump.

'Good evening,' he said wearily, noticing that Yannic had crept in to eavesdrop on them before he announced himself.

'News!' Yannic went on. 'Well, that was illuminating. A day with the Brotherhood is always a joy.'

'You're drunk!' Tiago said accusingly, as the whiff of unwashed flesh and old rum floated across to them.

'I had to join in, didn't I? Would've stood out like a sore thumb if I suddenly gave up the grog.'

'So, what did you learn?' Joe stroked Ren's back as she leaned on him, listening intently.

'There is some good news.' Yannic waited.

Winter crossed her arms and said, 'Go on then, tell us?'

'They're going to hold a feast tonight – they usually last till dawn. And I know where they keep the barrels of rum. How about a little light tampering? A few rotten rats to spice their drink? They won't be able to move tomorrow, and they can blame it on the bad food.'

'How can we be sure they won't notice?' Conor said. 'I'd notice if someone gave me dead rat juice.'

'Here's the thing,' Yannic said gleefully. 'They're getting restless. Insecure, you might say. Surprise, surprise: power isn't quite the easeful dream they was hoping for, what with people objecting to, y'know, the murder of cityfolk and dragons.'

'And? Get to the point,' Tiago said.

Yannic gave them a wide grin. 'Morale is shaky, to say the least. There will be lots of drinking and rousing Norlander drinking songs.'

Joe remembered the meeting he'd sneaked into: how he'd sung along, how he'd almost been tempted to join them, till he heard their true beliefs.

'The youngest soldiers are skittish and scared. They'll throw gallons down their throats, not notice a thing. They are ready to fall apart, oh yes.' Yannic rubbed his hands. 'Right. Now I need to get back before they miss me.'

They watched him wobble away, back towards the tunnel entrance.

'I can't believe we're trusting him,' Tiago said in the silence that followed.

'It'll be fine, trust me instead,' Joe said. He knew Yannic wouldn't let them down, now he understood his thirst for revenge. The same impulse was pushing him onwards, keeping his focus steady.

The next day was strange and hot. From the moment he woke, Joe felt nervous. To calm himself, he talked to Ren. She'd slept pressed up against his side, her body almost as long as his when she stretched out.

'Morning, you.' Her head resting on his chest was heavy these days, and her warm breath smelled smokily of cinders and charred meat.

She opened one golden eye and her left ear twitched as he murmured to her.

'Can you spare me again, just for an hour? I need to work on our backup plan. You stay here with Winter and Fidell?'

Now Ren retreated from him, and curled up small, her wings folded, her ears flat on her purple scaly head. She could make herself surprisingly compact when she was unhappy.

'I'm sorry, but there's one other thing I also need to do.' Joe leaned over, stroking her scales.

Mraa, she said softly. She raised her head and looked at him through those golden oval eyes.

He felt terrible. 'I'm doing this for us,' he whispered, 'to make our island safe again. I'll be as quick as I can.'

She blinked once and he took that as reluctant agreement.

'Ren?' Winter called, stretching out her hand. 'Would you like to join me and Fidell?'

Ren slunk over and let herself be cuddled, while Winter dug out scraps of dried meat from her pockets for both shadow dragons.

Joe left without looking back, while Ren was distracted. He knew the tunnels well enough now not to need his map. He used the western beach entrance and crept past the warehouses into the dock area.

He had only seen Arcosi like this once before, on Hatching Day. The busy harbour and the surrounding streets were almost empty, baking in the hot morning sun. The heat radiated up from the earth. He wore the plain old clothes that he'd grabbed on his visit home – nothing to connect him to dragons – and his shirt was soon sticking to his back with sweat.

245

Each street corner had a couple of black-clad members of the Brotherhood, nervously shifting from foot to foot like a pair of crows.

He had to walk straight past two of them. One looked only a bit older than Joe, so he couldn't have been one of the old duke's men – he would have been a young child in the last war. This young recruit had red-rimmed eyes, Joe noticed, and his skin looked waxy yellow. He was sweating visibly as he struggled to hold a sword that was too big for him.

Joe kept his eyes down. He didn't want to be recognised. There were ordinary people around, but they hurried along in twos and threes. No one was out alone, except him.

He made it past the Brotherhood's men, and circled the deserted marketplace next. There were no stalls out today. How were people feeding themselves? Food supplies must be getting low in every single house. The island felt like a keg of firepowder, ready to blow.

Just a little longer, Joe thought, *just till tonight.*

Even the harbour was almost empty: a handful of fishing boats tugging gently at their moorings and a merchant vessel, which must have docked without knowing the news. It would soon be on its way, he was sure.

Joe waited in the shade of a warehouse at the edge of the dock area. The blue sea was sparkling and dancing, as if nothing had changed. Before long, Joe saw a fishing boat heading for its usual mooring. It was the *Dolphin*, and he recognised the old man at the helm as Simeon Windlass, Thom's father. Joe hoisted himself up, palmed three gold coins and wandered out into the light.

He leaned on the harbour rail, whistling tunelessly, staring off into the far distance. He was aware of a curious glance from a pair of black-clad men, but he held his nerve and waited, waited, waited.

The sun felt hot on his face. Seagulls gathered in a screaming cloud above Simeon's boat, waiting for their chance.

As soon as the soldiers' attention was diverted, Joe started walking along the worn stones that edged the deep harbour, heading towards the *Dolphin*.

He paused by Simeon's boat and pretended to drop something. He bent down, so that his head was level with Simeon, working on deck.

'Simeon,' he greeted him.

Startled, Simeon examined Joe with his bright blue gaze.

'Thom asked you to tell Isak that I survived, didn't he? I'll always be grateful to you for that.'

The old man nodded.

'I need your help again,' Joe told him.

Simeon waited, keeping his hands busy as he listened.

'Where are Thom and Milla?' Joe whispered, keeping his eyes on the men of the Brotherhood now, to check they weren't watching.

'They went to look at that volcano.' Simeon followed Joe's lead, not looking up as they spoke in whispers. 'Thom was getting worried about it.'

Joe cursed. He'd been counting on Milla's help. 'Please can you get word to my brother on Sartola again? Tell the dragonriders to return – this evening?'

247

'You're fighting *them*?' Simeon's tone told him exactly what he thought of the Brotherhood.

'Yes, and we'll need all our dragons to join in, sunset tonight.' He explained their plan.

'Aye.' Simeon nodded once. 'I'll just unload this catch. Since this lot crept out of the gutter, they take it all off me, no payment. That's reason enough to go straight back out, and I'll go direct to your brother.'

'Here, for your trouble. And in case anyone needs persuading to join us.' Joe put the gold coins on the stone slab and walked away, just as a new group of black-clad men came to seize Simeon's catch.

From the corner of his eye, he saw Simeon's hand shoot out, grab the coins and return to unloading his crates, without a break in the rhythm.

He trusted Simeon, and he trusted Isak and Luca, but he had no way of knowing if they'd be able to reach them in time.

No, Joe and his friends were alone, putting all their faith in a man who wore the old duke's black uniform. He prayed that his plans would work. His sister's life depended on it. And the duke's. And their child's.

CHAPTER THIRTY-FIVE

As the day wore on, the strange unreal feeling grew stronger, a mixture of dread and fear and determination. They had to do this, Joe was certain. But he also knew the risks. This could be his last day with Ren, so he spent as much of it as possible talking to her, soothing her, telling her what they planned.

'We're going to free the duke's soldiers,' Joe whispered to Ren. 'So they can fight back.'

With her deep purple scales, she blended into the darkness, but her eyes were like little mirrors, reflecting the lamplight, and they widened as she listened.

'It's going to be dangerous, but I can't see there's any other choice.'

The cavern felt warmer than usual. Its air was muggy and full of murmuring anticipation as the children prepared themselves to leave, covering their clothes with the black fabric that Amina had brought from home to help them stay hidden.

Winter came over to speak to Joe. Her face was composed and serious. 'Joe, I'm sorry, about before. You were right. I was just so scared, and I couldn't lose Fidell, not after . . .'

'It's all right,' he said. 'I understand. You're braver than anyone I know, risking this, after everything.'

'I still haven't decided about today,' Winter told Joe next. 'I don't want to take Fidell up there, in case he gets hurt, but . . . but . . . I don't want to leave him either!'

Before Joe could answer, Ren made her feelings clear. She nipped his hand – not quite drawing blood – blocked his way, then burrowed her head under his jacket.

'Ow, Ren! What did you do that for?' Joe was hurt.

'Hmm. I don't think she wants to be left behind again, Joe,' Conor said, seeing what had happened. Ariel was already positioned next to him, ready to leave.

Joe took a deep breath. 'All right, Ren. If you don't want to be left, you'll just have to come along.'

'Are you sure? She's never been aboveground before!' Winter said. 'Nor has Fidell!'

'Her choice, I think,' Joe said. 'Ren, would you rather come along, or stay here and wait for me? If you come, you have to be quiet and do as I say.'

Ren pulled her head out, raising herself tall so her head was level with Joe's, and chittered softly. She understood. It was a risk, but so was every choice he made right now.

'We go together,' he said firmly. And he shouldered his way through to lead everyone through the tunnels with his dragon by his side.

Fidell made the same choice, padding along next to Winter as if he really was her shadow. Winter had one hand resting on his neck, as if she were glad not to be parted from him after all. Joe could see her lips moving as she spoke to Fidell under her breath.

The heat of the tunnels seemed to increase as they filed silently through them. Joe could feel Ren walking close against his hip. The deep comfort and strength he drew from her presence was plaited tight with terror that anything might happen to her. All his senses seemed heightened with tension. He could feel the coarse texture of the tunnel walls, the way it snagged on his sleeve and grazed his fingertips. The familiar weight of his father's compass in his pocket felt reassuring, like a link to his past. The noises were subdued: occasional whispers, the steady tramp of their boots and sandals on the sandy rock.

And then relief, as the cool air hit Joe's face, smelling of damp earth and straw and horses, as he poked his head out of the little iron gate behind the palace stable block to find no one there waiting for him.

'This is for you, Dad,' Joe whispered quietly, climbing out and putting it all in motion.

They'd gone over their plan, time after time, till everyone knew it by heart, scrawling pictures in the sandy earth of the cavern to show where they would hide. To the north-east of the palace, beyond the stables, sprawled the barracks: rows of low brick buildings, the bunkhouses and the burned-out armoury. A shadowy figure peeled itself away from the side of the armoury: Yannic, there to meet them.

Joe felt his world shrink to this: his breath coming fast, his feet moving across damp grass.

Winter and Fidell were fastest – they sprinted ahead, searching for patrols, greeting Yannic as they passed him.

Their courage gave Joe speed and strength. 'I hope your idea worked,' he whispered to Yannic as the man fell in at his side.

'Trust me,' Yannic muttered back. 'They've been puking since daybreak. Weak as kittens they'll be.'

Joe didn't reply. So far he had no actual evidence that trusting Yannic was the right thing to do. Just how good an actor was he? They might be running into a trap.

If Ren found the new environment strange, she didn't show it. She kept up with Joe and didn't make a sound.

He stole a quick glance left. Conor ran lightly, with Ariel gliding silently next to him. Conor, who'd never won a fight in his life, daring to join this attack. And Amina, to his right. She was an artist, not a warrior. They were his best friends and they believed in him, even if it meant risking their lives.

'Stop! Down.' Yannic gestured as they circled and came to the edge of the barracks where the rows of huts were tightly packed in the flat circle of land.

They all crept low, with their dragons following, crawling right into some bushes to the rear of the buildings.

Winter and Fidell were there already. 'No patrols,' she said softly. 'Just a few guards.'

They peered out through the upper leaves. Joe kept one hand on Ren's back. The moon was hidden behind a bank of cloud, but its milky light spilled out and bleached the night blue and grey. Joe strained his eyes. It looked as if there was a guard pacing at each doorway, but he couldn't tell if there were more hiding behind the long low buildings.

'See, as I said,' Yannic whispered. 'A guard for each building.'

They'd agreed that Yannic would stroll out and cause a diversion. 'Stay low, you lot,' he told them, getting ready to move. 'If we mess it up, hide till you can flee to your tunnels and don't look back. Got it?'

They would work in pairs: Joe and Winter; Amina and Conor; Flavia and Tiago.

Yannic crawled on his belly in the opposite direction, till he reached the cover of some trees. Then he stood up and strolled out into the moonlight, as if he'd come from the palace. He called out in Norlandish, 'Evening, Brothers, in the name of the lost duke.'

The greeting was returned by the nearest of the guards. 'What you doing here?' he added. 'Did Asa send you?'

In reply, Yannic belched, undid his trousers and relieved himself in a long stream, with a loud sigh.

It worked. The guards relaxed. One jeered, others swore at him, a few laughed.

The children circled the bunkhouses, Joe taking the east side of one, Winter the west. They paused for a moment, hiding in the shadows.

'There's some of that fine rum left from last night,' Yannic was calling out. He buttoned himself up and started singing a bawdy drinking song, swaying as he moved slowly towards the first pair of guards.

The Brotherhood joined in, their voices filling the night air.

This was the signal.

The children attacked.

Joe flung himself forwards with his knife lifted, not sure he'd be able to use it.

The guard faced him. As he saw Joe coming, he swore and tried to draw his sword, but Winter jumped on him from behind, her strong fingers clutching at his throat. The man made a horrible choking noise.

Ren and Fidell darted in, biting his stomach and legs.

Joe reversed his knife and used its bone handle to bash the guard's temple, hard. The man crumpled onto the damp grass. He moaned once, filling Joe with relief that he was still alive.

He twisted round, checking for danger. In front of the furthest bunkhouse, a body slumped, sprawling out into the moonlight, with a dark patch of pooling liquid by its head. He couldn't see who it was and prayed it wasn't one of his friends.

'Joe, the lock! Hurry,' Winter urged him.

If they could just open one of the bunkhouses and free the duke's soldiers trapped inside, the Brotherhood would be outnumbered.

Joe knelt and peered at the fastening – it was secured with two heavy iron padlocks. The Brotherhood had spared no expense. He could do this, he told himself. He bent low, fitting the tip of his knife into the first keyhole. He closed his eyes, shutting everything else out. Forcing himself to work methodically, he felt for each tooth of the lock, letting out a sigh when the iron bar clicked open.

He took the first padlock off and threw it down, reaching for the second. He was so focused on his task he didn't notice the approach from behind them till it was too late.

There was the familiar leathery flap of huge dragon wings, and for a moment Joe's heart leaped in hope. 'Isak? Is that you?' Then he felt the draught and heard the *crunch* as the dragon finished its low glide, touching down behind the bunkhouse.

But this dragon was the wrong colour: it blended with the shadows, glaring down at Joe through cruel amber eyes. And two figures jumped off its back: a boy his age and a young woman in dragonrider clothes, all black. He knew her by that scowl of disapproval – Lanys, from the last Hatching Day. So the dragon was Ravenna, the mother of Maric and Ariel and the others. Another smaller dragon landed next to him, yellow in colour.

'Guess again, Thornsen.'

It couldn't be! Not again. 'Noah!'

Joe spun round, searching for shelter, but it was useless. There was nowhere to hide from a grown dragon. He felt Ren standing behind him, pressing against the small of his back. He willed her to flee.

'No, no, no,' Winter moaned.

'You didn't do your homework, did you?' Noah taunted them. '*The dragons knew; they always do*. The wise teachings of your own grandmother, Kara. Oh, wait, you're a waddler, you didn't get to learn that. Only dragonriders had that lesson, and your stupid friends forgot to tell you. Ravenna here let us know that trouble was coming our way. Good job it's only you, not a real threat. You can fail at being a rebel, just like you fail at everything else.'

Joe felt cold suddenly. With Noah's mocking and Ravenna glaring murderously at him, it was like the hatching ceremony all over again, but lethal this time. He'd made another terrible mistake, and once more everyone would witness it. He'd just brought all these people up here to die. He squinted out into the darkness and his heart stumbled.

Noah and Lanys stood there, side by side, with Ravenna towering over them. Behind them, dozens more black-clad figures poured over the grass. It was the Brotherhood, speeding towards the barracks, towards Joe and his friends. This was one battle that was about to end.

'I'm so sorry,' Joe said quietly. He'd failed his dragon. He'd failed his father. Who would avenge him now?

CHAPTER THIRTY-SIX

They'd been so close. Joe was filled with helpless fury, pinned to the spot under the gaze of the huge black dragon, Ravenna, and Lanys, with Noah and his dragon impatient for their revenge.

Joe could feel Ren hiding directly behind him, and he wished she would run to safety.

The worst thing was that he understood Noah, finally. That look on his face? Oh, that was familiar, all right. Noah wanted vengeance for his father's death. He might be blaming the wrong people, but Joe understood the impulse all too well. Wasn't he here for exactly the same reason – to stop Asa and the Brotherhood because they'd killed Nestan? He had no right to judge Noah for it, even as he prepared to die.

'Joe, we have to do something,' Winter whispered next to him. 'The Brotherhood are coming!'

The burly guard at the next bunkhouse dragged Amina and Conor forwards by their arms, and threw them down in front of Lanys. 'These two thought they were a match for me. *Huh* – funny.' He didn't sound amused. He stood there rubbing his head where they must have hit him.

Ariel and Maric limped out of the shadows. Something had happened to Ariel's left wing, and it hung down awkwardly.

Where were Tiago and Flavia? Joe prayed they'd had more success.

'Stop them, please,' Joe begged Lanys and Noah, watching the men of the Brotherhood coming closer, blades drawn. 'Don't hurt my friends – they're just children, ordinary children, no threat to you.'

'Oh, no, no, no. All the *ordinary children* are at home in their beds,' Lanys said. 'Obeying the curfew. These are rebels, led by Jowan Thornsen: a dangerous and unstable young man. You attacked our guards, not the other way round.'

'Yeah. We're only defending ourselves,' Noah added. He copied his cousin, eyeing her to see he was getting it right. 'And when we kill you, that's what we'll tell everyone. You attacked us. Everyone saw you on Hatching Day. They know what you're like!'

'I'm not like that! Not any more,' Joe said. But he knew Noah was right – he had a reputation now, and no one would doubt Noah's word when he was dead. No one would know that he'd changed. No one would know that he'd tried so hard to save the city from the Brotherhood. He battled against despair.

Noah took a step closer to him, but Joe held his ground, still praying that Tiago and Flavia might free some of the duke's soldiers in time to fight back.

Ren leaped out now, hissing angrily at Noah and Della. She looked so fragile and small, but she did her best to protect him.

Noah burst out laughing. 'Is she yours? Ha, what a runt! What's wrong with her?'

Joe watched Ren spread her wings defensively and nearly choked on the injustice of it – she'd never even learned to fly.

'Lanys, over to you,' Noah was saying, with puffed-up pride. 'This is my cousin Lanys, who had to put up with your Milla always grabbing the best for herself. Lanys? Can Ravenna flame them all at once?'

Joe started shaking then, remembering Hatching Day and the pain of his burns. Fear mixed with fury, but he could only stand there, powerless, as the black dragon loomed over them.

'But she's Maric's mother!' Amina wailed, bending protectively over her lilac-coloured dragon. Tears glinted silver on her cheeks.

'She won't hurt her own hatchlings,' Conor said bravely, but there was a wobble in his voice.

'She will if I command it,' Lanys insisted. 'They left her nest months ago.'

But Joe caught a flicker of doubt. 'Don't!' The Brotherhood had got to Noah, and force-fed his cruelty, but he spotted a chance with Lanys. 'Please,' he begged her now. 'Let the dragons live! Don't ask Ravenna to kill her own brood.'

Did the black dragon have any protective instinct left now her hatchlings had grown?

Lanys hesitated.

That was when the world exploded in a bloom of orange flame.

Joe went flying forwards, one hand protecting his face, the other reaching for his dragon. 'REN! Are you all right?!'

For a moment, there was only silence. Then horrible screams filled the air, along with fire and smoke.

'Ren!'

Mrrrt. She squirmed close, nudging at Joe with her long nose.

Joe felt the warm quiver of her body, safe and alive. He patted her up and down, but found no blood. He knelt, his head ringing from the blast, and then stood, trying to see what was happening in the swirling smoke, darkness and confusion. 'Winter? Amina? Conor?'

'Here,' Winter coughed. 'Fidell's all right.'

All noise was oddly muffled, as if coming from a great distance away.

'What was that?' Amina choked out.

'Firepowder: must've been!' That was Conor.

The smoke cleared, showing him Noah and Lanys crouching low, but they weren't looking at him. They gazed, horrified, beyond him, and Joe couldn't resist a quick glance over his shoulder.

Three enormous dragons had landed on the roofs of the first two bunkhouses, spitting flame in massive jets at anyone who dared challenge them.

In the livid orange light, he recognised Isak astride Belara; while the other two were riderless. It was Heral, Tarya's red dragon, and Petra, Duke Vigo's green one, come to reclaim their people. Simeon had found them! And there, in the air, were more dragons and their riders – all those whom Joe had freed from the dragonhall.

The ruined armoury and several trees were burning, utterly consumed by fire. They must have used firepowder in that first wave of attack.

He saw Ando, Rosa's dragon, roaring loudly and scratching at one of the bunkhouse roofs. He flew down and turned his fury on the building that contained his person.

The tide was turning: the fight was theirs again.

Ando used his enormous weight and plunged one of his forelegs right through the wooden planks of the bunkhouse. They splintered like kindling and the prisoners staggered out, finally, into the chaos of bright flame and cold moonlight and bloodshed.

Now they were free, Duke Vigo's soldiers picked up the fight, taking weapons from the fallen guards. There was a new surge as the furious soldiers, prisoners for three days, finally gave vent to their rage.

And as Joe watched, he realised that Yannic's tampering must have worked: the Brotherhood fought badly, slow to react, sometimes bending double in pain. Soon the ground was littered with their bodies.

When Joe spun round again, Noah had vanished.

Lanys was climbing back onto Ravenna. 'Up!' she told her dragon. 'To the palace.' The huge black dragon crouched, ready to launch.

'Isak!' Joe yelled, at the top of his voice, running towards his brother as Ravenna took flight. 'Quick: it's Lanys! She's going to warn the Brotherhood in the palace!'

Could he stop her? Lanys was Isak's former student. Would she listen to him now and change sides?

Isak and Belara reacted immediately. The huge dragon flapped her golden wings and sped after Ravenna in hot pursuit.

'Lanys!' Isak was shouting. 'Stop! Turn back. Join us! Belara is your dragon's mother. Don't do this to them!'

Joe saw the moment that Ravenna turned in mid-air. For a moment he thought Lanys was listening. And then Ravenna kindled and let out a jet of flame.

'Isak! Be careful!' Joe cried uselessly from the ground.

Isak flattened himself on Belara's back, pushing his dragon into a low evasive dive, missing the fire. Then Belara recovered smoothly, flapping hard to catch Ravenna from below.

Joe was shocked to see his gentle brother in battle. It reminded him of a hawk fighting a crow. The dragons' wings tangled together, gold on black, black on gold, and dropped so fast it seemed they'd both crash into the earth, only pulling free at the last moment. They spat fire, in hot bursts. Now Ravenna banked hard, avoiding Belara's flame, Lanys low against her neck.

No one had ever seen this before. Dragons didn't fight each other. Dragons were on the same side. Till now.

CHAPTER THIRTY-SEVEN

Ravenna attacked Belara with her talons, ripping into her chest.

Joe saw a gush of blood spring from Belara's ripped golden scales. 'No!' he cried. His brother Isak was in terrible danger.

But while Ravenna was so close to Belara, the black dragon was also vulnerable.

He saw Belara kindle, her chest blushing through the yellow-gold scales. She opened her mouth and a huge torrent of flame shot out, catching Ravenna full in the face.

Joe heard the unforgettable sound of a dragon in agony. Ravenna spun out of control, her wings folded to protect Lanys as she tumbled from the night sky, turning over and over, finally crashing into a stand of tall trees.

'Isak!' Joe yelled, running towards the trees. He couldn't see his brother, or his golden dragon. He was gripped by panic. He couldn't lose anyone else, not now.

Fear gave him wings, and he sped forwards, overtaking dozens of soldiers as the duke's newly freed army took the battle to the palace. Petra and Heral were attacking its front doors, with a mass of soldiers surging behind them. In the distance came a loud explosion, and the noise of shattering glass.

In the chaos, Joe searched breathlessly, shouting for his brother.

It was Ren who found them. The little purple dragon, almost invisible now in the darkness, went rustling into the undergrowth, and summoned Joe with an excited *aark aaark aaark*.

Then Belara struggled up, sending Ren skittering nervously away from her bulk, and Joe made out the familiar tall figure of his brother.

'Isak! Over here!' he cupped his hands to yell. 'Watch out for Ren. She's with me!' Then he ran towards him.

Isak was limping, his face smudged with blood and ash, his eyeglasses askew, with a crack across one lens.

'Are you all right?' Joe hung back, full of fear suddenly.

'Joe!' His brother hugged him tightly, speaking into his neck. 'Simeon told me you were alive.'

'And Belara? I thought she was hurt.' They both turned to look at the huge golden dragon. The gash on her chest was shallow, and most of the blood was drying stickily.

'She will be fine – she managed to pull back at the last moment, or else we'd both be done for.' Isak pounded Joe's shoulder with relief, emotion making his voice crack. 'You're really alive! Oh, when the message came, I was so relieved. What did Dad say? He and Josi must—'

'No!' Joe gulped. 'Y-you don't know? Y-you didn't hear . . .' he stuttered and stopped. Time did something strange, slowing down to a crawl. The world spun around them, all black sky and orange flame, but right here, there was an awful stillness.

Isak waited, studying his face in the dim light. 'Tell me.'

Joe couldn't speak. It was too much. It was too big. Ren whined and wound herself round his waist, sensing his emotion.

In the end, he didn't have to say it. His silence did that. He shook his head, then scrubbed at his face with sleeve.

'When?' Isak was hoarse with tears.

'Three days ago.' Joe choked out the words in horrible little chunks. 'As the Brotherhood took the city. We buried him. Josi and Matteo and me. I'm so sorry—'

Isak stumbled, and Joe caught him as he cried out, 'No! Dad, no, he can't be—' He covered his face with his hands and sobbed.

Joe held his brother, feeling his heart break.

After a while, Isak tried to speak. 'I can't do this . . . Not now . . . We must keep fighting.'

Joe watched Isak's struggle to tamp down his grief, putting his feelings somewhere deep and locking them away so he could carry on with this battle. His brother took a few breaths, swallowing it all down. 'And my sister?' His face turned hard, almost unrecognisable, lit by distant flame as the freed soldiers took their fight to the palace. 'What have they done with Tarya? I thought, when I saw Heral . . .' He couldn't go on.

'No, she's in there. We think. With Vigo. And their daughter.'

'Daughter?'

Joe nodded, with a fleeting smile. 'The Brotherhood were planning a trial, tomorrow. That's why we acted tonight.'

He saw Isak slump with relief. 'That's good. That means she's alive. They must've worked out how to block her thoughts from Heral using a yew barrier. That's the only reason he's not smashed that palace to pieces already. If we can just work out where they're keeping them . . .'

Just then Belara growled a deep *mrraaa*.

'And that's where I come in,' a new voice said. 'Didn't I tell you it would work?' Yannic was strutting towards them with his thumbs in his pockets.

Isak pushed Joe behind him and drew his short sword. 'Hold! Stop there.'

'It's all right, Isak, he's with us,' Joe cried, pushing past to stand between them.

'Oh, yes, I'd better ditch this.' Yannic stripped off his black jacket and tucked it under one arm. 'And don't forget to tell your sister just how grateful you are. She can turn that gratitude into gold. Now, shall we go find her?'

'Who is this?' Isak spat and swore.

'Yannic, Tarya's spy.' Joe hurried through an explanation.

Another explosion made them all turn back to the palace. The fighting had lasted hours now – Joe had lost all track of time. Surely it was almost over? The Brotherhood couldn't last long, outnumbered by the duke's army and more than a dozen fully grown dragons.

'I'm going to get my sister out of there.' Isak put one hand on Belara's back, and prepared to mount. 'You, Yannic? If you're really one of us, you can prove it now.'

But before anyone could move, a voice screamed in the darkness, filled with desperate fear. 'Joe Thornsen? Where are you?'

Joe was filled with dread. That was Winter's voice. 'Winter? What's happened, I thought the duke's soldiers were free, that they'd . . . I thought . . .' His words petered out.

Winter stumbled out into view, her arms outstretched, like a sleepwalker. Her face was a mask of terror, lit by the flames. Fidell ran at her side, eyes wide, ears flat, tail tucked down low.

Joe didn't want to ask. He wanted to hide his face in Ren's scaly back and pray to wake up, somewhere safe, somewhere else. He gulped, his mouth dry and sour with fear. He made himself ask, 'What is it? What's happened now?'

'Look to the east. The warning beacons are lit on the mainland.'

'Sartola?' Isak swore. 'But I left Luca there.'

But Joe wasn't listening. He went to meet Winter, taking her hands, sharing her fears. 'It's the volcano. It must be erupting,' he guessed.

'And that's where Milla and Thom went.'

She looked as horrified as Joe felt.

PART FOUR - WATER

AIR

FIRE

WATER

EARTH

CHAPTER THIRTY-EIGHT

'It's the volcano, Mount Bara!' Joe ran to the edge of the plateau that held the barracks. The burned and broken bunkhouses were deserted now, as the fight surged back to the palace. Joe saw a few black-clad bodies lying in the grass, but he didn't slow, searching for more clues to confirm Winter's news. Ren kept pace like his shadow, with Isak, Winter and the others following.

From this vantage point at the top of the island, he could see right across the Straits of Sartola to the mainland. And there in the distance, a line of beacons had been lit, little dots of fire stretching away to the east, like bones in a spine. Something was terribly wrong. Something that affected them all.

'The beacons!' Isak shouted. 'The beacons are lit.' And more quietly, 'I have never seen that. Not in my lifetime.'

All those within earshot turned, shocked. This was a new threat, bigger than war. It wouldn't care which side they were fighting on.

'We should've guessed,' Winter mumbled.

Joe saw the same expression of horror on everyone's faces, pale in the grey dawn. Conor and Amina staggered towards him, with their injured dragons. Yannic, Tiago and Flavia were behind them. Could it really be morning already? He swayed with fatigue.

He stared further eastwards, full of dread. He saw something new. There in the grey-blue sky, two dots grew larger all the time: dragons flying towards them at full speed. He strained his eyes, trying to pick out more detail. Who was it? They were hard to make out against the sky. Surely that was a crimson dragon. And a blue one? Yes!

'Here!' He waved with both arms. 'Land here! Not the palace!' He turned and shouted to his friends. 'It's Milla and Thom! They're all right! They're coming home.'

Aark? Ren asked anxiously, nudging his side with her purple nose.

'I don't know,' he told her. 'I don't know what it means.' He shielded his eyes, watching their approach. His relief faded with every wingbeat.

Coming into clear view, the dragons looked utterly spent. Their wings were streaked with blood and ash. Ruby landed first, with a heavy thump, her massive head crashing down and her eyes closing.

Iggie fell out of the sky next to him, slamming down, wings outstretched to soften the impact.

Their people were no better. Thom slumped forwards on his dragon's back, unmoving. Milla rolled off Iggie and collapsed on the grass.

'Milla! Thom!' Joe yelled, running to them.

Milla groaned, opening bloodshot eyes. 'There's no time. Must warn everyone.'

'Warn them what? What's happened?'

'It's Mount Bara,' Thom said. 'It's starting to erupt. Soon it will blow. We have to get everyone to safety.'

Joe held his water flask to Milla's mouth, and she drank, then choked, spilling water.

Isak was there too, lifting Thom's shoulders. 'He's exhausted,' he muttered. 'Oh, and he's burned! They need a healer, fast.'

'No, no,' Thom twisted away. 'No time. Get underground. Everyone must get underground. When it blows, it will make a giant wave. There'll be fire in the air, and a wall of water.'

'We can't go underground – that's madness!' Isak cried.

'Anywhere else, yes. But the tunnels were built for this.' Milla forced herself upright, almost slurring her words in her exhaustion. 'The city may be damaged, but we'll be safe down there. We read about it in some ancient texts.'

Joe felt panic rising up, like smoke, threatening to choke him. He looked out to sea again. The sun was rising clear of the horizon. 'How long do we have? How long?' he demanded.

Thom looked at him. 'Hours? Once it blows, the wave will speed over the ocean, faster than a dragon.' His eyes rolled back, as he slipped into unconsciousness.

'Hurry!' Milla croaked, leaning against her dragon's flank now. 'There's no time. The air will be full of fire and ash and debris. Get everybody underground . . .' She closed her eyes, gathering strength.

'Oh, Milla!' Isak fell on his knees next to the blue dragon. 'You need a healer – now!'

'No! She just told us to get underground – there's no time!' That was Winter, sharing Joe's alarm.

'Underground? How? The dragons can't go underground. I won't leave Belara!' Isak insisted.

'Listen to me, Isak,' Joe said. 'The dragons will fit – there's a huge cavern down there.'

'What about Tarya and Vigo and the baby? They're still trapped in the palace.' Isak stopped, daunted. 'And what will they do on Sartola? Oh, Luca!'

He was right: they had to save the whole city, but the battle still raged around the palace. Their sister and her baby were in there somewhere. How could they possibly rescue everyone in time?

Joe felt overwhelmed. He looked at the faces of everyone around him – Winter, Conor, Amina, Isak, Flavia, Tiago, Yannic – trying to think clearly.

Milla groaned in pain, making a decision for them.

'We need to get them to safety, now,' Joe said. 'Isak, listen. If you take Thom and Milla to safety, I'll get Tarya out of there.' He spoke quickly in his brother's ear.

Isak listened to it all, and nodded. 'We try your way first. But if it doesn't work, I won't rest till she's safe. Belara will let me know.' He took his glasses off for a moment, to wipe a tear that tracked through the blood and ash on his face. 'Right. Where are these caves then, Joe?'

'I'll go.' It was Winter, surprising him. 'I'll show you the way, if Ruby will let me ride her again. I can show you above the western beach, how to enter the caves. If you'll take Fidell, Joe?'

Joe was shocked. 'Of course.' Was she actually offering to take more people into the home she'd always kept secret?

'Thank you,' Isak said. 'Is it really safe, do you think?'

'That's what Milla and Thom said. We'll be protected by the rock.'

'It's not far.' Joe pointed at the lower western side of the island. 'Isak, can Belara manage Thom too?'

'I think so. Her wound isn't deep. If you lift him up, I can hold him.'

Belara raised her head, listening, and gave a soft growl of agreement.

'Let's go,' Winter said.

'Winter . . . Thank you.' Joe grabbed her hand for a moment and squeezed it, hoping she'd know how grateful he was. That he understood what this meant to her. 'We'll have to spread the word, get everyone from the city in there. All right?'

'Of course,' Winter said, nodding briefly. Then she approached the fallen red dragon and spoke quietly in her ear.

Ruby opened her eyes blearily, staggered forward and fell again. Then, with a second effort, she got up.

Winter slipped onto her shoulders, talking to her all the time. She was tall, but so slight that she couldn't weigh much.

Ruby flapped hard, harder. It seemed impossible, but

the huge red dragon managed to fight her way into the air. Then, with wide open wings, she soared down towards the western beach, with Winter on her back.

Together, Joe and Isak gathered up Thom's limp body, and slung it over Belara's shoulders with difficulty. He lay, face down, legs dangling. Isak clambered awkwardly behind him, his legs over Thom's body, holding him in position.

The golden dragon also struggled to launch, wings straining, but she finally made it. Isak lost his balance, lurching to the right, straining to keep hold of his precious load.

Joe sucked in his breath, fearing they would both tumble off. The dragon dipped, adjusting her flight, and tilting her huge golden wings. Then she glided down over the city, following Winter and Ruby, carrying Isak and Thom to safety.

Iggie was the last to launch. The blue dragon was so weary it seemed hopeless. He flapped once, twice. The wind stirred up dust and leaves, but had no impact on Iggie's vast bulk.

'Come on, my Ig,' Milla urged, bending low over his shoulders. 'Almost done. One last effort. You can do it, brave soul.'

Again Iggie flapped, with all his strength. He took a massive leap, pushing up with his hind legs, and finally he was airborne. He skimmed the palace walls, his feet dangling, and soared after the others, heading west.

One problem solved. A dozen more to go, Joe thought, as he turned back to the circle of anxious faces.

Time was running out. Would he have to choose between saving the city, and saving his sister?

CHAPTER THIRTY-NINE

Joe felt dazed, clutching at his dragon, while Fidell whined miserably at being left behind. He stared down at the trampled leaves and grass below his feet. It all looked so ordinary. Just another morning. Only this might be his last. He couldn't believe that all this might be destroyed in a matter of hours. He didn't see how they could manage the task ahead. He just knew he had to try.

'We'll have to split up,' he said, finally, choosing one idea from the jumble in his mind. 'Conor and Amina, Tiago and Flavia, can you go down into the city? Tell them the news – get everyone into the caves. You have your maps still?'

'Yes, but—' Amina gulped. 'They'll panic.'

'They mustn't,' Conor said grimly. 'Or we'll all be crushed.'

Joe had a vision of the narrow city streets packed with people, screaming and rushing.

'We need more people,' Tiago said. 'We can't reach everyone in time.'

Joe's gaze fell on the palace, where an uneasy stalemate held. The remaining Brotherhood had retreated inside. Vigo's army and the dragonriders now surrounded the palace. If they needed more people to help, there was an obvious place to start.

'I'll ask them,' Joe said, pointing. 'Wait for me, just a little while. Keep Fidell with you. And Yannic? Hang onto your black jacket and stay out of sight. I am going to need you soon, when the Brotherhood are distracted.'

With Ren by his side, he ran towards the palace, ignoring the weariness in his legs.

Vigo's soldiers swarmed the palace steps, filling the tiled courtyard, entirely covering the ancient black dragon mosaic. Heral and Petra were right on top of the palace, like heraldic beasts, up among the stone struts and gargoyles that decorated its roof. The other dragonriders kept watch in a wide circle dotted all around the palace grounds.

Joe saw a flicker of movement inside the palace, and he knew that the Brotherhood would be watching it all from inside. What about Tarya? Could she see him? Where were they keeping her?

He pushed through the mass of soldiers surrounding the palace, looking for a face he knew – his sister's second-in-command. 'Rosa Demarco!' he yelled. 'Where's Rosa?' She'd known him all his life. The last time she'd seen him was at the hatching ceremony. He prayed she wouldn't hold it against him now.

Two burly soldiers grabbed his arms before he got

anywhere near Rosa, reunited with her fierce orange dragon Ando. 'What do you want, kid?' one demanded.

'Ouch!' Joe yelped in pain. 'There's no time for this. Tell her Jowan Thornsen is here. Tell her it's urgent.'

Ren started attacking the men, biting their sleeves and earning a sharp cuff from one of them.

'Ren! No! Stop,' Joe cursed. 'Please, you have to listen. And leave my dragon alone!'

She ducked out of reach, hissing loudly.

'Yeah, who says? Look at him. He's one of them! Did the Brotherhood send you?'

'No, I promise!' Joe begged them. 'Hurry, or we're all dead.'

The men exchanged a glance. 'You go, I'll hold this puppy still. Let it be the general's decision.'

One of the men rushed off. The other twisted Joe's arms behind his back. 'Don't get any ideas meanwhile. And tell your funny-looking dragon to behave.'

'Ren, please! Be still.' Joe kept his eyes on her, praying she'd stay calm. He stopped struggling, trying not to burst with frustration. The sweaty stink of the soldiers filled his nostrils, and his feet slipped a little on the black mosaic, slick with mud.

Finally, the first man returned. From the way the ranks of men parted respectfully, Joe knew he was followed by Tarya's second-in-command, Rosa Demarco. He heard her raised voice before he saw her.

She did a quick double-glance when she saw him, recovering in an instant. 'You're alive: I see the rumours were true. Explain yourself, Joe Thornsen,' she called as she strode towards them. 'Make it fast! I am doing my best to rescue your sister.'

Rosa was tall, with a narrow cat-like face and high cheekbones. Her black hair was plaited in the dragonrider style, her uniform all crumpled and stained from her days in captivity, her boots were smeared with blood and soil.

'We're all in danger!' Joe shouted. 'Mount Bara will erupt – look over at the mainland if you don't believe me. Milla and Thom just flew in to warn us of the wave that will follow. There are tunnels we can shelter in, but we need to evacuate the city, *now*.'

The man holding Joe's arms scoffed, 'Nonsense!'

Rosa silenced him with one gesture. 'Release him. You, go check – confirm his story.'

The man ran off towards the barracks.

Joe fell forwards, rubbing his arms, and Ren ran to him, growling like a terrier.

'So,' Rosa said with a quick grin, 'is it you I should thank for our release back there?' She hauled him to his feet. 'And for rescuing Ando – some kids, that's what I heard.'

'Yes, we used the tunnels then too—'

She cut him off. 'But now you want us to abandon our fight, is that what you're saying? Go hide underground, like rats? So they can kill us down there?'

'Or you can die up here, when the wave hits. It's up to you,' Joe snapped back. 'But your city needs you. Will your soldiers listen?' He explained everything Milla and Thom had said, how they needed to lead the city folk into the tunnels, and fast, and how they were built for this.

'What about the Brotherhood?' she said. 'I don't think they're the listening kind.'

'Leave them to me,' Joe said, 'and Heral and Petra.' The green and red dragons were still perched on the top of the palace, waiting for the chance to free their people.

'Oh, so you're staying up here?' Rosa sounded suspicious. 'Why should I listen to you if you're not willing to try these tunnels too?'

Joe bit down his retort, fighting a wave of impatience. They didn't have time for this! He knew he had to choose his next words carefully.

'Milla and Thom risked their lives to warn us. We only have a short time left. When the volcano erupts fully, Arcosi will be in great danger. I know it's hard to believe, so far away, but we need to get everyone into the tunnels, now. Without your help, we're lost. They'll listen to you, to the army. If you help us, I think we can do it, we can save everyone. Look, I've got maps here.'

The first soldier sped back towards them, skidding in the mud. His face had turned grey and taut with fear.

'All right,' Rosa said, before the man even had a chance to speak, 'we're in.'

'The beacons!' the man yelled. 'He's right. Hurry!'

'And there's enough room for all the dragons, in these tunnels?' Rosa demanded. 'Even ones as big as Ando?'

Joe nodded. 'Yes, the city people can use any tunnel, but there's only one entrance big enough for adult dragons. Ando and the others will need to go to the western beach, here' – he showed her on the map – 'when everyone else is safe.'

'What about your sister and the duke? We just leave them here, at the mercy of the Brotherhood?'

'I've got an idea . . .' Joe explained it to her.

There was a pause then. Joe watched Rosa flick her eyes back towards the palace, then over the ranks of soldiers. Everyone was listening, without seeming to, and she must know it. How long would they remain obedient if they knew disaster was headed their way?

Rosa sighed, and turned back to Joe. 'Right, Thornsen,' she said, 'we will do as you ask. Give me those maps.'

'Thank you.' He tried to show how grateful he was.

Joe was astonished how quickly everything changed then. With Rosa bellowing orders, repeated down the lines, the soldiers organised themselves into small groups. Each was given a map, a tunnel entrance to aim for, a neighbourhood to lead to safety, and a dragonrider to herd the city folk. They beetled off to evacuate the city.

Joe felt as if a weight had been lifted from his shoulders, as he and Ren hurried back to the barracks. He found Yannic and the others where he'd left them.

When he explained to Yannic what he wanted him to do, the ex-soldier burst out laughing, rubbing a hand over his badger-stripes of white hair. 'Oh, Joe,' he said, wiping his eyes with his knuckles afterwards. 'I thought you just said you wanted me to walk in there, rejoin the Brotherhood, when there's only hours before this whole island floods or burns, or whatever your mate said—'

'Yes,' Joe said steadily, interrupting, 'that's what I want you to do. There's a whole pile of gold in it for you. That villa on Sartola? It's yours.' *And your revenge*, he thought, but didn't say the words in front of his friends. 'Look, here's a little taster for you.' He dug around in his pockets and brought out all the gold he'd taken the other day, gesturing for his friends to do the same. 'Hold out your hands?'

Yannic did so, not laughing now. They piled his outstretched palms with all the gold coins they were carrying, till they were slipping from the top of the heap and his fingers grasped at them desperately.

'Do we have a deal?' Joe asked.

'Deal,' Yannic said, still looking stunned. He hurriedly found homes for all the coins, slipping them down his boots, under his shirt, in his pockets, till Joe was surprised he didn't clink with every step. 'Now tell me again, what do I need to do?'

So Joe told him, very slowly.

CHAPTER FORTY

When Yannic had sneaked off to the kitchen entrance at the back of the palace, Joe, Conor and Amina, with Tiago and Flavia, hurried after the soldiers heading down into the city. There was no need to hide now that the remaining members of Brotherhood were all gathered in the palace. Speed was everything. Joe pushed himself on-wards, his friends keeping pace, and for a few moments they only spoke to their dragons in a low murmur.

'Ren, whatever happens today . . . you're my best friend. Ever. You know that, don't you?' Joe began, but a lump formed in his throat, and he couldn't carry on.

She reached up, and bumped her head against his chin, chittering softly.

They were on the main road into the city, and the side streets were already filling with people fleeing from their homes. Soon Joe could barely think over the din. The dragonriders were yelling down instructions to their groups.

Children were crying. People were calling frantic farewells and questions.

Flavia and Tiago split up, heading to their own streets to evacuate their families.

'Stay with your neighbours! Follow me,' one dragonrider was yelling, struggling to keep her dragon steady as she circled above them.

'No, bring only food and water, they said,' a woman was shrieking at her young daughter, who was holding a struggling cat.

'I won't eat then! I can't leave him.' The girl stuck her lip out and refused to move.

'Don't rush! Steady now. We still have time,' the dragonrider was shouting down.

Joe hoped it was true. If Thom was wrong, and the volcano blew now, everyone would be caught in the open. He pushed the awful images from his mind and threaded his way through the growing crush of bodies, heading home.

When they reached the gates of the Yellow House, Joe found his mother and Matteo ready to leave, laden with bags of food and water.

'Mum! How are you feeling? Are you better?' Joe flew to Josi, his arms round her broad waist, resting his head down on her shoulder and breathing in the comfort of her.

'Almost,' she said.

Prrt? Ren was asking.

Joe pulled back. 'Mum, this is Ren, and here's Winter's Fidell.'

'Hello, Ren, Fidell. Aren't you something?' Josi smiled at

the shadow dragons, then winced. The bruises had almost faded, but she was holding herself so carefully that Joe guessed she was still in pain. It kept his fury against the Brotherhood simmering inside him.

He led them to the nearest entrance to the tunnels and held the door open. 'Where's your map?' he asked Conor, taking the time to show him exactly where to go. He didn't want his mother wandering for ever in the tunnels.

'Wait, why are you showing *me*?' Conor asked. 'Why don't you just lead the way?'

Now came the hardest part.

'I'm not coming,' Joe said. 'Not yet. Take everyone to safety. Take Fidell to Winter. I need to get Tarya and Vigo out of the palace first.' He looked away so he didn't have to see his mother's expression when he said that.

He busied himself saying goodbye to Fidell and his friends instead. He and Conor slapped each other awkwardly in a half-hug. Finally, things were back to normal between them.

'I'll look after them,' Conor said in his ear. 'Just keep safe, all right?'

'You be quick, Joe Thornsen,' Amina said, throwing her arms round them both. 'Don't make us lose you again.' Her eyes were huge and glittery, and when she closed them tightly, a few stray tears squeezed out.

'Hurry!' Matteo urged them. 'Josi can't walk for long – she needs rest.'

'I'll see you down there,' Joe said to his mother, who was trying very hard not to cry.

'I know you want to help your sister,' she told him, 'but I

need you safe. I cannot lose you too. Promise me again – you run when you have to? For your dragon's sake? And mine?'

'Promise,' Joe managed to choke out. 'Now go!'

He watched them disappear into the tunnels, Conor and Amina leading the way. They made a strange procession, laden with flasks and bags of food, an old man, a limping woman, two children and their dragons, Fidell looking backwards, torn between staying with Joe and Ren and finding his person.

The longing to join them and save himself was almost overpowering, but Joe tore his eyes away and focused on his next task. He returned to the Yellow House just long enough for them both to gulp down spring water from the well – somehow still fresh and cool. He felt light-headed and realised he hadn't eaten since yesterday.

He and Ren were going to need their strength, so he risked the delay to gobble down some stale bread while Ren swallowed some dried fish. He stuffed more food in his pockets for later. Then he was running back up the hill to the palace, praying that he would have time to finish the job.

CHAPTER FORTY-ONE

Joe felt like he was walking through a nightmare. The dust from the volcano had reached Arcosi. The morning was hot and still, tinted grey-orange like some endless dusk. The birds had fallen silent, or fled. The watchtowers at the entrance to the palace grounds were deserted, and the huge iron-studded gates hung ajar.

He slipped through the gates and into the gardens. The ornamental flower gardens were scarred now from the dragonfight earlier that morning. He saw trampled hedges, blackened leaves, branches twisted down like broken limbs. He stuck to the shadows, telling Ren to stay hidden too. He would need her soon.

He crept as close as he could without breaking cover, crouching under a tree and peering out at the palace for the sign he was hoping for.

Had Yannic managed his part? Did the Brotherhood suspect him? Joe was gambling they'd be too distracted by their enemy leaving to notice Yannic's return.

He looked at the palace, now silent and watchful. Heral and Petra still waited on their desperate vigil. Joe wondered when they had last eaten or drunk anything. They wanted to be close to their imprisoned people, and he knew they'd never leave, even now that danger threatened. He'd never leave Ren like that, either. So for the dragons' sake, as well as his sister's, his plan had to work.

He forced himself to be methodical and took his time searching from west to east, checking every single window, every turret, every annexe, every passageway. He was almost losing hope when he saw it – finally! A tiny square of red and green fabric, the colours Tarya and Vigo always wore to match their dragons, pressed up against a window high in the southern turret. Yannic had done it! He'd managed to discover the exact location where Tarya and Vigo were being held and send a signal.

As Isak had suggested, something must be blocking the connection between his sister and her dragon. What had he and Winter said? Only a yew barrier or a certain herb could do it? Or Tarya might be dead already, but Joe wasn't going to consider that.

Now for his part. 'Ren?' he whispered, turning to her and bending close to her long purple ears. 'I need you to do something for me. I know you're new to this. I know you're only young, but I have faith in you.'

She looked up at him, huge golden eyes unblinking. She tilted her purple head to one side, listening hard. Her long ears twitched as he spoke.

'You're connected, each dragon to each dragon. You're

289

all connected.' Joe remembered Noah's smugness as he'd thrown that in his face. *The dragons knew; they always do.* He might be late to this particular lesson, but he would make it count. He focused on Ren again. 'Tell Heral that Tarya is in that southern turret.' He focused on it very strongly, the image of the window with the green and red banner showing. 'Tell him about the western cave. Then tell Petra. All right?'

Ren closed her eyes. She stood very still. Was it too much? Was she too tired? How would he know if it had worked?

A strange ripple passed through Ren's purple body from nose to tail, then she opened her eyes and said proudly, *Aark!*

Joe stood staring at the palace, craning his neck, praying Heral and Petra would hear and understand.

For a moment, nothing happened. What else could he do? Joe was out of ideas and almost out of time. Then Heral launched into the air. He was still the largest of all the dragons, bigger even than Thom's Ruby. The huge red dragon flapped higher and gave a bellow of rage. He lifted, circling up and up, and then suddenly turned in the air and plunged like a hawk, hurtling down, gaining momentum, faster and faster as he levelled out finally.

Heral braced his head like a battering ram and went smashing, forehead first, into the southern tower, skimming the cone of the turret clean off, like the top of a boiled egg, scattering bricks and glass in every direction. A shard whizzed past Joe's face. He had to jump for cover, hands over his head.

When he looked up, Heral was swooping low, talons

outstretched, lifting something, lifting *someone* from inside the tower.

Tarya! Heral gripped her tightly by the shoulders. Joe's sister had curled her body up, protecting something small in her arms. Then they were gone.

Petra went in next, the green dragon diving fast and flapping hard, retrieving Duke Vigo in her claws.

Joe stared hard as the dragons carried their people away to safety.

That left Yannic inside. He'd be like a cat, Joe hoped, and find his own way out.

'You're amazing. Thank you!' he told Ren, hugging her tightly.

They'd done it. They'd freed the duke's army, saved Tarya and Vigo, and begun the evacuation. The only thing left was to flee.

Joe looked at the palace. Asa was in there. His men were in there. The Brotherhood showed no signs of leaving. Did they even know about the volcano?

'It's not my problem!' he muttered, turning, ready to run back to the tunnels. Hadn't he wanted his revenge? Well, here it was, and he wouldn't even get his hands dirty. The volcano would do his work for him.

He stopped. He wasn't that person any more. Joe realised he didn't want them to die. Not even Asa. It wouldn't bring his father back to life. He couldn't do it. He couldn't leave those men to die, not without a warning at least. Some of them, he remembered, weren't much older than himself, just drawn in by the Norlander songs and sense of belonging . . .

291

'Ren, hide, please?' He waited till she'd crept under a dusty shrub and was completely out of sight. Then he stepped out into full view, holding up his hands to show they were empty. He walked across the tiled courtyard, over the black dragon mosaic and up the steps to the double doors, trying to ignore the fact that there were probably a dozen hidden archers all aiming at his chest.

His hands were hot and sweaty, but he made a fist and rapped loudly on the wooden doors. 'Asa?' he called, alarmed to hear his voice trembling slightly. 'Asa!' he tried again. 'You need to hear this.'

The door opened a crack, and a voice said, 'You again? Are you their message boy now? He'll see you. Come in.' The door opened fully.

It was the ginger-bearded man who'd handed him the ale at the meeting.

'I won't come in.' Joe took a step back. 'He'll talk to me here.' He had to stay safe, for Ren's sake. Even coming this near was a terrible risk.

The door slammed again. He waited. The heat intensified. He rubbed his fingers against his trousers, slippery with sweat, then cupped his hands round his mouth.

'Mount Bara is erupting!' he bellowed, up at the palace windows, where he knew the Brotherhood were watching and listening. 'There's only an hour or less to take shelter. If you stay here, *you will die*!'

That got their attention. He saw traces of movement beyond every window, like fish in deep water.

The main door opened again. This time Asa stood there

himself, sword drawn. It was the first time Joe had seen him in full daylight, face to face. He was just an ordinary Norlander man, the same age as his father perhaps, with white bristle on his hollow cheeks. And yet Asa stood here, untouched, while Nestan lay buried in his own garden. What was Joe even thinking, risking his life for this man?

'You're in danger,' he began. 'You need to get everyone out of here.'

'You expect us to believe you? I don't know how you pulled that trick last night, sneaking past our guards, but we won't fall for your lies.' Asa had heavy brows, a sailor's lined face and sun-bleached eyes, with that little boat-shaped scar underneath. He also looked exhausted.

'I'm not lying,' Joe said through clenched teeth. He felt for all that anger he'd been saving up, ready to tell Asa exactly what he thought of him. But now he reached for it, there was nothing there, except pity.

Asa raised one eyebrow. 'Really?'

'Hurry! Just leave, now. Even if you don't want to follow me, you could take a ship – they say the open ocean is safer.'

That was the worst thing he could have said. Asa's mouth turned up in disgust. 'A ridiculous story. As if we would abandon the island now. Nice try, Thornsen. No. We have the palace, and we're holding it. The dragons might have taken your sister back, but we are winning and you people are desperate.'

'Asa, no. Look at the sky. You can see the warning beacons with your own eyes.' Joe was pointing over his shoulder now, realising he was losing his attention. Was he really so unwilling to listen? Would Asa rather die than admit he was wrong? 'And the histories are right there in the library – you can read for yourself how dangerous it is—'

'No.' Asa's voice was flat and hard. His hand flew to the hilt of his sword. Then he sighed. 'I'll let you go, Joe Thornsen. You remind me of—' He shook his head. 'Never mind. It's not your fault you've eaten up their lies. You could have been one of us. Remember that.' And he reached out and put his hand on Joe's shoulder.

For a moment, Joe held his gaze, and he felt sure he could reach him. No more people had to die. If he could just find the right words.

Then Asa pushed him hard.

CHAPTER FORTY-TWO

Joe fell backwards, right out of the doorway, breaking his fall with both hands. Pain shot up his wrists.

The doors slammed shut again.

'Asa! Open up! You have to leave, now!'

The door stayed closed.

Just then there came a distant rumble, like thunder, coming from the east. Mount Bara! Joe had no time left. The volcano was starting to erupt. How long before it blew? He glanced once, seeing the sky stained with a spray of orange lava.

'Save yourselves!' he yelled at the palace, hoping Yannic at least would hear him. He clambered to his feet, ignoring the pain, and sped back to where he'd left Ren, fear lending him speed. 'Come on, Ren,' he told her. 'Can you run?'

Aark! she said, darting after him.

Joe checked over his shoulder. Could Ren keep up? He couldn't carry her, she was too big now. And he wouldn't leave his precious dragon behind. He peered backwards, anxiously. She'd never flown before, but by spreading her purple wings, Ren managed to do a strange mixture of running and jumping, flapping and clambering after him. She was keeping up.

Spurred on by relief, Joe ran faster than he'd ever run in his life, arms pumping, legs stretching, eating up the ground with every stride.

He didn't know how long they had left. There was no time to reach the city. Instead, he veered round, heading for the stables and the tunnel entrance there.

His breath was burning in his throat now, his chest heaving. He flew round a corner – only a few more strides. He reached the stables and slackened pace, momentum carrying him forwards. Then he stopped, bent forwards, catching his breath and checking for danger.

Something caught his eye: a strange yellow wing, fluttering in a low bush. But hadn't all the birds gone? There was something bulky dumped under there.

Ren rushed awkwardly past him, falling head over tail and righting herself again.

Mrraa? Aark? She sounded as though she couldn't decide if it was danger or not.

Then, with a flap of wings, the yellow dragon, Della, ran out of the bush, behaving strangely, dipping her head low, wings wide. She came straight to Joe, caught hold of his trouser leg with her teeth and tugged him.

'Della, no! Get off me. We have to leave!' He pulled himself away, ripping away a shred of fabric, and turning back to the gate.

But Ren stretched up and nipped his ear lobe, gesturing frantically with her head towards the yellow dragon.

'Really? Now?' Ren nipped him again. 'Ow! All right,' he sighed, and followed Della back towards the bush.

With a shock he realised there was a person there, sprawled facedown in the dust: a person wearing a yellow dragonrider jacket and leggings.

Noah.

He must have been caught up in the fighting – Joe saw a shocking bruise on his face, where someone must've hit him. He bent and touched his wrist: it was still warm, with a faint thready pulse.

Ren growled, glaring up at him.

Joe couldn't leave Noah here: he would be a murderer. He would be worse than him. But time was running out.

Ren flicked her purple tail, blocking his way.

'Argh!' he cried in frustration. 'You may be right.' He bent down and rolled Noah over. 'But if we die saving *him*, it's not my fault!' Then he grasped one foot in each hand and leaned back with all his weight, managing to heave Noah's body along the ground, his head bouncing alarmingly.

They reached the stable building, and he kicked open the metal door to the tunnels.

'In!' he ordered the dragons.

Then he crawled in backwards and dragged Noah after him. Jumping down into the passageway, Joe positioned himself below the unconscious body of Noah and pulled him down over one shoulder, while Ren went ahead and Della crawled behind, making distressed sounds.

Grunting with effort, Joe just managed to shut the gate behind them. Taking deep breaths, he staggered down the tunnel in darkness into the heart of the island.

After twenty paces, Joe fell on his knees, ready to collapse. He rolled Noah off, as gently as he could manage, and rested there, gasping. 'That's it, Ren. I can't carry him another step.' It would have to do.

She seemed satisfied enough, and they left Della guarding Noah, while Joe stumbled on, dripping with sweat, legs shaking with exhaustion, ready to drop. Ren guided him all the way.

Every time he paused, uncertain of the way, Ren chittered in the dark: *aark* for the right way, an alarmed *mraa* if he tried to take a wrong turn.

After stumbling many times, Joe finally heard the distant buzz of voices and the perfect darkness was pierced by light. He'd made it. He reached the bottom stone step, and stood there, trembling, looking down on the crowd in the cave he always thought of as the dragonhall underground.

Where was his mother? There she was! Tarya and Vigo! They were alive, their heads bent low over the baby in Tarya's arms. Isak was with them. And Matteo, sitting with Amina and Conor. Winter was there, helping Milla and Thom. All the dragons were there, from Ando and Ruby, Iggie, Petra and Heral to the smaller Ariel and Maric. Tiago and Flavia, with Lina and Elias. Simeon and all the fisherfolk. Rosa and the duke's army. He saw his friends from school, all the market traders. There was a group of black-clad Brotherhood soldiers, with their hands tied, who must've surrendered when they heard the news.

Somehow, they'd done it. They were safe.

He swayed where he stood, overwhelmed with relief. His legs finally gave way and he sank down onto the lowest step and put his head in his hands.

He checked again. Yannic wasn't there.

'It's Joe and Ren!' Isak's voice pierced the hubbub. 'They made it!'

There was a loud rush of applause and cheering.

He looked up, hardly able to believe his ears. Were they laughing at him? What had he done now?

But no, they were smiling, waving, beckoning him down.

He was too stunned to move. His cheeks were burning and his eyes prickled, then a slow grin spread across his face.

CHAPTER FORTY-THREE

Joe staggered down into the crowded cavern. 'Noah's back there – can someone carry him in?' and then he was bobbing along in the sea of bodies as people he didn't even know wished him well.

'Well done, Joe!'

'That's Joe Thornsen. He sent the army for us.'

'Josi's son, he's got a dragon now.'

'He deserves it, after what happened to him.'

He was known for something good, something new. His cheeks burned.

And then, finally, he reached his family and his friends: Amina and Conor, beaming; Winter, giving him a nod that was better than any words; his mother, wrapped in a blanket, looking crumpled but relieved; and his sister, at last, sitting in a huddle with her family.

'Tarya!' Joe fell forwards. His chest felt tight and heavy, and he prayed he wouldn't have to break the bad news about Nestan once more.

She looked different. Her face was puffy, and her skin had a greyish-white pallor, with huge blue shadows under her eyes.

Vigo, next to her, looked nothing like a duke, just a tired man, broken with worry.

When Tarya saw Joe, her eyes filled with tears.

'Are you all right?' he asked.

'We will be. Oh, Joe, Josi's been telling me about Dad.'

Joe wedged himself in next to his sister and leaned on her shoulder. 'I'm sorry.'

'No, I'm sorry. I should have been there.' She hugged him tightly with her free arm, pulling him close. 'It wasn't your fault. You sent Heral for me, didn't you? They lined the room with yew panels, so Heral and Pete couldn't sense us.' Her tears flowed freely now, dripping down her face, as she looked down at her child. 'Dad won't get to meet her, Joe. That's the worst of it. He'll never meet our little survivor: Serina. Look, here she is.'

Joe peered down at the bundle in his sister's arms, seeing only a wisp of black hair, bushy little eyebrows and a rose-bud face, tightly closed in sleep. He felt a rush of warmth towards this tiny new person. 'Ah, she's lovely.' He gave a hiccupy gulp. 'Dad would've loved her.'

'He couldn't wait to be a grandfather.' That was Josi, shuffling in on Joe's other side, so he was surrounded by family again. 'He joked he'd had the beard for it for thirty years.'

Isak was there too, next to Vigo. They all circled Tarya and Serina, all talking about Nestan, letting their tears flow, till the weight in Joe's chest eased a little.

'Oh, Joe. We missed you so much. Now, haven't you

301

got someone to introduce me to as well?' Tarya said after a while, looking past Joe. 'What's this about fire dragons?'

'*Shadow* dragons, the books say. Ren, come on.' She'd been hiding with Fidell, nervous of so many new faces in her nest, but now she came forwards to meet Tarya, her ears pricked forwards. Winter and Fidell followed cautiously.

'Thank you, Ren,' Tarya told her, handing her daughter to Vigo so she could greet Ren properly. 'You spoke to Heral, didn't you? You told him where to find me.'

Ren stretched her neck out, nostrils flaring. *Prrt?*

Joe watched them get acquainted. 'And this is Winter, who saved my life, and Fidell, the other shadow dragon.'

Winter smiled now, no longer hiding behind her hair. 'I'm glad you're back with us, Your Grace.'

'Thank you.' Tarya opened her arms. 'May I hug you?'

Joe found his eyes prickling as he watched his sister embrace his new friend.

'I think you've got lots to tell us, Joe,' Tarya said. 'Come find me later? I need to feed Serina.' And she headed back to Vigo and their child.

Joe searched the packed cavern again. The city's healers were at work, tending to all who needed their help.

'I can't believe we all fit in,' he said quietly to Winter. 'It must be true: the tunnels were built for this.'

'Built to save the city,' she smiled, a sideways flickering grin. 'Not just ours, after all.'

For a long moment they looked steadily at each other, as if they were the only people in the huge packed cavern that was their true home.

Joe grinned back. 'Come on, let's rest, while we can.'

Ren and Fidell sank down in a heap on the floor with their necks entwined. Following their example, Joe and Winter found a free section of cavern wall and settled themselves against it, next to their dragons. Winter tilted her head and let its weight fall on Joe's shoulder. He stretched out his left arm so she could lean on it.

They stayed like that for a long time.

Joe realised later that his arrival had given people something to focus on. That was part of the reason for the welcome. After the flurry of interest died down, everyone resumed their waiting. Tense anticipation grew. Joe and Winter moved to sit near Milla and Thom, who told them in tired whispers about their journey to the lands around Mount Bara.

It was unbelievably hot. Silence fell. Baby Serina cried and was comforted.

Joe could see the sweat trickling down Thom's face, as he sat leaning on his dragon. He wiped it away with his sleeve, and new drops formed in moments.

'Are you sure we are safe in here?' Joe asked quietly. Amina and Conor were nearby, with Maric and Ariel curled up together at their feet; Ren and Fidell did the same.

'Yes,' Milla murmured. 'It's happened before: that's what the people who live near the volcano told us, when they shared their precious archive and their folk tales.'

'Think about it, Joe: where is the main entrance to the tunnel?' Thom propped himself up, speaking urgently now.

'The western beach.' Joe took out Nestan's compass,

waiting till the needle settled. He lifted it, so everyone could see.

'And where will the wave be coming from?'

'Mount Bara, in the east.' He took a reading from the compass and pointed, then tucked the metal case away safely.

Conor understood first. He made a fist with one hand, and then cupped the other, bringing it closer and closer and slamming it against the first. 'So it'll crash over the island, like this. And whatever damage it may do, the wave will pass on, travelling west. The tunnel entrances all face west, don't they? Joe, these tunnels must have been built for this! Maybe the whole of the shadow strip was built where it is, to be protected from the wave?'

'So it won't flood, not in here?' Amina said anxiously.

'We'll be fine, if we stay here.' Winter sounded as if she almost believed it.

That's when they heard it. The silence in the cavern thickened with listening. And then – distant at first, but getting louder – there came a fierce rushing noise, coming from the east, just as Joe had said. The volcano had erupted and finally blown its top. Joe pictured the unleashed wild wave, galloping over the sea, gathering strength, faster and faster, louder and louder.

There was a vast boom, an echoing crash of mighty force.

The huge wave must have broken over the island, slamming down with all the weight of gathered water, amplified through the rocky tunnels into a wall of sound. Joe heard a deep groan, as if the island itself was in pain.

Joe braced, gripping Amina and Winter's hands either side so tightly that his knuckles showed bone-white through his brown skin.

His ears were filled with confused noise. Dragons growling their alarm call: *mrraaa, mrra!* Someone was screaming.

Gradually it eased, breaking up into other noises: smashing, splintering, swirling. Joe pictured all the island's boats stolen from the harbour and flung high, where no boat should ever be.

And then it was gone. He sighed out a shaky breath, relaxed his fingers.

Was that it?

'Look!' a voice cried. 'The water – it's rising! Help!'

No. Everything in Joe denied it. No, no, no. This couldn't be happening. He couldn't have led the whole city down here to drown like rats in a barrel.

CHAPTER FORTY-FOUR

Joe grabbed one of the storm lanterns and hurried over to see, with Winter following, their dragons close behind. They knew these caves better than anyone. At the eastern edge of the cavern, where the underground stream vanished, bubbling away underground, something had changed. The stream was still flowing, but the water was getting higher and higher. Soon it would overflow. It must be hotter than ever. Steam rose from its surface, filling the air with heat and dampness.

'It must be stuck further down!' Winter spoke in Joe's ear.

'That wave – it must've blocked the flow of the stream.'

'We need to get people out, quickly,' Winter said.

The people nearest the stream were backing away. There were cries of alarm – 'It's flooding!' 'Get back!'

In the enclosed space, dimly lit and crammed full, panic spread fast. People started swarming higher up, grabbing children, abandoning everything else, rushing to higher ground.

Joe peered closer. They had moments left before the stream spilled its banks. It was still bubbling up from its underground source, super-heated like a geyser, from the volcanic jets deep below the island.

Ren and Fidell hopped down, leaning over the water.

'Wait,' Joe said, watching their dragons.

'Careful!' Winter said. 'It's hot.'

Joe could feel the heat rising from the stream. But Ren wasn't careful. She dived straight in, splashing them. Joe jumped back as the water hit him, scalding hot. 'No! Ren!' he yelled. He stared down at the water, unable to follow. 'What's she doing? Come back!'

Winter put one hand on his arm. 'Wait – look! She's swimming. She's fine.'

Fidell dipped his nose in, looking below the surface, then he too glided in smoothly, barely rippling the surface.

'How can they bear it? Why aren't they hurt?'

'They're shadow dragons, aren't they?' Winter said, growing excited now. 'Born from four elements: they can do this. They're trying to help.' She brought her face close to the water, muttering softly, 'Go on, Fidell. Go see what's happened.'

Both shadow dragons swam away, sleek as otters, vanishing under the water.

Joe and Winter waited, eyes on the bubbling stream, getting higher and higher every moment.

Moments passed. Joe held the storm lantern over the water and paced up and down. The water trembled on the lip of the channel, and then poured over its edge, splashing onto the floor.

The people of Arcosi were still clambering out of the way, but the dragonriders and the duke's soldiers had gathered each neighbourhood again, and there seemed to be order within the chaos, as they moved higher in turn and started filing into the tunnels.

But there was one problem. The fully grown dragons couldn't enter the upper tunnels – they were too large – and the rising hot water now blocked the main entrance from the beach. The adult dragons were stuck here, till they could leave the way they'd come in.

'Joe!' Amina called from the other side of the cavern. 'Come on, you two! We can't leave without you.'

Tarya and Vigo, Milla and Thom, Isak, Rosa and all the other dragonriders waited with their dragons at the far side of the large cavern, watching them intently.

'We can't!' Joe shouted, feeling the heat of the water through the leather of his shoes. 'We can't leave Ren and Fidell.' He didn't need to ask Winter – he knew she felt the same.

'No! Save yourself, Joe, please!' His mother huddled on the top step, refusing to leave, though Conor and Amina were there, begging her to move to safety.

'Mum, I'm sorry. I can't.' Joe kept his eyes on the place where he'd last seen Ren. There was a tight knot in his stomach. All the people he loved most in the world were here, climbing the stone steps up to safety, or watching the waters rise.

He waited for Ren. He had faith in her. He did. But he was being eaten up by desperate fear. Surely it had been too long?

Winter took his hand, and they backed away from the pooling water, just a step. They didn't speak. They waited, in the intense heat.

Soon the cavern was empty of anyone else, except for Josi, the grown dragons and their riders.

Joe pictured Ren stuck underground, the weight of rock and water crushing her. Every moment that passed, the tension tightened in his stomach, till he could barely breathe. The water rose around his ankles. It cooled as it poured from the stream, but it was still hot. He felt like a lobster, waiting to be boiled alive.

'Look!' Winter said. 'Look, it's not rising any more.'

It was true. Joe fixed his eyes on a spot and watched to see if the water rose higher. Instead, after a long moment, a new stretch of rock was exposed. 'It's going down!' he cried. 'They've done it. They've cleared the blockage!' He let out a long breath of relief. The water stopped splashing from its rocky bed, and instead, it flowed harmlessly through the cave and disappeared again.

'Where are they then?' Joe whispered. 'Come on, Ren, come back to me!'

The next few moments felt like the longest ones of his entire life. Ren might have saved all of them, with Fidell, but how could he bear it if it cost her life?

He tried to stay strong, but he felt his throat tighten, and his eyes grow damp. The only thing that helped was

Winter's hand in his, knowing she felt the same, knowing she'd faced this before – faced the very worst – and that she was still standing.

And then it happened: two streaks of bright colour shot towards them, green and purple, iridescent and full of life.

'There they are!' Winter gasped.

'What's happened?' Joe could see they'd changed somehow.

The dragons were swimming, more strongly than before, so fast that they broke the surface of the water and shot right out, up into the air. With their wings spread, they flew up, up, up, high above their heads, circling the upper reaches of the cavern.

Joe was laughing. 'Ren! You did it! Oh, Ren!'

Tears streamed down Winter's face, but she was laughing too.

Nothing had prepared them for this.

Joe tipped his head, trying to see clearly, but the two dragons darted around like two huge dragonflies, so bright and buzzing with energy, restless and quick.

'Do you remember?' Winter was saying. 'We read about this, in that book.' And she recited the words again:

'A broken heart will dare it all,
Take the leap and risk the fall.

From ash and bone, new life will rise,
Shadow dragons roam the skies!'

'From ash and bone – maybe that meant the volcano, its lava, all the heat below the island? And now somehow it's changed them, made them fly – they've taken to the skies, or the next best thing, down here . . .'

'It's you, Winter,' Joe saw it suddenly, and clearly. 'It means you. You're the broken heart. After Jin died, you were broken-hearted, weren't you? But you were so brave and you risked everything to try again with Fidell.'

'Why me?' Winter said, with new light and mischief in her eyes now. 'It could also be you, Joe Thornsen. When I met you, when you'd fallen, you had nothing. You'd given up on life, till you found the eggs.'

Then Ren and Fidell came fluttering down to land near their people, and there was no more speaking for a while.

Joe reached for his dragon. Ren stood in front of him, filling his vision. She touched her nose to his, and quivered her open wings, showing him their new power and gleaming fiery sheen. She was transformed. She seemed sleeker, more powerful. Her eyes, always golden, were now swirling with orange fire. Her purple scales were crystalline and dancing with light. He gasped when he touched them: they felt hot and cold at the same time, like ice, confusing the fingertips. He got used to the zinging thrill of it, and stroked down her muscular neck, getting to know her new self. She was dazzling.

Winter turned to him then, her face alight, her smile so wide that she looked as transformed as Fidell and Ren. 'Let's tell everyone it's safe to return.'

'Thank you, Ren; thank you, Fidell.' Joe felt a giddy

mixture of relief, pride and hope. He couldn't stop looking at his dragon. 'You saved us.'

Ren gave a proud *aark*, and sprang into the air again, her strong purple body glinting in the lamplight and filling the cave with swirling shadows.

EPILOGUE

A year later

Joe loved swimming with Ren. They played hide-and-seek off the western beach. Ren gave him a head start, and he swam his fastest, through the waves and out past the rocky fringe of the bay into the ocean. He looked under the surface for the telltale swift shadow, hoping to find only her and nothing more deadly. He'd once chased an orca, mistaking it for his shadow dragon. It had chased him back, almost costing Joe his life, till Ren joined in and scared it away. Now he surfaced and took a deep breath, filling his chest with air, then dived once more, eyes wide in the blurry light-filled sea, feeling out for her with his hands. She wouldn't take him by surprise again.

But of course she did.

She came from behind, fast as a hunting shark, rising swiftly right underneath him, so they both came shooting out of the water, and he was left gasping and flailing, only just managing to hook both legs round her shoulders and grip her neck with his hands, before they were rising, up into the air and circling over the deep blue sea.

Joe spat out salt water and shook it from his hair. 'Eeeeee!' he yelled into the clear air. This was the best. Ren was the best! Joe and his dragon flew together. Holding on with his legs, he spread his arms wide, loving the feel of the wind against his bare skin. Below them, the sea stretched like twinkling silk as far as he could see.

Ren turned her head, keeping her wingbeats steady. She was amused – he could see it in her golden eyes. *Prrt?* she said.

He always knew what she meant, even without words. He felt it. He understood it. 'Yes, you're right. We won't go too far. If we're not back in good time for the festival, Conor and Isak will be furious.'

Isak had taken on Conor as apprentice dragonguard, and they'd both been involved with planning the festival from the start. It was meant to celebrate the island's recovery from the eruption of Mount Bara and the wave that had smashed into Arcosi afterwards. The other purpose, less discussed but just as clear, was to unite and celebrate all the different people of Arcosi, so no one ever felt as angry and left out as the Brotherhood once had.

Joe arrived in the palace gardens, just a little late, as everyone was getting ready for the opening parade of the festival. Ren would find him soon – she'd gone to snooze in the cavern meanwhile. Joe and Winter had moved permanently into the dragonhall underground: Ren and Fidell saw the cavern as their home and they loved having the stream – even if it was cool again now and they were far too big to swim in it these days.

They'd all had to live down there for ten days after the volcano blew last year. Everyone shared food and water, forced to get to know each other more than ever before in such close quarters. Joe had used every part of the shipwreck kit and been grateful to his father for that life-saving gift all over again. There'd been tense moments and a few scuffles, he remembered, but the people of Arcosi had worked together and they'd survived. By the time it was safe to go back into the city again and the ash cloud had cleared, the people of the island were more tightly knit than ever.

Joe wandered through the buzzing crowd of people who were adjusting their costumes, tightening the straps on their stilts, and having their faces painted in bright colours. He called out greetings to people he knew – people of all ages and from every quarter. Today they were celebrating all the rich and varied strands that made up the fabric of island life.

People of Norlander ancestry clustered round a huge paper sculpture of a longship. Children had made boat-shaped hats, with waves painted on their cheeks, to celebrate their origins in the far north and the long journey their ancestors had survived sixty years earlier. Joe recognised a few Norlander men as former members of the Brotherhood. Some had remained on Arcosi: the younger ones, the ones who were willing to change. But Noah was missing. He and his mother had left the island in the confusion after the volcano's eruption. Back in the cave, Noah had avoided even looking at Joe, unable to bear the fact that he owed him his life.

Next came the Sartolan families, walking behind a huge paper fish, silvery blue, an intricately detailed sculpture carried on six poles, with a tail that moved, flicking from side to side. The children here wore paper fish heads and fish tails made of stiff shiny fabric. King Luca joined in too. He'd led his people to shelter in the Sartolan uplands that terrible day last year, but the harbour and low-lying streets had been badly hit by the wave.

Then came the Silk Islanders. They wore flowing red robes and walked behind a paper-crafted silk loom.

And so it went on. There were ten different sections. It would look like a living rainbow from dragonback, Joe guessed. He was glad he didn't have to choose which section to belong to. He and Winter had their own section: the shadow dragons were honoured with the final position and would close the parade.

'Joe!' Winter called when she saw him. 'You're late!'

'Sorry, we were swimming. Flying, I mean. You know . . . Anyway, we're last, there's no rush – we can always catch them up on dragonback.' He held his hands up defensively, laughing.

Winter pretended to be cross. 'Isak's looking everywhere for you. I said you'd be late. I also said you wouldn't miss it for the world.'

'Where else would I want to be?' he teased.

Winter wore dragonrider robes and a scarf of emerald

green, dotted with gold sequins in stripes to reflect Fidell's adult colours. Her grey eyes seemed green today too and full of laughter. Her long black hair was plaited ornately, with green ribbons through it. Her smile was wide and bright, lighting up her whole face.

Joe paused long enough to flash a grin back, then hurried and found his own costume: a fine woven silk jacket of dappled purple, with gold buttons that his fingers struggled to do up now. Amina had helped her father design them. On the back of his jacket and Winter's there was a circle, half made of waves, half of flames, to signify the shadow dragons' special gifts, able to move seamlessly between the elements.

Now the music started up, and the drummers began, beating out a rhythm on the drums they wore on thick bands round their necks. Joe felt his excitement rising. People stamped on the spot, practising their dance moves, or waving their ribbons and banners in circles to watch them shimmer in the sunlight.

Ren and Fidell arrived at the last moment, circling down over their heads, with their wings spread wide like silken canopies. People scattered as they landed, quite used to this behaviour.

'You're late!' Joe called up to Ren in his turn. She blinked at him through those golden eyes, and he could swear she was almost laughing too. He came forward and leaned on her, his cheek against her scaly hide, breathing her in, while Ren snorted smoky breath down his neck, whiffling into his hair. He smoothed his hands over her back, checking she was warm enough.

And then it was time! The parade moved off slowly, down through the palace gates, along the main street that coiled the island like a snake. The roadway was lined with people watching and waving, some city folk, some visitors, all smiling and ready for the festival. Dragons walked among the groups, carrying their riders and extra children on their backs, glowing with pride.

Finally it was their turn. Joe turned to Winter. 'Come on then, let's show them who the most beautiful dragons really are.'

'Fidell, my love,' Winter said, 'will you lead the way?'

The green shadow dragon stepped forward, shimmering gold and green, with Winter at his side.

Joe and Ren followed, the very last part of the parade. It was their honour.

As he walked through the city, the sun hot on his face, the noise of cheering in his ears, smelling the delicious street food – orange cakes, sweet caramelised nuts and roasting meat – Joe couldn't help recalling that other day last year when they'd first emerged from the tunnels.

The skies were dark grey that day, and the air had tasted of smoke and death. It was still carrying ash, though the main cloud had dispersed to the north. It was heart-breaking to see what the flood had done to the island. The streets were full of thick black sludge and heaps of flotsam from the wave, with broken wood and glass scattered everywhere. It stank like blocked drains, and Joe couldn't see how they'd begin to clean it up. It felt like a giant had picked up the island, turned it upside down and shaken it, before casting it away.

There was a broken boat on the roof of a house, smashed shutters and broken flowerpots leaking soil. He saw a dead cat, its body swollen with sea water. Windows were broken, curtains torn and the mud covered everything. They streamed out, a forlorn band of survivors, each heading home to discover how bad the damage was there.

In the end the palace was spared – except for the southern tower, which had been destroyed by Heral as he'd rescued Tarya. But the library was safe, and all of Isak's precious books. No one ever saw the leaders of the Brotherhood again, though rumours swirled about their disappearance. Some said that they'd fled to the harbour at the last possible moment; others claimed that they'd been seen heading north by the captain of a Sartolan ship. They'd taken their chance on the ocean, rather than joining the people of Arcosi in the tunnels, and that told Joe everything he needed to know.

Six months ago, he'd received a package, delivered by a trader from the north. He'd unfolded a piece of purple silk to discover a tiny purple dragon carved of marble and a note that read: 'From your friend, Y. Thank you,' scrawled in Norlandish.

So Yannic had survived. He'd saved Tarya's life, and Joe hoped that gave him peace. And that the gold made him happy. He wondered if he'd found the vengeance he sought, before the wave came. Was Asa still alive? He should be brought to justice. But Joe found he didn't mind, as long as he stayed far away from Arcosi.

As for the rest of the gold he'd found with the eggs? It was all gone. Joe had taken it to Tarya and the duke, and begged them to divide it equally among the city folk, so everyone could rebuild their homes. They'd all worked so hard, everyone pulling together in those first desperate days when food was scarce and the spring water wells were the most precious resources on the island.

Now he glanced around him at the streets full of people and life again. The houses had new shutters, freshly painted in bright colours, all the buildings scrubbed clean, inside and out.

'Look, it's Joe and Ren!' a small boy shouted in excitement.

Joe waved, feeling shy, still not used to the way he was recognised now, but Ren purred comfortingly, and he knew it was all worth it to have her in his life.

Then they were arriving at the marketplace for the festival finale. The drumming sounded louder here, echoing off the sides of the surrounding buildings. Joe found a sunny spot at the side for Ren to bask in.

A group of ten children, dressed in the different colours of each section, came forward and performed a dance with great concentration and solemnity that told the story of the eruption and the flood and the long, slow clean-up.

After the applause died down, Duke Vigo stepped forward, smiling.

For a moment, Joe was taken back to the day of the hatching ceremony, and a shudder of horror pulsed through him as he remembered what he'd done and said. He made himself take slow calming breaths: that was before he'd changed. That was before Ren.

She moved towards him, wrapping her long neck around his shoulders, and he leaned on her gratefully. The huge bulk of her next to him, the gleam of her scales, her dazzling beauty, this told Joe how far he'd come. That awful day had begun his journey here. Each painful step had been worth it.

'Friends,' Vigo was saying, 'I hope you're enjoying the first festival of Arcosi. My daughter is!' A huge cheer went up, for Tarya at his side, wearing baby Serina in a sling to face the crowd. The little girl's huge brown eyes were round and wide. She flapped her arms and squeaked in excitement, her wispy black hair dancing in the breeze. 'I won't speak for long,' Vigo said. 'I just want to say how proud I am of the way we worked together . . .'

Joe half-listened to the speech, focusing instead on Winter, a few steps away. The way she was smiling at him made his cheeks warm.

Next, it was time for the feast. Everyone had brought their favourite dishes down to the marketplace, all striving to outdo each other. Joe's mother and Matteo had both been cooking for days.

They'd all mourned Nestan, this past year. When they returned home, they'd given him a proper Norlander funeral, with full honours, though the burning ship was empty this time, while Nestan rested in peace under his olive trees. Josi had found solace in her garden and her cooking, and in her new grandchild.

Joe met his mother's eyes in the crowd and waved at her. 'Save me some of *your* food?' he mouthed.

She pulled a mock-stern face, and then nodded in reply.

'Nobody will miss us, will they?' Winter said.

'Never, we'll slip away like two cats,' Joe said, smiling. 'No one could possibly notice the island's only shadow dragons flying overhead.'

'They want a swim, and fresh fish. Don't you, Fidell? Not this mashed-up picnic . . .' Winter still wasn't keen on crowds and had a habit of melting away from gatherings, just as she used to.

'*You* need a swim, more like. I think you're amphibious now,' Joe teased, planning to come back afterwards and feast on his mother's cooking.

'Fidell's rubbing off on me – though I can't quite fly yet.'

'I'll race you to the western beach!' Joe said, slipping one leg over Ren's enormous shoulders. She unfurled her wings, making people back away, and moments later they were in the air, waving down and yelling their goodbyes.

As the city streets receded below them, Joe held tight to Ren's neck and looked around for Winter. There they were! Fidell was catching up, his green wings flashing in the sunshine.

'Come on, Ren! We can beat them,' Joe laughed, feeling his heart speed up, as they headed out to the open sea – and freedom.

ACKNOWLEDGEMENTS

Dragons might only live in our imaginations, but you don't have to look far in our miraculous natural world to find dazzling examples of power and transformation. From the dragonfly to pyrophytic plants, I have taken inspiration from real living things to make shadow dragons.

The tunnels also came from real-world examples, and the impact of a trip to Naples and a visit to Vesuvius are probably obvious here! There are many cities around the world that have underground tunnels or caves – from Edinburgh to Paris to Rome or Berlin – and they fascinate me. Having said that, I have stretched the limits of possibility in many many ways, so please do forgive and bear with me (and please don't try to shelter in caves if you should ever face a tsunami – it's only the very specific height and location of the tunnels in Arcosi that makes that even a fictional solution).

I'm not a scientist, but I'm lucky enough to be married to one, and I thank him most gratefully for all the help he gave me with research, not to mention everything else. Christoph, this one is for you (sorry there's not more geology). Thanks to all my friends and family for your endless generous support.

Thank you to everyone at David Fickling Books, especially Rosie for continuing to believe in me, and Bron, for allowing the dragons to fly far and wide.

Thank you to my agents Abi Sparrow and Phil Perry for their leap of faith.

Thanks again to Angelo Rinaldi for yet another stunning cover. And thank you Paul Duffield for more beautiful interior art. I am dazzled and inspired by the work of both of these talented artists.

Grateful thanks are due to The Society of Authors for the Authors' Foundation Grant which supported the writing of this book. Please see www.societyofauthors.org for more information on the work of this wonderful organisation.

The first draft of the story was written when I took up the #100DaysOfWriting challenge, inspired by novelist Jenn Ashworth's sharing of her own experience with it. I wouldn't have managed my 100 Days without my dear friend Tara, who joined me.

Thank you to all my beta readers, including Rosie Beyfus, A.M. Dassu, Mustafa Dassu, Hanna Kratz, Arlo Lloyd and Raffy. Thank you to Tom and Rosie for letting me continue to borrow your names; neither Thom nor Rosa is as cool as you, the originals!

Thank you to all the eagle-eyed members of my writing group, Story Mill, whose advice, support and insight is invaluable: Sally Ashworth, Brianna Bourne, Tara Guha and Kate Sims. Thank you to all my local writer friends, including Melvin Burgess, Chloe Daykin, Bec Evans, Harry Heape, Susie Lloyd – you rock and I'm lucky to know you!

To Fiona Sharp and Durham Waterstones Children's Book Group – thank you for your support, feedback and advice! I'm afraid I failed utterly in my homework, except I did sneak the words 'fire dragon' in there. Perhaps you'll forgive me if I visit you again and bring better sweets?

Heartfelt thanks are due to all the amazing booksellers who have supported me. Thanks to all of you, near and far, including the amazing folk of Bookwagon, The Bookcase, The Book Corner, Bradford Waterstones, Deansgate Waterstones, Imagined Things, Kenilworth Books, The Little Bookshop Leeds, Read Holmfirth, Seven Stories Bookshop, Simply Books and Tales on Moon Lane.

Library professionals, I salute you! Thank you to all who champion children's reading, especially Eileen Armstrong; Kirsty Fenn and all at Leeds Library Services; Alison Roberts and all at Calderdale Library Services.

Massive thanks to all the teachers and students who have welcomed me into their schools. I have loved travelling round the UK and hearing your ideas this year. Thank you, Susan Williams, for the teacher resources on my website. Thank you, Authors Aloud. And thank you to the Federation of Children's Book Groups and the extraordinary Ros Bartlett.

Thank you to all the book reviewers and book bloggers who have taken the time to respond so thoughtfully to the world of Arcosi, including Gordon Askew, Fiona Noble, Pam Norfolk, Anna McKerrow at BookTrust, My Book Corner, Book Monsters, Scott Evans, Mr Ripley's Enchanted Books, Serendipity Reviews – I really appreciate your fantastic reviews and support.

To everyone who has written to me with their artwork or reviews: thank you so much! I am very grateful to you. Receiving your letters is a joy and I've started a new part of my website to share readers' artwork, see lizflanagan.co.uk. I hope you enjoy this story too!

David Fickling Books

DRAGON DAUGHTER

LIZ FLANAGAN

THE DRAGONS WERE LOST AND FORGOTTEN, UNTIL NOW . . .

On the island of Arcosi, servant girl Milla witnesses
a murder and discovers four strange eggs. Dragon
eggs! And her world will never be the same again.

Fiery friendships, forgotten family and the struggle
for power collide in this exciting fantasy adventure.